FINGERS OF FEAR

JOHN URBAN NICOLSON was born in Alma, Kansas in 1885. He published several volumes of poetry, including *King of the Black Isles* (1924), *The Sainted Courtezan* (1924) and *The Drums of Yle* (1925), as well as translations of Chaucer's *Canterbury Tales* and the works of François Villon. His only novel, *Fingers of Fear*, was published in 1937 to positive reviews and is remembered today as one of the works included on Karl Edward Wagner's list of the top supernatural horror novels of all time. Nicolson died of coronary thrombosis in Mason, New Hampshire in 1944; his death certificate indicates that he was married to Ida Nicolson and that at the time of his death at age 59, he was working as manager of a storage warehouse.

FINGERS OF FEAR

J. U. NICOLSON

VALANCOURT BOOKS

Fingers of Fear by J. U. Nicolson
First published by Covici-Friede Publishers, New York, in 1937
First Valancourt Books edition 2015

Published by Valancourt Books, Richmond, Virginia
http://www.valancourtbooks.com

ISBN 978-1-943910-01-4 (trade paperback)
Also available as an electronic book.

Set in Dante MT

I

By June of 1933 my finances had fallen to so low an ebb that only sixty-eight cents stood between my pride and beggary on the streets. I had been hoping against hope that the professionally optimistic predictions of the country's financial and political wizards would prove to have been well founded. Like millions of others caught in the trap, I had waited from autumn till spring and then from spring till autumn. Always the return of prosperity was to be but six months hence, or it was "just around the corner." I knew, at last, that it was not coming at all—that is, it was not coming in any manner which would permit me to resume my old life of indolent preparation for the great work in creative writing that I was to do—some day. It had become plain, even to myself, that I must go to work.

Work? But at what? For weeks, since the break with Muriel, I had sought work, at first in the more sniffish and high-toned fields of endeavor, then sinking swiftly through brokers' and insurance offices to application at department stores, at corner grocers', and to foremen of gangs repairing the streets under political patronage. But nowhere had I succeeded in persuading anyone to put my name on a payroll. Bread lines were lengthening. Factories everywhere were closing down, or they were operating on reduced time and paying starvation wages. Men, women and children were streaming in ever-increasing multitudes from city to country, so that there was no demand for labor on the farms—if the farmers could have sold anything! Seized at last by a kind of fatalism, I sold for a few dollars a great sheaf of securities which had once been worth many thousands, pawned my few remaining trinkets and heirlooms, and sat down to wait indifferently for better times. If they refused to return, I fancied that I could starve as gracefully as another man. If they did. . . . But better times had not returned in June of 1933.

Nursing the sixty-eight cents in one fist tightly clenched and thrust deep into a pocket of my baggy trousers, I stood on a curb, rocking idly back and forth in a pair of worn shoes, wondering whether I should ever again dine at the M—— Club, the gray façade of which rose before me across the street. Men I knew entered its doors and men I knew came out. But always they sauntered along that opposite side of the street, intent upon their own affairs, oblivious of my near presence and unaware of my increasing need. I was an outcast. No doubt I had already begun to look the part. I am certain that the fear within me had stamped the name of Ishmael upon my soul, though, as yet, my indifference had not allowed the turning of my hand against my fellow men. I remember thinking that it could not be long before——

"Hello, Seaverns! Come over and have lunch with me."

I turned to find myself confronting Ormond Ormes, head of a small importing concern, a business he had inherited shortly after leaving college. We had been casual friends since our freshman year together. But now I smiled swiftly and grasped him by the hand. I had thought he would wince from the contact, but he did not. I told myself that I had never given this tall, pallid, shapeless, rather coarse fellow the affection he unquestionably deserved. Indeed I knew next to nothing about him. But I was hungry, with the terrible hunger of those who have only dreaded want and have never known what real hunger is; and I was not a little frightened, besides; and here was a friend. Here was an old friend. I could have hugged him to my breast. He was, moreover, already leading me across that busy street to the doors of the Club. I was no longer a member, but I fancied that it would be good to see some of the fellows again, and to lie at my ease in their comfortable chairs, imagining that, God being once more in His Heaven, all must, of necessity, have come right with the world.

I had not foreseen the poisonous courtesy I was to encounter. Everyone spoke to me. I rather fancied that several men were particularly careful to greet me—from a distance—as if they were afraid it might be said they were snobbish. Everyone inquired how matters were with me. Everyone was formally sympathetic. Everyone assured me that I was not alone in misfortune and had no reason to feel peculiarly discouraged. Everyone was certain that in the fall. . . . Or else everyone was sure that prosperity was just around the corner. But not one of the men who paused at our table or exchanged remarks from tables nearby failed to note that my clothes were rapidly verging on shabbiness, that they were out-dated, that my hair needed cutting, and that my face had already acquired something of the hangdog look of failure. Seeing all this, they were prepared to forestall any tale of need with another of even more shocking distress. They kept up appearances, those chaps. Oh, yes! Yet not one of them but was ready to declare that he knew nothing of where his next meal was coming from, in the event of my asking the accommodation of a loan.

I was more than a little glad when that most dreary luncheon of my life was ended. My friend Ormes led the way into the library, which was deserted then, as it usually was. We chose comfortable chairs in a far corner, lighted cigars and awaited upon digestion. I had nothing to say. After all I knew this Ormes only slightly. I could scarcely attempt an intimate conversation, and everything of a chatty or general nature that I could think of saying had been said at the table. So I was content to smoke and await that glance at the watch and that abrupt discovery that he must leave the club immediately, which would be notice enough that I must also leave. But after a few moments Ormes sank even deeper into his chair, blew a long stream of smoke from his lungs, and began to speak.

"Seaverns, I gather that you're pretty hard up. Been hearing about you, now and then. And that got me thinking that perhaps I can offer you something. Of course you may not want it. Quite up to you. But in fact, I was wondering where to find you when I ran across you downstairs. Want a job?"

"And how!" I replied, fervently.

"What," he asked, most surprisingly, "do you know about early American literature?"

"Nothing."

"I was afraid you wouldn't. Still, that's no insuperable barrier. There's plenty of time to pick up everything you'll have to know. I've a notion that your taste runs to such things. Briefly, then, I need a librarian."

"A what? When did you take to buying books?"

"I didn't. I haven't. I never did. Books are all right, of course. Culture and all that. Personally, I prefer the movies and maga-

zines. But there's always been a library at Ormesby, you know, and
I've recently inherited forty thousand volumes and the Lord only
knows how many pamphlets and old newspapers and forgotten
periodicals. Got 'em from an aunt, who got 'em from her father,
who died before he ever got 'round to writing his *Outline of the
Elizabethan Influence in Colonial Literature*. Well, if he *had* to write
a thing like that, I don't blame the old boy for dying. But Aunt
Matty left all that stuff to me, along with a hundred th— with a
nice little bit of money. However, she provided that unless and
until I completed the work her father set out to do, the money's
to go to a historical society. I forget which one. That's the sweet
little job the dear little old lady wished on me. And that's why I've
got to have a librarian, or, rather, a historian."

"What you really want, then, is a ghost," I said.

"A what? Ghost? Eh? Well—hardly."

He had started upright in his chair; now he sank slowly back,
exhaling at length as he did so.

"It's a word," I explained, "used for a chap who writes what
another chap signs."

"Eh? Oh, I see. Well, yes, something of the sort. What in
the world do I know of early American literature? I know little
enough about early American furniture, and that's worth while,
if you ask me. I read a book, once, by Hawthorne, and I used to
read Cooper, and in school they made me dig into Washington
Irving. It seems, however, that there were a lot of writers before
those fellows."

"Who," I asked, "is to judge of this monumental work when
it's completed? Who's to say when and whether you've complied
with the terms of your Aunt Matty's will?"

"Oh! Well, it's provided that a committee of professors from
Harvard and Dartmouth are to do that. More than that, the man-
uscript must be submitted to 'em before 1935."

"Not much time, then."

"What? Why there's a year and a half. You can knock something together in less time than that, can't you?"

"But will it pass the committee?"

"I don't know. It'd better!"

"Oh, I don't mind tackling the job, Ormes. I'm no student of early American literature, or any other early literature, for that matter. But, as you say, a fellow can read up, I s'pose. Shall I work at your place—I mean, where those forty thousand volumes are?"

"Yes. They're all at my house. Ormesby. Near Pittsfield. In the Berkshire Hills, you know."

"And will you give me a free hand?"

"Free as you please. All I ask is that you finish the job and get me that money. Boy! I certainly could use some of it right now. 'Course I'll take care o' you, too, when I get it. Meanwhile, what do you say to a hundred a month and live at my place?"

"When do I start?"

"As soon as you can get up there."

"I'll go tomorrow morning. Tonight, if you say so."

"Oh, the sooner the better. I'll go with you. We'll drive up tonight. Be there before midnight. But now I'd better post you on what you'll find there."

Ormes threw away his partly smoked cigar, lighting a cigarette to replace it.

"By the way," he said, holding his lighted match in mid-air, "there isn't anything to hold you, is there? I don't remember whether you ever married, Seaverns."

"No," said I. I saw no reason why I should tell him of the recent divorce. "No, I'm a free agent."

I settled back in my chair and assumed an air of attention. This Ormond Ormes had become my boss, you see. I stared straight into his eyes, which seemed to be of a nondescript blue, their blond lashes making them appear even lighter than they were. Yet I must admit that I paid very little heed, at the first, to what this new employer of mine was telling me, nor do I know, to this day, all of what he said. Of course there were words, phrases, a few entire sentences that struck through my preoccupation and remained in memory afterwards, though most of them are of small consequence now. I was congratulating myself upon this sudden and unexpected turn in the course of my fortunes. I was preparing to receive the returned prosperity, that prodigal, with a cynicism that would be somewhat in keeping with the heartless manner in which it had left me. I was wondering whether Muriel would be deeply affected if I were to leave town without seeing

her, and then I was suddenly remembering how her manner
had been unmistakably cold of late. No, she probably would
welcome a final break with me. I'd write her as soon as I found
myself settled in Ormes's house. If she cared to reply, all right.
If she didn't . . . I was telling myself that I had no good reason to
protest to this ignorant fellow that I could not possibly write such
a book as he had described. But Ormes was saying:

". . . and then there's Gray. She's s'posed to be beautiful. Maybe
she is. I reckon you'll lose your head—at first. But don't worry
'bout that now."

"Who," I interposed, "is Gray?"

"My sister. Didn't I ever mention her to you? Seems to me I
must have. Never mind. Gray's twenty-six. Four years younger'n
I am. Good lookin', as I said. Least she's s'posed to be. But queer.
Never goes anywhere. Never comes to town. Stays up there in
the country year in, year out. Men don't like her. I used to invite
fellows there, but it was never any use. 'Cause she's probably
handsome, if I do say it. That is, sometimes I think she is, other
times I don't know. She isn't a wallflower, either. Gray can talk,
dance, do anything else, and do it well, when she wants to. But I
guess she prefers the Ghost."

"The what?" I cried, starting upright, as Ormes himself had
started when I had used the same word.

"Yes, the Ghost. Gray and I always capitalize the 'G' when we
mention it in a letter. It's an old house, more'n a hundred years;
in fact the original wing was built in 1767. And so it's got a ghost.
Personally, I've never seen the family goblin. Supposed to be that
of a woman. Fact is, there used to be two ghosts, though Gray
says she's seen the other one, a man, only once."

"So your sister sees such things!"

"Oh, yes, the place is haunted, all right. My parents were
always very proud of our spectres. Used to get up parties to sit
and watch for 'em. But nobody ever saw anything. Except my
father's sister, Aunt Matty, when she was a girl. She's the one who
wished this history job onto me, you know. She claimed to have
seen both the man and the woman. Twice. But never mind that.
The man, according to the legend, always looks like the owner
of Ormesby, and the woman always looks like his wife. But never

mind all that. It's mere moonshine and romance, of course. The thing is . . . What will you need in the way of equipment?"

"Have you a typewriter there?"

"Yes, I think so. Fact is, Gray uses it, now and then. Don't know what shape it's in. But all that sort of thing I'm leaving entirely to you. Order whatever you need. Tell Gray. She'll see that you get it. Now I'm due at the office. Suppose you meet me there at six. We'll dine, then go get my car and drive up to Ormesby. It'll be moonlight. We can do it in five hours. That'll put us there by midnight, or a little past."

Now came the glance at the wrist watch, the suddenly evinced animation, the attitude of being restrained from vast and important affairs only by the courtesy due to a guest. We arose and left the club, and I have never entered its doors since that day. I have no wish to go there.

My preparations for the journey to the Berkshires were simple and few. I went to my room in ——th Street, the rent for which had fortunately been paid, packed my single bag with such of my better shirts and other haberdashery as could be squeezed into it, then sat down to wait until it should be time to go to the offices of the Ormes-Paget Importing Company. My waiting was punctuated, however, with several fruitless attempts to reach Muriel by telephone. Her hotel had no information as to when she might be expected to return.

I had a job. I had awakened that morning with a depressive feeling of dread of the day before me. I had roamed the streets, idly and guiltily, unable to rid myself of a feeling that the job I needed, and didn't want, somewhere awaited me, if only I could summon up courage enough to go look for it and get it. Then, without the slightest effort on my part, it had come to me. I should have a hundred dollars a month, a room to sleep in, a place at the family board. There was a girl for companionship, maybe even for—well, companionship. There was a Ghost for romance. There was a lot of reading to do. Knowing nothing of the difficulties of such a work as lay before me, I shrugged them away. Fortunately my employer knew even less of such matters than I. For more than a year to come I should be safe and warm. If, by some lucky chance, I should succeed in putting together a his-

tory of the Elizabethan influence in Colonial literature which
would meet the demands of the committee from Harvard and
Dartmouth, then I might expect to be rewarded out of the hundred thousand dollars I should thereby have secured for Ormond
Ormes. He had plainly hinted as much. Prospects were bright.
I began to feel that, after all, prosperity might be "just around
the corner." Maybe the financial and political wizards did know
a little of what they were always talking about. I sat indolently
before a window in my room, looking down with good-natured
pity upon the idlers in the sunlight on the street below. There was
probably a job for each and every one of them, if only he took
courage and energy enough between his hands to go get it. I was,
I suppose, being as tolerant and virtuous as most men are when
they are safe and fed and warm.

And all that shows how little one can foresee of what the
future holds. For I know today no more of the Elizabethan influence in early American literature than I knew that afternoon
in June. And a scientific classification of the books, pamphlets,
periodicals and newspapers in the library at Ormesby has never,
to this day, been made.

II

As Ormes had predicted, there was a fine moon that night, and
we drove between hills and along valleys turned by the magic of
that moonlight into vistas of fairyland. It was a night for dreaming. To have talked would have been no less than sacrilege. I do
not know what passed in my companion's mind, but in my own
revolved more dreams than one, all of them inextricably and
quite pleasantly woven in and around the name of Gray Ormes.
When Muriel's name obtruded, I laid it gently yet firmly aside.

Muriel Piercy had been my wife. We had had two years of
what, in retrospect, I could call happiness, before the crash in
common stocks reduced me from a position of ease and indo-
lence to one of wretchedness and to the necessity of working for
my bread. When that happened she sought her old place on the
stage, first, however, demanding a divorce.

"It isn't," she said, "that I *want* to divorce you, Selden, because of any other man, or because I'm tired of being your wife. But I feel that it's the best thing to do. I must be free. When things pick up ... in two or three years, perhaps ... we'll still be friends, I hope, and then we'll consider marrying again—if you still want me."

"Of course I'll want you!" I cried.

Muriel smiled.

Nevertheless I continued, for some time, arguing against this step, and I had at the first refused to consider it. Muriel, however, was firm. She did not point out to me, in brutal words, that I had no longer a right to claim her allegiance. I was not so great a fool as to be unable to see that without having to be told. And so at last I wavered. Under the circumstances I could not very well continue to insist that she remain tied to me. What if she were offered marriage by some wealthy man? She was still handsome enough to command that much of any admirer. The upshot of it was that she went to a western state, resided there the necessary brief while, made her application, and was awarded an absolute divorce. Then she returned to New York and secured a small part in a new play. During the long period of rehearsals we continued to meet occasionally, since we remained good friends. But in the several weeks past I had noticed a growing coldness in her attitude toward me. She denied having on hand any love affair more "serious" than usual. Yet it was more difficult for me to find her unoccupied and ready for a supper or a quiet dinner at some inexpensive restaurant. And that, at the first, had hurt a little. I think it would have hurt a little even had things been well with me in the world of money. But now, setting forth upon the adventure of this new job, when I considered that I ought to feel a pang for what promised to be a long separation from Muriel—I had, as I said, telephoned her repeatedly that afternoon, but had been quite unable to find her—I realized to my own mild astonishment that there was no pang at all, nor more than a ghost of any pain.

And I found, also, that I was forming and re-forming mental pictures of Ormes's sister Gray, the girl who might be beautiful, or who might not be—for her brother did not seem to know—

but who preferred the quiet of Ormesby to the gay life of town, and who could remain alone in a country house among the hills, unterrified of goblins and unacquainted with such gamins as rule the modern world. And I wondered less then, thinking of that, at the foolishness of my friend Ormes in being willing to trust me in his house with such a girl. Of course she and I would not be quite alone; there must be someone else in the place, if it were no more than a servant or two. All that, however, did not trouble my dull brain during our drive into the Berkshire Hills. I had gone with the current and it had washed me here. Let it do further whatever it wished. And so far as his sister's reputation was concerned, I certainly felt no call to worry over what apparently worried her brother not at all.

We entered Pittsfield about half past eleven. The streets were awake and echoing with the laughter of young people, though it was after theatre time. But on such a night the youth of Pittsfield and of that beautiful country surrounding the town still strolled and chattered and made love; and Ormes drove very slowly through the city, his eyes turned, like my own, upon those happy walkers in the moonlight, and probably a bit wistful, even as I was, remembering the ten years which separated him from that time of carefree beauty and romance. Let the broken fabric of the country's economic life crumble into nothingness if it would. What should those boys and girls have cared for such a thing as that?

Then we came to the eastern edge of the town and took the road to Ormesby, which lay at a distance of nine miles into the hills, being also a mile and a half beyond the little village of Tiltown. The latter place straddled a narrow gravel road, unmolested by the constant automobile traffic which thrummed and rumbled along the great highways through Pittsfield.

Ormesby itself stood upon a hill some hundred feet above the road and well back from it. Below the road fumbled a noisy brook, tributary to the Housatonic. This hill had been formed of wash from the peaks surrounding it, so that it lay hemmed in by them on three sides, like a delta, its nearly flat top covering an area of twenty or more acres. Great old trees stood about the house. They were maples and elms, for the most part, and they increased in density as one left the immediate neighborhood of the residence and walked toward the hills rising steeply behind it. All this, however, I was to see clearly only in daylight of the next morning. As we approached the place I was aware merely of a huge bulk towering gloomily up through heavy shadows, a bulk dark and mysterious save for a single lamp that burned above the lintel of the wide double doors in front.

As we had left the road, and before we had come in sight of the burning lamp, Ormes stopped the car and, alighting from it, opened a great iron gate. I drove the car through it, wondering, as I stopped and shifted my body from under the wheel, at the haste made by the usually lethargic Ormes in closing the gate and regaining his seat beside me. But I did not long wonder on that. Suddenly the night was made hideous by the angry voices of dogs. They came rushing toward us from all directions, and it seemed to my startled nerves that there must have been scores of them. Large dogs they were, judging from the tones of their barking and baying, which quivered with a ferocity quite out of keeping with one's usual notion of animals tamed and become the companions of mankind. In an instant there were monstrous gray forms leaping about the moving car on all sides, and more of them shot from beneath the trees, snarling in savage rage. Their fierce eyes burned in the darkness like the red and terrifying eyes of circling wolves.

"Wait!" Ormes commanded, bringing the car to a stop before the doors. "Don't get out yet. I'm not at all sure those brutes will recognize me."

He spoke to the dogs through the lowered window of the car, calling several by name. But they continued to snarl and dash themselves against the door beside him, oblivious to his efforts at conciliation.

"You don't need to fear burglars here, at least," I remarked, thinking that Gray must stand in deep fear of them, nevertheless, to keep so fierce a pack to roam the grounds by night.

Then I saw that the house door had opened, and that a woman stood within the portal, wrapped in a red robe of a thin and clinging silk, and I heard her voice raised in one word of deep command. But that one word was enough. The dogs dropped

to the ground and were silent, save for low growls and protest-
ing whines. Some of them slunk from sight around a corner of
the house, others disappeared beneath the trees. A few fawned at
the woman's feet, which were thrust bare into high-heeled slippers, her slender ankles and gleaming calves bright in the kissing
moonlight.

"Oh, hello, Gray!" greeted Ormes. "Good thing you heard us
and came down. The damned dogs . . ."

His voice trailed away. I marveled that he did not open the
door and descend from the car, since the pack had been cowed
and brought under control. But he sat there during the length of
almost half a minute, staring at the silent form of his sister, whose
face and shoulders were in deep shadow. At last she spoke again.

"Is it about the history?"

I cannot describe the voice I heard coming from that slender
woman's lips. It was a deep contralto. So much is easily said. And
such a voice is common enough to arouse no great wonder in
those who hear it. But how shall I turn into words the vibrant feeling I recognized, in this case, within it? It was a woman's voice,
unmistakably, and yet it was like the voice of no other woman
that I have ever met. Deep and commanding, it yet held a tenseness as of some strong emotion very near to utterance. A shallow
girl said of it, afterwards, that it was a "gorgeous voice." But it
was not gorgeous, if by that the girl meant that it was colourful.
On the contrary, it was flat, dull, opaque, and yet it was, as I said,
arresting. I think that no man, hearing it for the first time, could
fail to be stirred somehow deep within himself.

"Yes," Ormes replied, "I've a friend with me—Mr. Seaverns.
We were at school together. He will do the work."

"Come in, Ormond. Agnes is asleep. She complained of a
headache. Barbara's in bed also, of course."

So there were other female inhabitants of Ormesby! No doubt
my friend had told me of them. I vaguely remembered hearing the name of Agnes, during the first part of that recital at the
club, to which I had given so little attention. But I had come here
thinking, like a fool, that I was to be alone in the house with my
employer's sister. I remember suffering a momentary pang of
disappointment, unrelieved by knowledge that my expectation

had been but a vain and childish thing. I did not, however, find it necessary to regret having deliberately put Muriel out of mind during my late journey. Whatever other persons might surround me here, the voice I had heard and the slim figure of the girl in red were quite enough to solace me for Muriel's desertion, for the present, at any rate. Yet I do not think that I proposed, even then, never to dream of Muriel again.

We left the car and entered the silent house. And several snarling dogs lunged toward our heels just as Ormes closed the heavy door behind us. I wondered whether I should have difficulty in making the acquaintance of those brutes.

Inside, the hallway was in darkness. I stood waiting for light during the few seconds Ormes needed to shut the door and make it fast. And though I am not certain of it to this day, I could have sworn, then, that as I stood there something touched my throat, something cool and seemingly sharp, as of thin metal or of delicate, polished claws. It might have been mere imagination; it might have been a bat; but it was no such touch, if touch it was, as one could expect a woman to make. Still I had reason to think that a woman stood near me in that darkness. Then Ormes groped past, muttering something under his breath, and found a button and pressed it.

His sister had disappeared. I had not heard her move away, but now she was gone. I threw a glance over every corner and surface, but I could see nothing of an intruded bat or night bird. Perhaps I had imagined that sensation of being touched.

"Come, let's get a drink," said Ormes, preceding me along the hallway toward a closed door at the end of it.

Passing through that door, we found ourselves at once in the dining room. Ormes went to the sideboard, an ancient thing, beautifully carved and appointed. He turned back toward me, placing a decanter and glasses on the table. We poured and drank good whiskey, saying little until after we had lighted cigarettes. Then——

"I'll show you where the library is," he said, speaking in low tones, for all the world as if he were somehow afraid, here in his own house, of letting his voice be heard beyond that room. "I'll probably be up and off before you wake in the morning. But you

won't need me. The thing's going to be entirely up to you. Do
you want anything? If you do, tell Gray; she'll see that you get it."

"It was your sister who opened the door for us?"

In an instant I had remembered that it must have been his
sister, since I had heard him call her Gray. He did not answer me
directly, but asked a question in his turn.

"What did you think of her?"

He asked his question swiftly and furtively, with a sidelong
glance at me, as if the words had tumbled from his lips in spite of
a wish to refrain from uttering them. And as he spoke he glanced
here and there about the room and then toward the door by
which we had entered, for all the world like a man who fears that
he may be overheard and does not wish to be.

"I think," I said, "that she must be rather an uncommon
woman. But I couldn't see her face. You didn't seem to be sure
whether she's handsome, when you spoke of her at the club in
town."

"No. However, I do know. She's good-lookin', all right. You'll
find out in the morning."

"Who," I asked, "is Barbara?"

"My aunt. Didn't I tell you? Thought I explained all that. A
kind of invalid, you know. That is, she's had a nervous shock and
gets about very little, though she's not actually ill. You won't see
much of her, it's likely. But I'm sure I told you about my wife."

"I remember you mentioned Agnes," I said, "and I thought
at the time that she was your wife"—as a matter of fact, I had
not known the man was married—"but you didn't say enough
to——"

"Well, you'll see her, too, at breakfast, no doubt. Sorry I can't
stay to introduce you to all of 'em. But you'll get acquainted. You
probably won't want to see very much of Agnes. She's a kind of
hellion. Prefers living here to staying with me in town. It's Gray
you'll deal with. She's boss of Ormesby, Seaverns, even when I'm
here. Fact is, the property's been put in her name since the depression. See?"

I nodded.

"But come! Have another drink, then we'll go look at the
books, and then to bed."

We drank. He led me out of the room through a door standing at right angles to the one we had entered. Thus we came into a long passage which, when my host had pressed a button and flooded it with light, appeared to run the entire length of the house from east to west. Almost at its eastern end we came to a door giving into the library. It was a very large room. Ormes lighted a single lamp that stood on a table near the centre, and I judged that the room was fully sixty feet long by half that distance in width. The ceiling was so far overhead as to be lost in the gloom, though I made shift to see that it, like the walls, was covered with paneling of some dark wood. Cases for books lined the walls, save for a few breaks in their ranks to permit of doors, windows and a great fireplace that rose from the middle of the northern wall. The windows to the east, giving onto the lawn, were doors in reality, being casemented to the polished floor, the kind that are called French windows. I saw that the shelving extended from floor to ceiling, and I made out that the shelves, for the most part, contained books that appeared to have been tossed upon them with no regard for order. Doubtless these were the volumes recently acquired, which had been unpacked and piled there, awaiting the arrival of a librarian and historian. Other cases, indeed, bore heaps of dusty papers which must be the old newspapers and pamphlets of which Ormes had spoken. A glance told me, however, that this room had been a library since long before the birth of its present owners.

"Some job!" I said.

"Eh? Yes, maybe so. I'd hate to tackle it. But then you writing fellows like that kind of thing. All these books are just the way I unpacked 'em. Our older ones—I mean, my father's—are all down at that farther end. Don't think you'll need to dip into them. But the new ones will have to be looked over and catalogued, I s'pose. Maybe you'll have to read right through a lot of 'em. Over there are the magazines and so forth. So there's your job. You've got a year and a half, but maybe you'll need most of it."

For my part, as I stood looking at the thousands of books in that huge room, abruptly and for the first time I realized something of the enormity of the stupendous task before me.

Stupendous? It was simply impossible. A decade of reading would be necessary before a book could be compiled that would even approach the exacting demands of a committee of professors from Harvard and Dartmouth. And I had a year and a half! That period of time scarcely allowed for the actual writing and printing of such a work. It would be very fraud to permit Ormes to go on thinking that the task could be accomplished in time to secure his legacy for him. I roused to such honor as poverty and disappointment had left within me.

"Look here, Ormes," I said, turning toward him, "I need a job, sure enough, but I can't take your money for such a thing as this."

"Why can't you?"

"Because I can't write the book in the time we have. What's more, I don't believe that anyone else can."

"Nonsense."

"No, I'm serious. It can't be done."

"Well, Seaverns, if no one else can do it any better, you may as well go ahead and try. Maybe a mere lengthy essay will do. I don't know. The will says nothing about that."

"But even so ... Tell me, could you read through all those books in——?"

"Hell! You don't have to read 'em all. A lot of 'em haven't got anything to do with your subject. Sort 'em, skim through 'em, do the best you can. I'll go back to town and come up here next week, after you've had a chance to look things over. Then we'll talk about it. Besides, keeping busy at this job will cheer you up."

I saw him smiling in the vague light, though it did not strike me as a pleasant smile. His lips came down at one corner and he shrugged slightly, as a man may who has no belief that the thing he speaks of will come to pass. But I was not thinking of Ormes. I was considering that if I did not make the vain attempt to help him, another man would be procured to do it. I did, for a moment, consider that a real scholar could be hired whose background would have been already established and who might be able to catalogue this library and set forth his thesis in the short space of eighteen months. But I needed the job. Ormes's last words recalled to mind how badly I needed it, not only for physical maintenance, but also to lift me out of the mental slough into which I had fallen. I decided swiftly that I would at least take advantage of my host's offer to work for a week and then, if it should be still necessary, "talk about it."

"All right," I said, "I'll see what I can do."

"Good! Then let's turn in. I'm tired, after that drive. I'll show you the room I want you to have, since all the servants seem to be in bed."

I had left my bag in the hallway near the front door. I picked it up as, following Ormes, I passed through that passage and up the broad winding stairs. At the top a small wall lamp was burning. The wide hallway on the second floor ran the length of the house also, from east to west, though it evidently did not continue across that wing in which the library was situated. Ormes indicated a door near the front of the building.

"That's my room," he said. "My wife's is just across. Gray sleeps on the third floor. My aunt's there at the back. You may have this room. There's an individual bathroom in it."

As he spoke he opened a door next his own, slid his arm around the frame of the doorway as if to press a button. To do this, it was necessary that he lean far forward, nearly out of my sight, because, as I was soon to learn, the partition was just short of being three feet thick.

But my host started suddenly backward, straightened, cleared his throat.

"What do you want?" he demanded.

His voice was harsh. There was a note of defiance in it, as though he had addressed his question to some unwelcome, strange intruder in his house. It flashed into my mind, during that second, that he must have surprised a burglar within the room.

"What is it?" I whispered behind him.

And I moved closer to him as a man moves when he wishes to assure a friend that he will not be deserted in danger.

"Oh! I— That is, I was thinking——"

I could see something of the man's face in the light from the landing. I observed that he continued staring fixedly at something, or someone, within the room.

"Where the deuce is that button?" demanded Ormes, abruptly

and peevishly. "Ought to be here. Funny how it—ah!"

He pressed the switch, spreading a softly shaded glow of light across the floor and walls. I was directly behind him, now, looking into the room over his shoulder. Then he moved aside, as if to allow me to pass him. I did so. There was no one within the chamber. Well, then, to whom, or to what, had he addressed that question? Then he spoke again to me.

"You see, Seaverns, I was— Well, I was just wondering whether you'd want anything for—for your work, you know."

I turned and stared into his face. He had voiced that question several times before. He had told me repeatedly to seek what I might need of Gray. Why should he have asked such a question again?

Nor, as I continued staring at him, did I believe that his stridently startled "What do you want?" had been directed at me. He had addressed someone else. Of that I was certain now. And yet, since the room was quite empty, to all appearances, at any rate, to whom had he spoken? Or to *what?*

But now his face was a mask. I knew that I should learn nothing by questioning him. Therefore I turned from him. I looked about the room, seeing with one glance that I was to have as comfortable quarters as a man could reasonably ask. The chamber was a very large one, containing some good old furniture, a vast four-poster, a heavy carpet of a dull red tone, and a great case full of ancient books. Ormes had followed me.

There was defiance in his bearing, now, and I am certain that there was fear in his face. But he had regained control of his nerves. Once more I felt intuitively that I could gain nothing by asking the meaning of what he had said and done. He would lie to me; he might even grow angry. After all, what right had I to suspect him, here in his own house?

"O.K.?" he asked, lifting one eyebrow in the way he had.

"Could I want anything better?"

"Then I'll say good night. Hope you sleep well! If I'm gone in the morning, just make yourself at home. As I told you, ask Gray for anything you want and don't happen to see. I'll be back on Saturday, a week from day after tomorrow. Good luck, Seaverns. Hope you sleep."

"Thanks, Ormes. Good night."

He turned away. He had twice expressed a hope that I should sleep. He must be in a very nervous state. Were the ghosts of the house wont to walk in the room he had assigned to me? I shuddered. *What* had he seen? To *whom* had he spoken before pressing that electric switch?

Gradually, however, my tenseness went away. I was not in darkness. Whatever happened, I should have light to see by. So then I shrugged, drew off my coat and threw it onto the bed. Composure came swiftly after that. Going, as one naturally does when entering a bedroom for the first time, to one of the windows, I saw that it looked out to the eastward over a stretch of lawn. By reason of the moonlight I could make out that the road ran in east and west directions past the house. The place fronted toward the south. Northward from my window extended a wing which I took to be that housing the library we had lately quitted. But there was nothing of great interest to be seen outside, so I turned back and started to unpack my bag.

In the midst of this operation, I wheeled, darted toward the door of the single closet in the room, and dragged the door open. The closet was quite empty. Then I ran to the bathroom, switched on the light in there, and carefully examined the little room, even stooping to look under the tub. Nothing of a suspicious nature was to be seen.

And I do not know, even now, why I did these things. I had thought myself calm and composed. Perhaps my composure was of the body only, and not of the mind. Perhaps I was still as tense, mentally, as I had lately been physically. I can only say that I did what I was impelled to do. Having done it, instead of breathing easier for the relief of learning that I was alone in the apartment, I became again conscious that I suffered from conscious fear. But of what, I did not know.

Slowly I undressed. I entered the bathroom, shaved, bathed, and was ready for bed. I stood still in the middle of the room, looking about me and carefully noting the position of every article of furniture. And I grew aware that I was now harboring an unaccountable feeling of being watched. I listened intently. Not a sound was to be heard within the house. The silence seemed deeper than it should have been, since I knew that four or five persons lay in the rooms about mine.

I could not throw off that feeling of being an object of scrutiny. Yet I asserted my will against it. I struggled to regain courage. I was alone in the room. I would not allow superstitious fancies to overcome my reason. Nevertheless, when I passed a hand across my face, I felt it to be wet with a cold and clammy dew of perspiration.

The bed, when I approached it and extended my length upon it, was an excellent one. I told myself that if a man could sleep anywhere it must be here, ghosts or no ghosts. And at last, safely under the light covering, I felt I might laugh at the fear which had driven me—to my shame I confess it!—into bed more expeditiously than strict dignity would have allowed.

I lay in the middle of the bed, forcing my thoughts to take hold on Gray Ormes. I had not yet seen her face, since my eyes had not penetrated the shadows in which the upper part of her body had been wrapped while she stood in the doorway downstairs. What would she be like when we met tomorrow morning? And what, also, might Agnes Ormes be like? Her husband had called her a hellion. That, coming from a husband, might mean anything, or nothing. I amused myself with fancying that Gray was dark of eyes and hair. Tall I knew her to be, and slender, and I supposed she would be rather dark, with regular, haughty features, very red lips and large expressive eyes. Agnes must be an Amazon in appearance. It seemed strange that the owner of the voice I had heard at the entrance should be called Gray, while the hellion of a wife bore a name of such undeniably feminine gender as Agnes. It meant chaste and gentle, didn't it? It would be amusing to compare my present notions with realities over the breakfast table and through the days to come.

I considered that I'd probably not be here over a week. But a week is a week, and to a man so nearly cast upon the rocks as I had been it is leisure in which to seek a permanent haven, leisure for which he ought to give due thanks. He ought to give thanks. He ought to give . . .

The damned house was so very *still!* And the night outside was too still, also. The dogs were perfectly silent. It was only by listening very intently that I could hear the faint murmur of the distant brook. Not a bird of the night called anywhere. For all my urban existence I had spent enough time in the country to have, ordinarily, no fear of the quiet. Yet I could not rid myself of the weight of that stillness now. It weighed upon me as a material thing might have weighed. I wrenched my mind away from that oppression and turned to a deliberate thinking that Muriel . . . For a long while I lay there, thinking that Muriel and Gray . . .

I awoke to find myself struggling to a sitting position, convinced that someone had but now been very close to me.

But no. When I turned on the light at my bed's head, there was no one. Nothing had been disturbed. Nothing was in the room. I must have been dreaming.

After some minutes of hesitation, I snapped the light out. Since my windows opened toward the east, the moonlight did not, of course, stream directly into them, but the world outside was so well lighted that my room was far from being completely dark. No sound reached my ears.

"Fool!" I thought. "You've been dreaming of the Ormesby ghosts. You're afraid. Go back to sleep."

I lay back again on the pillow. My own angry explanation for the mysterious sensation which had awakened me seemed, in the light of such reasoning as I could at that time summon, to be quite sufficient. Somehow, though only after a long while, I fell asleep again.

When I next awoke it was full day. My watch showed it to be nearly seven-thirty, an unconscionable hour in town, but not too early for rising in the country, or so I thought. I slipped out of bed, yawning and stretching luxuriously, then staggered sleepily toward the dressing table and confronted my tousled reflection in the mirror, thinking that wives must be quite anesthetic to manly ugliness, since they can look upon their husbands in the early morning and still make shift to love them.

And then, abruptly, I was fully awake and trembling. For there, on the left side of my throat, just where I had fancied I had felt the faintest of faint touches in the hall downstairs, and just where I could feel the great artery throbbing against the tips of my fingers, was a vivid scarlet mark.

I *had* been touched, then, upon entering this house.

But no! I had shaved and bathed before getting into bed. I could be sure that no such mark had been upon my throat before I slept.

When I bent closer toward the mirror and examined the mark with care, I saw that it had been made, or appeared to have been made, by the pressure of a pair of thickly rouged human lips.

But when I had rubbed that place with my hand, and then with a moistened towel, and then had washed it thoroughly with soap and water, I knew that the mark was not a mark made by rouge. It was the mark of blood. It was of blood which had been drawn almost through the skin of my throat. And it seemed to have been drawn there by the sucking action of a woman's young and evil mouth!

III

I have set down "a woman's young and evil mouth" and I do not know how to account for the words. There was nothing to indicate that the mark might not have been made by a hag; and there was nothing to indicate that it might not have been made by a man. I can say only that I have written that which was indicative of the conviction which swept upon me as I stared into the mirror.

I dressed hastily and not so carefully as I might otherwise have done. Leaving that chamber I shuddered, glad to be out of it.

Downstairs there was no one to be seen. An odor of cooking came from the kitchen, however, telling me that the servants were abroad and that I was hungry and ready to do justice to my first meal in these mountains in spite of the depression which weighed upon my spirits. I strolled about the house. I was too nervous to sit still. So I pretended to be making myself familiar with the arrangement of the rooms and their furnishings. As to the rooms, there was nothing remarkable about them. They seemed to be all of ample proportions, furnished in haphazard fashion, though such pieces and carpets and pictures as I paused to examine were good enough for any man's house. I was thus engaged in one of the rooms near the library when a servant came to me. He was tall, lean, middle-aged; he squinted villainously; he wore a coarse apron in place of a coat; and he bade me good morning in a high-pitched nasal twang.

"You can have breakfast at any time, sir," he informed me.

"Oh! Oughtn't I to wait for the ladies?"

"Mrs. Ormes never rises before noon, sir. Miss Barbara always takes breakfast in bed. And I don't think Miss Gray would want you to wait for her, sir."

"Very well. I'll have it now. Has Mr. Ormes gone back to town?"

"Yes, sir. He left at daybreak, sir."

I supposed Hobbs's statement—the fellow had given me his name, adding that his wife cooked for the household and that there were no other servants—that Miss Gray would not want me to await her coming had been prompted by some feeling of reticence against meeting me for the first time so early in the day. But I was scarcely seated at table when the door opened and a young woman entered. It must be Gray herself. After one searching glance at her, I did not need to be better informed of her identity. Whatever else she was, she was an Ormes, for the family likeness to her brother could not be mistaken.

"Good morning, Mr. Seaverns," she greeted me.

I started inwardly. The voice in which she addressed me, though it was a full rich feminine voice, was certainly not the heavy commanding tone I had heard from her lips last night. She had spoken then under stress of some emotion. I had caught the tenseness of it vibrant within her words. But it is natural for a person, certainly for a woman, to raise the pitch of the voice in excitement or under strong emotion, not to lower it. As I say, I was startled, and I fear that I rose and bowed more awkwardly than I might otherwise have done.

While she murmured a commonplace about hoping that I had slept well, she came to the table and seated herself across from me.

"Without a break all night," I lied, wondering whether the wide lips I was seeing had been pressed against my throat while I lay asleep.

I thought, also, how little she resembled the mental image I had made of her. She was not beautiful. That is, I at the first thought that she was not. Afterward I could not be sure of that impression, and I began to understand something of the difficulty under which Ormond had labored in describing her to me. For when she had seated herself and had turned her head sidewise to speak to Hobbs, who served us still wearing his apron, I noted that her face, in profile, clean-cut, proud, almost classical, telling of poise and grace, resembled an Englishwoman's of good birth. Yes, seen in profile, her face was beautiful enough. She wasn't dark, as I had thought she would be. On the contrary, she was so blond as to present an altogether startling appearance. Her heavy hair, which she wore long and caught into a great knot at the nape of her neck, was of that peculiarly white color known as ash, though her brows and lashes were somewhat darker than the hair of the head, nor could I discern that they were artificially darkened. Her face, seen fully, as I was not seeing it, was far from being regular in cast. The eyes were large and they were yellow, like the eyes of a cat. Had I been in love with her at the moment, I suppose I should have said they were golden; and indeed they were not opaquely yellow, but were translucently so, the color seeming to come from far depths and not to be plainly seen when one looked steadily into them. But her face was too broad through the cheek bones, and her mouth was far too large. I do not mean that the lips were gross or badly shaped. They were, on the contrary, exquisitely carved, and the teeth were very white and even. Even so, the mouth was too wide for a pretty woman's mouth, though this feature was not particularly noticeable, save when she spoke or smiled. The skin of her throat and hands, I noticed, was flawlessly white and gleaming.

She made some remark about the work I was to do, repeating her brother's statement that if I needed anything she would see that it was provided. From this the conversation ran, for some minutes, on the same subject, and I could not but marvel at the way this girl, even as Ormes had done, accepted my purely theoretical literary ability as sufficient guaranty that I was competent to write an *Outline of the Elizabethan Influence on Colonial Literature*. From her manner and words the thing seemed as good as accomplished. I marveled, but I was not yet ready to admit to Gray what I had hinted to her brother.

"It will mean that I've got to dig in and work like—well, pretty hard," I said. "But if I'm not interrupted, perhaps——"

"Interrupted? By what? By whom?"

"I don't know. I wasn't thinking of any thing or person in particular. I merely meant——"

"But I'm thinking of particular things—persons, too. You'll probably be interrupted, Mr. Seaverns."

"Indeed!"

"Didn't Ormond tell you about our ghosts?"

She asked the question without the slightest appearance of levity. She said it in the most casual tone in the world, just as she might have asked whether I had been informed that they kept a kennel.

"Yes, he mentioned them. But are they ... do they interrupt one?"

"They are. They do. They will. You'll probably not be allowed to work very long in peace. I hope you're not afraid of such things. I'm not. They try to influence me—oh, often and in many ways. But I usually pay no attention. You'll be wise to ignore them."

"This *is* interesting!" I cried. "I'd no idea your ghostly companions were so much in evidence."

Now I had been kissed in my sleep last night—well, call it a kiss!—and I could not believe, in broad daylight, that a ghost had done the kissing. Upon discovery of the mark on my throat, I had at once concluded that one of these mysterious women who preferred the quiet of Ormesby to life in New York had been on the prowl. Which one? Yet I had locked my door and I had bolted it, before getting into bed, and the bolt had not been shot, nor had the lock been turned. The windows remained as possible means of exit and entrance. Therefore I had carefully examined them, each of them, finding that the screens fastened on the inside. How could they have been replaced by anyone leaving the room that way? Moreover, the wall beneath those windows was of brick and it fell sheer to the ground, and the distance could not have been less than fourteen or fifteen feet. How could a living person have kissed me, then? But the blood drawn near to the surface of the skin of my neck was real enough.

Gray attempted to change the subject of conversation. She began to speak, in a general way, of literature and of the work I had agreed to do; but, as may be imagined, my answers were perfunctory and not always quite to the point. What occupied me to the exclusion of every other interest was the possibility—could I call it the probability?—that it had been Gray's graceful and yet inordinately large mouth which had lain against my throat just where the artery throbbed nearest under the skin.

"I think I understand," I was saying, "that you mean to tell me your ghosts here are subjective phantoms, as perhaps all ghosts are everywhere. If I understand you, it is the life one leads here, the routine one falls into, the habit of going back into the past for companionship, and perhaps the persisting influence of all the dead and buried Ormeses that——"

"Indeed I don't, Mr. Seaverns. I don't mean anything of the sort. The Ormesby ghosts are as objective as ... well, as I am They walk and you see 'em. After you have seen them, or one of them—the woman, perhaps —you'll know better what I mean."

"You think, then, that they'll appear to me?"

"If you remain here. You may even speak with them. I have."

"What?"

"Yes. So now you see that I'm not speaking of subjective visions. But enough of ghosts! What a splendid day it's going to be! I'm for a ramble over the hills. Want to come along?"

"I wish I could."

"Can't you?"

"No, I ought to start work. Your brother will be back in a week, and——"

"No, I suppose you can't. It's too bad."

Whatever else she might be, I told myself that this wholesome, healthy young woman of mixed ancestry and doubtful beauty was not the intruder who had left the print of her sucking mouth on my throat. She claimed to see ghosts and to speak with them, but what woman does not? Surely such an absurd confession was not to be imputed to any particularly deranged mentality in Gray Ormes. Her laugh was hearty enough, her eye and complexion

as bright as one could wish for. I decided that I must look farther for my nocturnal visitor. Besides, what had Ormes told me
about Gray? That she was "boss" at Ormesby, even when he was
present. Well, it was plainly to be seen that she was boss. Hobbs
had been entering and leaving the room, serving us, and whenever she interrupted her talk with me to fling him the scrap of an
order, as she did repeatedly, he snapped into attention as rigid and
immobile as a soldier's, every line of face and figure and every
movement of his manner bespeaking respect and a desire to understand fully so that he might perform her will without error. It
was scarcely possible that such a woman went a-prowling at dead
of night into the bedrooms of strange men.

But Agnes? The hellion? The woman who would not live
among Ormes's friends, but preferred this haunted house in the
hills? The woman of whom I had never heard her husband speak,
in all the years of my casual acquaintance with him? Undoubtedly it was to my employer's wife, rather than to his sister, that
I must look for a solution of the mystery of that kiss. I became
so convinced of Gray's innocence, and further, so convinced of
her ability to deal with any situation that could arise, that it was
several times on my tongue to speak of the matter to her. But I
refrained. After all, and be it given in what manner it may, a kiss
is a kiss. What right had I to inform Gray of her sister-in-law's
doings?

But we had finished our breakfast and taken a second cup of
coffee. She rose and left me, smilingly and with a renewed invitation to forget books and ramble with her across the hills. Do you
think that I was not tempted? I refused, but I freely admit that
it was because I knew so little of the girl, not because I did not
wish to learn more. Everything, even the manner and purpose
of my employment, was mysterious at Ormesby. How could I be
sure that she was not testing me? I sighed and watched her leave
the room, her long slender legs swinging gracefully beneath her
short brown skirt. Lighting another cigarette, I sought the library.

It was damp and cool in there. It should not have been cooler
in that room than in any other, for it had been built against the
eastern wall of what had been the main part of the older house,
toward the rear of it; and the morning sun fell unhindered

upon it and entered its gloom through five or six tall windows. Nevertheless, the air in there was almost too cool for comfort. Certainly the damp and musty odor pervading the place reminded one more of a tomb than of a study in which to do creative work. I shivered, surveying the chaos before me, wondering where to begin upon it. I knew that I must first manage to catalogue everything. I said to myself that it would be best to start with the bound volumes; by the time I had completed the labor of listing them, I should perhaps be sufficiently familiar with the task to tackle the pamphlets and other papers. And then I sighed again.

The front door opened and closed, rather noisily. I was perhaps a hundred feet away from it, yet the fact that I heard it so distinctly told me that whoever had entered or left the house was careless of waking others who might be still asleep. It must have been Gray. And I wished again that I might join her and forget the unwelcome toil awaiting me. Probably she'd take one or more of the dogs. Probably she'd wear breeches and a man's shirt, with her light hair covered by a man's cap or sombrero. How fine it would be to roam those green and wooded hills with her, returning tired and happy to the house just before the twilight. The things we two could find to talk about! There might be just a hint of sentiment (certainly not more, not enough to spoil the day for comradeship), only a recognition of the difference in sex, but never a giving way to its demand. That is, today. Well, and why not for many days to come? For I was tired of the feminine in women. Muriel had done enough to sicken me of their ways, their wants, their weaknesses. Away to the rearward of the house I heard dogs barking, suddenly and joyously, filling me with added bitterness because I was less free to follow my inclination than a dog. Why should I not run after Gray?

I believe that I might very well have yielded to the temptation assailing me had it not been that by the merest chance my attention was momentarily caught by a typewriter. This must be the machine used by Gray herself, the one of which Ormes had spoken. It stood on a little table, and it was very dusty from lack of use. I had paused beside it but a moment, idly allowing my fingers to touch the keys which had been touched by Gray's fingers, noting that the machine was of a make with the operation of which I was quite familiar.

But I was not touching any of those keys now.

Yet now, and though I saw the thing with half an eye only, yet I saw it plainly—I knew then, as I know now, that I had not been mistaken—*the "O" key of the typewriter moved sharply downward and the type clicked against the roller!*

So I became aware—once more!—that though I stood alone in one of the rooms at Ormesby, yet I was in company of a *thing* which was not to be seen but which was quite capable of moving material objects.

A moment later I saw the woman.

I straightened and half turned toward the south wall. I had not heard the door open. Nor had I heard it close. Nor had it opened, nor had it closed. A moment before, looking at the typing machine I had been alone in that long room. Now I saw the woman.

She stood before me, distant perhaps twenty feet. She was a young woman; certainly her years could not have been more than thirty. It flashed across my mind that this was about the age of the female spectre at Ormesby. Was this really the ghost, then? We of the modern world fear these things . . . oh, yes! But we have been taught for so long that they are but creatures of our imagining that even in the midst of fear we somehow doubt. I remember thinking, even then, that I must be dreaming and that it was time to rouse myself out of sleep.

The figure stood between me and one of the long windows, far from the single door of the room; and the north light, spilling in through the window, spread round her hair and clothing, seeming to throw an aura about her and perhaps intensifying the appearance of unreality she exhibited. At least, that is the way I tried, in that moment, to account for the look of her.

She was not very tall, but she was slender and graceful, and I do not think I have ever seen a living woman's face that was more beautiful. I am still of that opinion to this very day. The hair rose on my scalp—or seemed to be doing so—and I shivered in swift fear. I would not give way to fear. I was resolved to conquer it. Yet I shivered in spite of everything my will could do to prevent it. Incongruously, I thought, I was seeing the first ghost of my experience on a bright and wholesome morning in June, not in the dead of night and not in mysterious and eerie surroundings.

And still, for all that the eastern and southern windows of the room were flooded with warm sunlight, which flowed in bright streams over the parqueted floor and set the dust motes dancing, the air of the library was cool to the point of being uncomfortable, so that again I shivered involuntarily as I stood and watched that visitant.

"Good morning," said the vision, her voice low and musical and anything but ghostlike. "I hope you don't mind our ways here. And I hope you'll do just as you wish, without interruption."

Rather fatuously I remembered that the ghosts of Ormesby were able to speak and hear. Gray had told me so not half an hour since. But if one must be visited by a spectre, then let it be so beautiful a vision as that before me now, and let it come at such a time and into such a place.

"I expected to be interrupted, however," I managed to say.

"You did?"

"Oh, yes!"

"But by whom?"

"By you, I suppose. And by the other."

"The other? Which other?"

"What," I cried, "are there more than two of you?"

"I'm afraid," she said, her eyes widening in a queer, old-fashioned, staidly modest manner, though she barely breathed the words loudly enough for me to hear them, "that I don't very well understand you."

I was delighted with her! I had no leisure, at that moment, to analyze my feelings, nor any time to consider the preposterousness of this ghostly visitation, and I was, besides, still rooted to the floor by the mere physical fear which everyone experiences in presence of the unknown, but nevertheless I repeat that I was delighted with the appearance and words of this gentle goblin. She wore, I remarked, a little silken mauve-colored scarf about her neck and shoulders, and under this a long robe or gown of a slightly darker mauve, which just escaped touching the floor as she moved. Her hair was a dark brown, though there seemed to be gray streaks within it, and I could have sworn that her deep eyes were brown also. She was pale, though not so deathly pale and livid as I should have expected her to be. But she was certainly not transparent, for all that the north light shone round her and made an aura on her robe and hair. To look at the figure was almost as if one looked at that of a living woman. Even in the moment I found time to marvel on this opacity. But she was speaking again.

"I'm sorry to have disturbed you. I was looking for . . . but I see she's not here."

She glanced at me, a fleeting, modest, shy little glance. Then she turned and walked away toward the west end of the room, not toward the door, which was in the south wall and gave into the long transverse passage, as I have said. I watched her going, wondering whether I should see her disappear before my eyes. Her little feet made not the slightest sound as she moved across the dusty parquetry, though I fancied that I caught the faint rustling of the silken robe. She held on without pause until she had come to the very end of the room. Then she drifted slowly toward her own right and vanished into the wall!

But there is this to be said for seeing ghosts by day: the net of terror and horror they weave about one is dispelled sooner and far more easily than by night. Whatever had just happened before my eyes, and however incredible it may have been, I was not troubled by fancies of nameless creatures creeping and swooping behind me. After a few moments I mastered fear and followed the figure to that spot where it had vanished. There was no break in the line of deep-shelved bookcases. From where I had stood, she had seemed to walk into the bookcase and merge with it. And it was only then, I think, that I really began to believe, for all the fear that had unreasonably gripped me and made me shiver like a man with ague, that I had actually seen and held converse with an uncorporeal being from beyond the grave. I had already begun to rationalize the entire proceeding, as I walked the length of the library, following the Lady in Mauve. "Fool!" I had reasoned, "The woman couldn't have been any other than Mrs. Agnes Ormes. Why, her first words were words of greeting and they were expressive of the hope, perfectly natural in your hostess, that you should be comfortable and able to work without interruption. And you answered her like an idiot of the first water. And yet . . . and yet . . . there's nothing of the hellion about that little thing." So thinking, I had followed her very slowly to the spot where she had disappeared. Of course there would be a door of some kind there, some kind of panel in the wall, at any rate, some means of egress of which I had not yet learned. But there was nothing. There were only the deep-lined book shelves. How could any living creature have walked *through* those?

And how could any living creature have pressed down that "O" key of the typewriter without touching it?

Then I heard another voice. It came from behind me, and again it was a woman who was speaking.

"Good morning, Mr. Seaverns! I am Mrs. Ormes."

IV

I whirled and confronted the speaker. She was large, pale, red-headed, not a little coarse, rather loud, certainly vulgar. I knew in a flash why Ormes had never told me of his marriage. Apparently, also, he had mentioned it to no one in town, else I must have heard of it from one or another of our mutual acquaintances. But why he had called his wife a hellion was not so clear to me. I supposed the woman had a temper; her heavy eyebrows and chin indicated as much. But it seemed to me that she may have been a bit justified in asserting it. For it was plain that she was lonely here. I had not listened ten minutes to her talk before I had formed the opinion that she wanted to be in New York, but that she was compelled to remain at Ormesby for some reason over which she had no control. Maybe that reason was her husband's reluctance to have her by him. He would unquestionably have been ashamed of her in town. Perhaps he had married her to avoid a scandal. I judged that she was not above forcing a man to do such a thing.

All this passed through my mind while she talked volubly of everything under the sun—my projected work; her husband's business affairs, which kept him so much away from home, es-

pecially since the beginning of this horrible depression; Gray and
her dogs, a dozen, it appeared, all large, always hungry, and all so
fierce that everyone was afraid of them, except Gray herself and
. . . and Barbara. She had hesitated just a little before pronouncing
the name of her husband's aunt. Then she was off again. Now
that summer was fairly come, she was positively afraid to venture
out of doors because her skin freckled so easily; she had a new
car, but didn't like it and was thinking of trading it for another,
to which Ormond objected; the servants were incompetent, but
what could you do; it was so hard to get any kind of servants
to remain steadily in the country, especially during the winter;
and then these horrible hills, all about, hemming one in till one
couldn't breathe.

Hearing all this, and taking advantage of the verbal torrent to
collect my own somewhat scattered fancies, I put this creature
down as a gossip too silly and inconsequential to be harmful, a
woman merely lazy and useless, born to bear children without
any knowledge of what to do with them or how to rear and edu-
cate them after giving them birth. I did not think she could be
much of a hellion, save perhaps in her husband's imagination,
and that may very well have been warped and prejudiced against
her at the time of their marriage.

"And Miss Barbara?" I asked, when the woman's tongue had
slackened, at last, for I wished to be given more detailed information than I then had—"And Miss Barbara? Is her last name
Ormes?"

"Yes. Oh, yes. She's Ormond's aunt, you know. She never married. She's such an odd little old thing, though I guess she's only
thirty-one at that."

"Only thirty-one? But Ormond's about that age, isn't he?"

"Yes. I think they're the same age. She was about thirty years
younger than her only brother, Ormond's father. But she's certainly a queer one. Sometimes I wonder whether she's . . . well,
she's so *queer*, Mr. Seaverns. Hardly ever leaves her room. I don't
s'pose you'll see very much of her. Not that you'd want to. She's
a kind of an invalid, Ormond says, though I tell him it's just foolishness. I say she's a hypochondriac. I don't hesitate to tell her so,
too."

"What is her ailment?" I asked then, as casually as I could.

"Oh, she's had a shock of some kind. I don't know much about it. These people are all as tight-mouthed with me as though I was a perfect stranger, Mr. Seaverns."

"Indeed!"

"And then, you see"—though I was far from seeing the connection between the statement and the fact she had just enunciated —"there are ghosts in this house."

"No!" I thought it well to pretend ignorance on this head.

"Oh my, yes! Didn't my husband tell you? But that's just like him."

"And have you seen . . . anything . . . Mrs. Ormes?"

"No, never. Still, I must say, things happen. I don't see why Ormond didn't warn you. I don't see why he doesn't sell this place. These Ormeses seem to think it's nobody's business, but I always say a person ought to be told, so he'll not be caught unawares, don't you see? Don't you think so, Mr. Seaverns?"

"Oh, undoubtedly! But you say that things happen?"

"Yes. Queer things. Sometimes I think the place is bewitched. I'm sure I'd sell this house, if it was mine, and move out of these hills."

I questioned her again as to the happenings she spoke of; but evidently she had caught a breath of caution and wished no longer to pursue the subject. Her mouth closed tightly. The lips, I thought, were far too thin and straight to have been the voluptuously heavy lips that had lain sucking against my throat the night before, though why I persisted in supposing that that mysterious mouth had been a voluptuously heavy one, I do not know.

"Oh, some other time we'll talk . . . after you've been here a while and had your own experiences," she assured me.

"You think, then, that I'm likely to have experiences of that sort?"

"If you don't, Mr. Seaverns," she said, smiling upon me in what she apparently wanted me to think was a kindly and hospitable fashion, "you'll be the only one who's ever missed 'em at Ormesby. I only hope they don't disturb you too much. But now I must go to see about lunch. You'll excuse me, won't you?"

I rose—we had been sitting—and bowed. She started away

from me toward the door, but hesitated, turning toward the shelves, picked a novel from one of them, blowing dust from the edges of its leaves and squinting nearsightedly at the title.

"Phooey! It's too old and out of date. They did use to write such disgustingly tame and uninteresting novels, didn't they? A person has to read through page after page and chapter after chapter of the dreariest description before ever finding out what the man and woman are going to do. I like to . . . well, just plump right into the middle of things, all at once. Don't you? Who's your favorite author, Mr. Seaverns?"

She had probably remembered that I made pretension to literary knowledge. But she did not wait for me to reply to her question.

"Personally," she continued, "I like Booth Tarkington, don't you? Don't you think he's too sweet for anything?"

I murmured assent, marveling upon the swiftness with which she had dropped her pose of the busy housewife and assumed that of the gushing girl. Besides, I saw no reason to differ from her in her characterization of that maker of popular confections. Nevertheless, I doubted that Mr. Tarkington was this woman's favorite novelist. I rather fancied that she was endeavoring to impress me with the soundness of her literary taste, and that she really read fiction of an even more evanescent kind than that she had mentioned. Somehow she reminded me of the Molly Bloom revealed in that final pitiless chapter of Joyce's *Ulysses*.

But her chatter had certainly driven the ghosts out of that chilly room!

She left me, at last, after informing me that luncheon would be served at one o'clock. I flung my coat aside, rolled up the sleeves of my shirt, and prepared to make a start on the books. All chance of catching Gray and idling through the day with her was now quite lost. It would be necessary to clear some shelves at one end of the line of bookcases; then, as I noted down titles, authors, and the contents of each volume, I should have a place at which to begin my work of sorting and arranging the books. I did not suppose I should be troubled by any further unexplained noises or motions of the typewriter, unless I should be again visited by the Lady in Mauve.

However, I was interrupted, this time by the entrance of the man Hobbs, who came to inform me that I was wanted on the telephone. It was Ormes, calling me from his office in New York.

"Hello? Hello, Seaverns! I called to tell you about——" a noise of static or of clicking terminal plugs drowned his words during several seconds, then I heard again——"yes, just got in. But remember my aunt's illness. You must be very careful not to startle her in any way. If you see her about the house, always be sure to call yourself gently to her attention, not abruptly. Understand? It's her nerves. Doctor says she mustn't be frightened. Liable to cause ... well, you understand. By the way, Seaverns, I've got a coop in the stable that you can use. Prob'ly needs some fixin'. But Gray'll tell you 'bout it. You can use that car whenever you feel like it. That's all. Everything O.K. so far?"

"Yes. I'm busy sorting books. Can't tell you anything about 'em yet."

"Oh, no, I didn't expect you to. Met Gray yet?"

"Yes. Yes, I met her at breakfast."

"Sure it was Gray? But of course it was. She's all right. You'll get along with her. Well, that's all, I guess."

"And I've had a chat with Mrs. Ormes. So now I'm acquainted all 'round."

"Good. I'll be seein' you a week from Sat'day, I guess. So long."

"Good-bye, Mr. Ormes."

I put up the receiver, wondering why I had called my old friend "Mr. Ormes." Yet I knew in my heart that it was due to the fact of my employment by him. I was working for him, taking his money, being ruled by his orders. I had known him since college days, and it had never previously entered my head to address him by such a title, save on the more or less formal occasions incident to "introducing" people. The fact that I had just called him "Mister" rankled within me, making me ashamed of my servility and furious with the instinct which had called it into evidence. The trouble with us in America is, we are too close to the peasantry from which all of us have sprung. We love a lord with the love of a woman for protection, and for precisely the same reason, though we largely do it under the guise of respecting "success," that idol of the underdog.

But my mood of self-condemnation was changed by catching a first sight of Mrs. Hobbs, a wizened little creature, gray-haired, and with an even more evil squint than her husband boasted. She crossed my path, carrying broom and dust pan, bowed slightly and shyly, and was gone. But someone had shown an outward respect toward me. My spirit was lifted up at once, and my ego swelled and was proud.

I turned back toward the library, entered it and picked up my coat. I was in no mood for work upon the listing and ordering of Ormond Ormes's books. I would go out to the garage and see what kind of car he had placed at my disposal. Besides, I wanted to ponder on a fresh mystery that troubled me. Why had Ormes telephoned me? I could not believe that it was for the foolish reason of warning me to be careful of his Aunt Barbara's nerves. I was not a blundering booby to go frightening ailing females into nervous fits. No, that specious excuse had been given to cover a deeper reason. Why had he asked whether I was "sure it was Gray" I had met at table that morning? Was he jealous, then, of his wife's company? Good Lord! Did the fool suppose that I felt any urge to flirt with that wife of his?

The car proved to be a coupé of fair quality, not above two years old, and still presenting an appearance of shiny respectability, which showed that it had been driven always along the safe and comfortable roads, doing its little job without protest and avoiding collisions with opposite opinions, I mean, of course, opposite powers. No one was about. The dogs had been penned in the kennel. The door of the car (I smiled, remembering my college mate's use of the vulgar pronunciation "coop") was unlocked and the key in place over the ignition switch. I got in, pressed the starting pedal and was rewarded by an instant firing of the motor. The engine ran smoothly, silently, efficiently. I backed out and ran down to the road, turning away from Pittsfield, wondering why Ormes had said that the machine stood in need of repairs. There were a few small rattles and squeaks, such as are never absent from the body of a car of this value, but I could discover nothing seriously wrong.

I wanted to be alone for an hour or two, and not only alone in the physical sense. I needed to be out of reach of the influences of Ormesby. I must come to a decision without further delay. As I had told my friend Ormond, I was no scholar, and I knew only a few of the most obvious facts concerning New England's early literature, or its later literature, for the matter of that. That its present-day writing is representative more of an imaginary than of a real people is a thing known to every literate man. I was vaguely conscious that there had been a real beginning in New England toward an independent esthetic, but that it had been suppressed or snuffed out, first by the rise of the magnificoes of Boston and Hartford, later by the migration of intellect to New York and to the West. Beyond that I knew nothing. More, I cared nothing about it. I was lazy, and I had not yet found the work I really wanted to do. It seemed to me that I ought to tell Ormond Ormes plainly that his job was not for me to undertake. Then, though I should be without a roof to shelter me and without prospects of a single meal to follow my last, I should at least be a free man once more. I need not feel impelled to address an old schoolfellow as "Mister."

I had not been twelve hours at Ormesby, yet the mysterious influence of the place had already got its grip upon me. Undoubtedly there were ghosts in the house. I was quite willing to believe that now. Whether the Lady in Mauve had been a spectre, a living woman, or a figment of my disordered imagination, I was now convinced that something of evil haunted the place, and that no one who lived there could escape its influence.

There was Gray. I wanted to see more of Gray. It was not that I was in love with her, nor that I felt inclined to be in love with her. I told myself that I must soon tire of that asymmetrical face, and that the will I had sensed within her must soon clash with mine. Nevertheless there was a mystery about the girl that provoked solution. There was mystery in plenty about all the inmates of Ormesby, but about Gray there was a deeper problem to be solved. Gray was different. I wondered where she had wandered to, scanning the hilltops about me in the hope of catching sight of her tall, lithe figure, surrounded by her dogs. It would have been a delightful thing to have roamed those hills with Gray. Why hadn't I done it?

My speedometer showed that I had ventured above twenty

miles from Ormesby. Therefore I sought a convenient place at which to turn the car about. I was more than half resolved to resign (by telephone) as soon as I should have reached the house; and I did not feel at ease in this borrowed car. It would have been different had I been motoring over the countryside for the sake of relaxation after long hours of honest effort and diligent toil.

It was too bad, I thought, that I must be soon leaving the Berkshires. I was not now seeing them for the first time, but no one who has ever seen them can weary of their loveliness. I knew, moreover, a little of the legends and traditions to which they had given birth. I had once climbed Monument Mountain and pried into that cave which was reputed to have given refuge to Herman Melville, Nathaniel Hawthorne and Oliver Wendell Holmes during the sudden fury of a mountain storm. I had visited friends throughout the country now famous as having been the scene of William Cullen Bryant's earlier efforts in verse and prose, where he had written "Thanatopsis," which he had never bettered in all his long life of writing. I had heard of Catherine Sedgwick and had even read a part of her *Hope Leslie*. I knew the people Mrs. Wharton had saved from an utter oblivion in her *Ethan Frome*. And I still had friends—that is, I knew people—in and about Great Barrington, Lenox and Stockbridge. I felt myself at home in the Berkshire Hills. I certainly was not averse to summering among them. Nevertheless I drove back toward Ormesby firmly resolved to call its master on the telephone and resign my job.

I do not know, to this day, why I had come to this decision so abruptly. I do not think that I had really intended deciding upon anything. But I am inclined to suppose that the mystery of Gray presented itself to me as a mystery that I should never be wholly able to solve unless and until I gained back the freedom which had been mine. I might interest her, but somehow I felt that her pride would never let her love entirely her brother's servant. And I wanted to know much more of Gray than her brother's servant could be likely ever to learn.

It seems that I had been expecting to find Gray before reaching Ormesby. I had not been fully conscious of this expectation, barring my brief period of scanning the hilltops for sight of her figure; but when I saw her sitting on a bank beside the road, distant from the house about a mile and a half, I knew that I was in no wise surprised at finding her there. She was clad, moreover, as I had fancied she would be, in masculine shirt and breeches, with a hickory staff in her hand and three savage-looking dogs at her feet. I slowed the car to a stop before her.

"I was waiting for you," she said, unsmilingly, but yet pleasantly enough.

"Were you? How did you know I was going to come here?"

"Easily enough. I saw you leave the house. I was coming down the hill back of it."

"Well, I wanted to think before plunging into that work. Your brother telephoned, telling me to use this car whenever I wanted to. So I came out, hoping I'd find you."

"Indeed? Why didn't you accept my invitation this morning?"

"Naturally I thought I ought to go to work."

"Come, Mr. Seaverns, are you really intending to start that ridiculous job?"

"Ridiculous? Perhaps it is ... considering everything. But I'd intended starting it—yes."

"And now you've changed your mind?"

"But how did you know that?"

"Haven't you?"

"Yes."

"Why?"

"Because I'm not competent to perform it."

"What's your real reason?"

Her questioning irked me. It was not that, as a sister of her brother and his representative here, she had no business to ask such questions of me. I think it must have been the tone in which she asked, which seemed definitely hostile and disdainful, as if she doubted my ability as much as or more than I myself doubted it. And if that were the case, what right had this ugly girl to doubt? Looking steadily into her face at that moment, I saw that she was not at all handsome. I wondered indeed how I could have been led to think her even pretty.

"What's your real reason?" she repeated, arrogantly, when I hesitated for want of words in which to answer her.

"I think," I said, slowly—and where I found such a thing to say

I do not yet know, since I had not intended saying anything re-
motely like it—"I think it must be because of the ghosts that walk
by night at Ormesby, rather than those one sees there by day."

"Oh! You've seen . . . something?"

"I have."

"Tell me about it!"

Her manner had undergone an abrupt and a complete change.
She rose from her seat on the flowering bank and came down to
the road, standing beside the car and staring into my eyes. She
was no longer the mistress of Ormesby, haughtily questioning an
employee about his reasons for leaving her house and her brother's unfinished work. She might have been a girl of twenty, or she
might even have been a child, so naïve and frankly eager was she
to hear what I might have to tell.

But I was not yet ready to take her wholly into my confidence.
She had too recently showed me her will to dominate. I had been
thinking of telling her about the Lady in Mauve. Now I altered
that intention.

"There isn't much to tell. I was in the library. I had been stooping over some books piled on the floor. When I looked up a man
was standing before me."

"A *man*? Are you sure?"

"Why . . . yes. Yes, I'm sure, Miss Ormes. A man about fifty
years old, I should say."

"Oh! How was he dressed?"

"In black."

"Not in buff and wearing high boots?"

"Should he have been?"

"I really don't know."

"Then——"

"I do know, however, that you're lying, Mr. Seaverns. You
haven't seen the man you speak of. You're making fun of me."

I opened the door of the car.

"Thank you," I said, coldly. "Will you let me drive you to the
house?"

I had expected a refusal; at least, I should not have been surprised had she refused to ride beside me. But she got in and sat
down without a word. Her manner had changed again. Yet she

was not again the arrogant, supercilious woman of wealth putting an inferior in his place. There was a little frown of thought between her brows. She appeared to have forgotten me and her own incipient anger. Nothing was said during the greater part of the short drive to the house, but when we had almost reached her private roadway she turned toward me, and without warning of any kind laid a hand upon my wrist.

"Don't leave Ormesby, Mr. Seaverns!"

I looked into her face, but though it was turned fully toward me her eyes did not meet my own. Instead she gazed steadily at that place on my throat where I had found the mark.

"Well, of course, if you put it that way——" I began.

"Yes, I do. I ask you to stay, for a little while, a few weeks, at least. I can't tell you why—anything—just now. But you are wrong to laugh at us. There's really . . . something . . . in that house. It walks. It comes into rooms at night. It's there in the day also. And I—I'm beginning to be afraid, Mr. Seaverns."

"Then of course I'll stay—Gray!" I cried.

I saw her lashes move in the merest flicker when I thus used her Christian name. But she gave no other evidence that she had noticed it. Why, after all, should I not have called her by that name? I had known her brother long enough, even if I had inadvertently called him Mr. Ormes that morning, to adopt an air of informality toward his sister, especially after the request she had just made of me and the confession of fear she had just uttered. And yet it came over me that it would have been far better manners to have continued calling her Miss Ormes until the effect of that strange request had somewhat passed away. I seemed to be peculiarly unfortunate today in my choice of names and titles. But she was speaking again.

"Tonight, after dinner, when Agnes has gone to her room, I'd like to have a talk with you," she said, seriously. "Will you wait for me in the library? There are things I want to tell you about that house . . . and about us who live it in. Also I must tell you something you don't appear to know about yourself. Will you meet me?"

"Of course!"

Her yellow eyes stared into mine unseeingly. Then she turned away. I stopped the car, at her bidding, nearer the garage than the house itself. She descended immediately and called to the dogs which had been trailing easily along, since I had not driven above ten miles an hour. They were fierce gray brutes, of the breed erroneously called "police dogs" by nine Americans out of ten. Yet they cowered before this woman, at her sharp word of command, and left off trying to nose me out of the car and into the open where they could fairly have got their fangs into my legs. I drove into the garage as she disappeared with the beasts behind a clump of cedars that grew at the rear of the house.

"Something to tell me about myself, eh?" I mused, taking my way toward the library, conscious that I had missed by an hour the luncheon which was to be served at one sharp, if Mrs. Ormes's warning meant anything. "I wonder, now, whether she intends telling me anything about a certain kiss? And I'm beginning to wonder whether my role here isn't properly that of protector of lonely women, rather than that of amateur historian? Gray sneered at my work, asking whether I really intended going on with the ridiculous job. One thing is certain: if Gray asks me to stay here, wild horses can't drag me away. I hate her. I'm afraid of her. There's something about her that's somehow all wrong. But oh, Gray! I am beginning to be more in love with you than it is wise for a man to be in love with any woman!"

I think I remember that I was not, after all, too late for lunch. And during the afternoon, without thinking of what I was doing, I actually listed nearly a dozen books, by title, date, publisher and subject matter.

V

Both Agnes and Gray were present at the dinner table. Conversation, while not animated, was general and sufficiently interesting to be easily maintained. A few remarks were made, desultory and evincing no interest in their makers' minds, on my supposed labors toward an understanding of New England literature. It was said that the Coddingtons probably would not open their big house that summer. Agnes querulously found fault with something the servants had done or had not done. For the most part the talk was of such happenings as had been reported in the daily papers, of this, that or the other radio entertainment, of Hollywood's doings and of Broadway's. Nothing of any consequence was put into speech. Mrs. Ormes's usual volubility was evidently being held in leash, doubtless owing to her sister-in-law's presence, since the woman was obviously afraid of Gray.

Nevertheless I was not bored. A play of some kind was going on beneath the surface. That was plain, even to perceptions less quick than mine. The eyes of the two women did not concern themselves, adversely and quietly critical, with details of each other's costume and make-up. Disdaining concern with such purely feminine jealousies, their eyes plunged straight forward, thrusting and fencing like rapiers in the hands of bitterly hostile men, while their courtesy was just as poisonously exact. Hatred between the wife and sister of Ormond Ormes was too openly evinced to be mistaken. It was not the petty, childish, unreasoning hatred that one would not have been astonished to find existing between two women condemned to live together in such surroundings; rather it was an emotion of a far higher and more deadly sort. They knew why they hated, and they knew how they would have liked to glut their hate. I passed from secret amusement at having been thus made privy to a sight of these raw passions, held with difficulty in control, to a state of nervous expectancy induced by fear that the pair must, in the next moment, yield to suppressed fury and fly at each other's faces like a couple of Gray's dogs. I was relieved indeed when, without waiting to smoke, Agnes arose and left us.

It was only a little past seven o'clock. The day had been fine and the evening was warm and still, though thunder rumbled somewhere off among the hills and, as the twilight deepened, the darkening sky was lighted by an occasional flash of distant lightning. Not wishing to suffer an interruption during the early evening, I was on the point of proposing a stroll to and from the village of Tiltown, since I supposed that, even in the event of rain, we could find shelter somewhere along the road. But Gray forestalled my proposal with a refusal to accompany me. It was almost as if she had read the intention in my mind.

"Why don't you amuse yourself for the next hour or so by walking down to Tiltown?" she asked.

"I was about to ask you to go with me."

"No, I can't. I've something to do. But you go. I'll give you a few letters to post for me. Then meet me in the library at ten-thirty."

Walking very slowly, I was able to make the journey of three miles to and from the village occupy me for the next two hours. I returned to Ormesby in the heavy sweet dusk of the long June evening. It would, however, have been even darker in the valley had it not been for a glow that bathed the mountain tops, aftermath of a sunset which was near to being the latest of the year. A storm was gathering headway over the hills to the east and south.

There seemed to be no one about as I neared the gate and looked uphill toward the house. I remember having a feeling of uneasiness as to the dogs, for if they had been loosed I should probably be forced to swing myself into one of the trees to avoid being mauled by the savage brutes. But they had not been released from their kennels. The front door stood open, protected from invasion of insects by a screen. I entered and went at once to my own room, where I bathed my face and hands. Then, cooled and refreshed, I made my way downstairs and along the passage leading to the library. Everything was in darkness. The house was silent and seemed as deserted as it had seemed last night when I lay awake in my bed, unable to sleep because of the preternatural stillness. I groped along the hallway until I had come to the door. It yet lacked more than half an hour of the time of Gray's coming to meet me here, but I had chosen to await her in that room, rather than spend the time in my own lonely bedroom.

There was no light in the library. I entered—after a moment's hesitation. Say what you will against it, a man who goes in darkness through a house in which ghosts are confidently said to appear does not conduct himself with the fearless assurance of one to whom goblins are only faint tales out of half-forgotten books. There was a lamp, I knew, standing just within the doorway, the light of which could be switched on by pulling a tasseled cord depending from the switch. I went in and groped for the cord. I had just found it and was about to twitch it downward. But

I dropped it, instead, as if it had burned my fingers, darting back and scrambling out into the passage with the haste of quick and heart-clutching terror. For a hand had closed, ever so lightly and ever so coldly over the back of my own hand, even as my fingers found the cord; and though I had felt no force at all in the feathery touch of that soft cold hand, yet I knew that its compulsion had been against the lighting of the lamp.

I did not run quite away. Once out in the hallway again, I halted and stood listening. I do not know how long I stood there, the open door before me seeming to show as an oblong of deeper darkness than that surrounding it. But I could not remain there for ever, motionless and shiveringly expectant. Gray might be coming to join me, though it was not yet time for her to come. But suppose she was even now within the room, that it had been her hand which touched me. It might be—well, why not? For I had my full supply of masculine vanity, I suppose—that she wanted to receive me in darkness. I mastered my fears, not caring to have them betrayed in voice or manner.

"Gray?" I called, speaking the word as naturally as I could.

There was no answer. Listening intently, I seemed to catch a faint—oh, a very faint!—rusting of silken garments, just as I had seemed to catch such a sound in the morning, when the Lady in Mauve had left me. The slightest of air currents moved against my cheek. I called the girl's name again, less confidently, I am sure, this time. Still there was no response. It was not Gray Ormes who had bidden me, without words, to leave the room in darkness.

But the ghost, if ghost it was, had done me no harm. More, if it were the Lady in Mauve, I reasoned that I need not be afraid of so gentle a spectre as she had shown herself to be. Abruptly I gathered together my shaken resolution and stepped once more across that threshold, stretching out my hand for the cord. I found it. I pulled it. The soft light of the lamp sprang about me and spread instantly across the room. There was no one within the circle of its beaming. I stood still again, listening again, relieved that I had so far conquered my fears as to have entered the room and lighted the lamp, despite the mysterious hand which had so lately forbidden it. Then I heard someone—it must be Gray —approaching along the passage.

She came garbed in a thin robe of some very dark color, though I do not remember that it was black. Her light hair was piled against the nape of her neck, and within it was a single small ornament of gold, while her silk robe was fastened at the breast by another little golden pin. Except for these, she was dressed so simply as to heighten the redness of her painted lips and the smoldering light in her yellow eyes. That afternoon, seeing her beside the road in breeches and shirt, I had thought her not even pretty, despite the grace of her movements. At dinner I had been absorbed in watching the play of passions beneath the surface of her manner, and I had not then given my masculinity to admiration of her youth and charms. But here, in the subdued light of the one shaded lamp, with the sleazy robe clinging to her breasts and thighs, and with the faintest of perfumes reaching my nostrils from somewhere about her body, I found her beautiful. I even remember thinking it a pity that she could not always appear to a man under such conditions and in such circumstances as those surrounding us at the moment. Indeed, it is the tragedy of most women that they seldom are able to heighten the allurements of sex by settings adapted to their endowments of its charms.

"I'm glad you came," I told her.

She said nothing, but stood before me, looking into my face and eyes as if she had never previously seen them. I went on to relate, frankly, what I had lately experienced.

To my surprise she shuddered. She drew closer to me, by ever so little. I would have sworn she was afraid, had I not, in the next instant, caught her eyes, which seemed now to burn with a fire that was somehow dully red, fastened upon my throat. And then I shuddered also, though I was able to hide the involuntary twitching from her eyes. She slunk across the room to a chair that stood just at the edge of the circle of light, motioning me to find another and be seated near her. I did so. I saw, then, that she wore no stockings on her gleaming legs and that her feet were hidden in slippers that matched the sombre gown.

"You didn't expect me, then," she said.

I was about to reply that I had not expected her so soon, but I did not. I said nothing at all. Now, again, I was hearing the voice that I had heard when she stood last night in the shadowy portal to welcome her brother and myself to Ormesby and to drive the dogs away from us. Deep as a man's it was, and yet it was not the voice of a man. There was little of masculinity within it. I had not heard it all day, though I had spoken much with her and heard her say many things.

"You've been here long enough," she continued, not seeming to expect a reply from me, "to have learned that things happen queerly here and that queer things are to be seen in this house. I used to think the place was haunted by impersonal ghosts."

"Impersonal ghosts?"

"Yes. Ghosts outside of and foreign to ourselves—to us who live here. I know now that the things one sees are the ghosts of the things one has done."

This was in direct contradiction to what she had said in the morning, as we had sat together at breakfast. Then she had maintained, against my own suggestion that her ghosts were subjective, that they were real and exterior to herself. I could not think why she had changed her opinion. In the vague light I saw her shudder again, and this time, without caring that she might notice it, I shuddered also. But she was speaking once more.

"Please don't interrupt while I tell you. Queer things are done here. Murder has been committed——"

"Murder!" I could not have suppressed the cry, regardless of her admonition to maintain silence.

"Yes. Murder. There's a man of fifty. I saw him . . . last night. It's my . . . it's my father."

The girl paused for a time, and now I did not find it necessary to break her command to keep silent. She leaned toward me, so that the robe about her breast fell forwards and I saw, vaguely and in deep shadow, yet alluringly enough, the curving of her delicate naked breasts; and I smelled again that hint of some exotic perfume, coming probably from the masses of her hair. It came to me that she was tempting me to put my hands upon her, yet because of the boldness of it I fancied that I must be mistaken. Moreover, what she had said about a murder done in the house had deprived me of all wish to meet her challenge, if challenge it was, with any answering passion.

"There's a woman. I've often seen her . . . oftenest here in this room. Others have seen her also. She was my ... mother. My father killed her."

I drew swiftly back, the legs of my chair screeching over the polished floor. Sheer horror choked me and held me from utterance of the words that clamored to be heard. Into what kind of den had I unwittingly fallen? Outside the sultry night was riven by a blinding flash and a tremendous peal of thunder obliterated all other sound. My taut nerves snapped, so that I sprang erect, trembling before her. But the woman remained as calm as if nothing had happened.

"He killed her because he was in love with ... he was in love with his own sister."

Horror piled upon horror! But the being before me seemed oblivious even of my presence, now, as she sat before me, leaning in my direction and with her burning eyes fixed steadily upon my throat. And I was no longer conscious of the nakedness of her white breast and gleaming legs.

"The girl—my aunt—was thirty years younger than my father. There were no children between the two of them. It happens that way, sometimes, I'm told. And my mother was ten years younger than he. But he forgot her and made love to Barbara, my aunt."

So *this* was the reason for Barbara's invalidism. This was the shock from which she had never quite recovered, the reason why I, perhaps any man, must be careful in approaching her suddenly. But the other continued:

"Mother learned of it. What happened between them I don't know. He killed her in the night. He killed her ... he killed her by tearing her throat out ... with his teeth!"

Her voice had risen almost to a scream. Gone was the deep commanding note of it. She darted to her feet and ran into the shadows at the place where I had that morning seen the Lady in Mauve disappear. I leaped up also, my own nerves a-jangle with the horror of this thing I had heard and of the eerie room in which I had heard it. And yet, remembering back upon that moment, I think that my greatest emotion was one of loathing. And it had been caused by the eyes, burning like those of a wolf in darkness, which showed me something of what this woman's soul must be. She had glared into my face with a lust that could not ever be content with less than blood. Outside in the night, swept to my ears by a gust of the rising gale, I heard the wild brutality of snarling dogs, as if they had coursed and borne down a helpless victim and were tearing it limb from limb.

This was the girl to whom I had thought to speak gently tonight of love! This was the woman whom I had even permitted myself to dream of marrying!

I stood beside the chair in which I had been sitting, grasping the back of it to steady my swaying feet. I was profoundly shaken. Seeing her approaching me again, I did not know whether to stand my ground or to retreat into the circle of definitely bright light under the lamp. For, loathing her passions as I could not help doing, I yet knew that I desired her! Evil she might be—evil she was!—as ever a hag of Hell, but in that moment she was beautiful. God help me, I believe that I held out my arms, ready to take her into them!

She came on, her feet as noiseless on the parquetry as had been those of the Lady in Mauve. And I awaited her, my nerves tense and the heart pounding in my breast, but in my brain a horror of what she was, and in my blood desire. She avoided my arms. I let them fall slowly to my sides, helpless to take her. She thrust her distorted face almost against my own. I smelled the faint sweet perfume of her tumbled hair. I smelled the hot and sweaty odors of her excited body. The eyes that held mine in a fierce stare of nameless passion were the eyes of a madwoman. They were no longer yellow. From somewhere deep within them rose a flame that was red, like the eyes of a wolf in darkness.

"Now you shall hear the rest of it!"

She leered at me. Her voice was no longer deep and commanding. It had risen almost to shrieking pitch, changed not less than her appearance was changed. She was not a young woman now, but an aging Thing withered by excess and writhen by the torment of quenchless and rioting lust. She had refused to come into my arms, for that would have meant surrender; but she came closer to me. All the while she was speaking she came steadily closer to me and closer, until I felt her hot fierce breath over my face, turning me sick as if it had been the breath of a beast, and at the same time maddening me. And I awaited contact with her, utterly unable to avoid her steady and stealthy approach.

"Now you shall hear the rest of it! Yes! He tore out her throat with his teeth. And he sucked her blood. And he gnawed the flesh of her throat. Meat! He was mad! I tell you that he was mad! But he knew well enough what he did. He knew what he wanted. He broke into Barbara's room and flung his body upon hers. My brother heard and ran there. I followed. Ormond was twenty, then, and I was sixteen. My father turned on us and knocked my brother down with a blow of his fist. I was afraid and I stood there, cowering against the wall and unable to do anything. He threw Barbara back again onto the bed. She screamed. God, how she screamed! I saw him hurl himself on her and tear at her throat. I saw him bite into it. I saw him throw his head this way and that way, tearing it. The red meat! I saw the blood spurt from between his teeth and lips and from her neck. She fell down under him. But Ormond got up and dragged my father away. And when my father turned on him again, Ormond hit him with a chair and knocked him down. Then he pulled a revolver and shot him. Twice. I saw where the bullet hit him first, in the forehead. It was all white skin, then the red blood was coming out of it, down into his eyes, and all over his face and into his open mouth. He fell forward. I saw it. I watched him falling. I saw him catch breath, then, and then he struggled to get up. He slumped down and lay still. Just one finger moved. It was a finger of his left hand and it moved, and it kept crooking itself. I don't know how long it moved. But it kept crooking itself. It was beckoning us—Ormond and me—to come to him . . . I saw all that. I see it . . . now!"

During this recital her voice had once more fallen to its usual low register, and the last words came from far down, with a tearing quality about them, as if they had been ripped and wrenched alive from living tissue. For the moment her eyes had gone dull and opaque. Now her knees doubled beneath her, and she sank slowly downwards and remained kneeling on the floor. To my shame be it said that I did not at once offer her my aid. I was standing, looking upon her as I might have looked upon some hurt and unreasoning animal. And I allowed her to remain kneeling there on the ground before me. It was only after what seemed to have been a very long time that I put forth a hand to help her to her feet.

"I'm all right," she said, still speaking in that harsh, tearing tone. "Let me alone. You don't know why I've told you this? Listen!"

She held up one hand for silence. The storm roared over the house and beat against its walls and windows with a fury which threatened to throw them down. Yet from far away, rising above the howls of the wind and rain, came the cry of the savage dogs.

"The dogs! Yes! They're my dogs! We buried them—my father and my mother. We never reported the killings. We gave out that they'd sailed suddenly for England. My brother has friends there. He forged papers and bought other forgeries. It was told about that they'd both died . . . of influenza. No one questioned it. No one's ever suspected. But the servants—they know. Barbara knows. I know. And Agnes knows that something's here . . . something that won't die . . . in this house. Now you can see why it's full of ghosts."

Yes, I could understand that now. How should the house have failed to be full of bitter and grisly ghosts that would not die and be buried so long as these Ormses lived? But I did not so readily understand why she had told all this to me, a stranger to herself, comparatively, and certainly not an intimate even of her brother. She had this morning informed me that of late she had been afraid. Looking upon her now, recalling how she had so recently stood before me, showing forth her soul shamelessly naked in the fierce passions of madness, I could very well believe that in her saner moments she was in truth afraid of the Ormesby ghosts. Once more she read my inmost thought. She spoke again, and now I was to learn the meaning of it.

"I've told you," she said, rising swiftly to her feet and glaring again into my fascinated eyes, "because, whether you know it or not, and whether you like it or not, you've become a part of all this. You've seen something of the Things that won't die and be buried, here. You're a part of it, now. Everyone who ever has come here has become a part of it. I know that you were hired and brought here for a purpose of my brother. Perhaps I know more about that purpose than you think I do." Her eyes flashed with a cunning leer. "Maybe, even, I know more than he himself does. What of all that? I know well enough that you'll never write any such book."

She crept closer to me, and her eyes blazed at me, and her mouth leered.

"You're in love with me! You fool! Do you think I don't know that? They're all fools here, except me. But I'm not so great a fool as not to know that you're caught. I saw you looking at me last night. I knew the moment you arrived—yes, before you got out of Ormond's car, that you—oh, I know you, Selden Seaverns! I know you, and I'm— So you can't leave Ormesby! The dogs out there won't let you. The ghosts won't let you go. And I—*I* won't let you go . . . now that you've come to me . . . at last! You're mine! Now I want to kiss you!"

I said nothing. I drew back, seeking to avoid her steady approach. She came on, not swiftly, but without pause. Something behind me, a chair, perhaps, interfered with my retreat. I endeavored to move sidewise. And then she sprang upon me. It was not the spring of a human creature. She stooped, snarled, then leaped at my throat as a wolf might have leaped!

Her open mouth sought my throat! Even now I see the red tongue darted between the bared white fangs of that slavering mouth! Her head drove swiftly forward to reach the flesh of my neck and tear it . . .

I remember flinging her hands from my shoulders. I remember hurling her heavily off me and down onto the floor. Then I turned and ran blindly out into the passage and somehow up the stairs. I reached my own room and locked the door behind me. And while I leaned against it, panting hard and seeing the world outside as a vast sheet of rain through which leaped and twisted the fire of constant lightning, I heard a woman laughing somewhere down on that lower floor, a wild maniacal laughter that tore at my soul like fangs.

And from very far away, as if in answer and as if in obedience to that unholy mirth, rose again the nearing cry of the pack.

VI

From the manner in which I have set it down, I think it likely that I shall be thought to have fled from the library and Gray's presence there because of some physical fear that drove me. This, however, was not the case. Why should I, a man in the prime of life, without bodily weakness or disability of any kind, have been afraid of what a madwoman might do? No, it was not that. But I freely confess that the insanity within her horrified me and sent me flying to the security of my own room as from something far more terrible than danger. The woman was a wolf! There was that about the lust of her which wanted blood. I had sensed it and I had seen it in her blazing eyes. Besides, she was daughter of a man-wolf, as she had herself confessed, and she had seen her father kill in the terrible fashion of his kind.

But over and above all this, stunning me and making it necessary that I be alone for leisure to adjust my hurt emotions, was knowledge that I had loved this girl. I had not thought, during the day, that the thing went so deep in me. One never knows such a thing until it is too late. I had loved her and, as I stood leaning against my bedroom door, panting, and striving to collect my faculties, I somehow knew that I had not lost all feeling for her merely because I had seen that I could never indulge it. Pity came slowly to me now, driving out loathing. If she was mad, yet she was not always mad. How horrible it must be for her, since I could not believe that, in her sane intervals, she would not remember the deeds of her frenzy. Yet the wild laughter that I had heard told me that she might never again be sane.

Getting a grip on myself, I opened the door and stepped out into the lighted hallway. She might do herself an injury, or she might rush out to her death somewhere in the storm. I listened, but heard nothing. Not a sound rose from below stairs. Surely some of the others in the house had heard that peal of laughter, yet the house, save as it creaked and groaned under assault of the elements, was as silent as the tomb. I wondered whether she had

climbed the stairs to her own room, which Ormes had told me
was on the third floor. A desire to know came over me. I would go
up there and listen and thus learn about it. If I heard her moving
within the room, then I could come back to my own room with
a quieter mind.

Carefully I passed Agnes's door and tiptoed up the stairs, cursing every creak and certain that my presence must be detected,
though under cover of the storm it is not likely that any listener
could have heard me. And I gained the top of the stairs without accident. No lamp burned there, though it was the custom
of the family to leave one always burning on the floor below.
Facing toward the rear of the hallway, my own room and that
of Ormond Ormes would be on the right. Instinctively, then,
I turned toward a door opening into a room just over his, supposing that his sister occupied it. I was not mistaken. The panel
stood ajar. By means of the lightning flashes, which were nearly
continuous, I could see well into the room, and though it was
beyond doubt a woman's bedroom, it appeared to be quite empty
of human presence. I pressed the door yet farther open, so that
I could insert my head and the upper portion of my body. The
bed had not been disturbed. No one was there. It was yet not
later than ten-thirty, the time of my appointment with Gray. But
that meeting had already become a thing of the past. I could not
remain there. No one, save Gray, would have forgiven me for
being there, had I been seen. Not even the excuse I had of wanting to investigate the madwoman's laughter would have been
sufficient, or so I thought.

Slowly descending the stairs, I came again in front of Agnes's
door. Was she awake? It seemed preposterous that she had not
heard the peal of furious laughter, even above the storm, and
that, having heard it, she could be so indifferent to the fate of the
laugher as to remain quietly in her bed beyond this door. Listening intently, I fancied that I heard sobbing. It might have been the
wind. No, for I caught the sound again. There was no mistaking
it this time. A woman wept in there, loudly and unrestrainedly,
though not as one weeps who is in need of a stranger's comforting. It was rather the forlorn and dismal wailing of one who
bemoaned her miserable lot, of one who cried in pity of her own

small woes. I felt my lips curl in contempt of the shallow creature
as I left her door and took my way down the last flight of stairs.

Everything was in darkness down there, as it had been when
I quitted the library. The storm's fury had suddenly abated, and
though the lightning still played on the hills, the flashes came
from a greater distance now and they were no longer so frequent.
I stood in the lower hallway for some seconds, hearing nothing of
consequence. Then I began to grope my way toward the library. I
did not want to switch on lamps. If the madwoman were a-prowl
down there, I did not want to see her until I had first become
otherwise apprised of her presence. But there was no sound to
indicate that anyone was near. In the library at last I could hear
nothing at all. I stood by the door, fumbling for the lamp which
I had been previously forbidden to light. No such coldly gentle
hand closed over mine, this time. I pulled the cord.

The room was empty. I walked softly into it, looking carefully into all the shadows and beyond the corners of the great
fireplace. No one was there. Wherever Gray Ormes had gone,
whether out into the storm or to some room not yet visited by
me, she had probably quitted the library soon after that peal of
her insane laughter had chilled my veins with terror. I retraced
my steps toward the opening. Suddenly I trod on something
and was down, sprawling on hands and knees. I searched for the
object which had caused my ankle to turn. It was a woman's slip-
per. Gray's? No doubt it was. And then a second later I saw her
crumpled silken robe, lying where she had dropped it from her
shoulders. All this did not greatly surprise or astonish me. It is
a common vagary of madness to strip the body naked. But this
evidence, added to what I had seen and heard, left within me no
doubt that Gray must be found and captured before doing herself or another some injury. I had crossed the building along the
passage, entered and left the dining room, and was in the short
hallway at the front, from which rose the stairs. Then I heard
voices outside, and knew that someone was approaching the
door. In a second I darted back through the door to the dining
room, standing there concealed in the darkness, but with the
door held partly open. Then the front door opened and two persons entered, shutting the door swiftly behind them.

"You're wet through," said a man's voice—Hobbs's. "Can I get you anything?"

"No."

I knew that the muffled word had proceeded from a woman's lips, but I had not been able to recognize the voice. Yet it could only have been either Gray Ormes or Barbara Ormes. Agnes lay weeping in her room. And Hobbs's wife would not have left him there and proceeded to mount the front stairs, as this woman was now doing. I drew back behind the door, knowing that the man must be upon me in the next second. I heard him snap the switch governing the lamp in the hallway. Then the front door opened and closed again. Had he gone again into the rain? Looking round the edge of the door, I saw that the passage was quite empty.

In an instant I was climbing the stairs after the mounting woman. Was it Gray? That question drove me to a speed sufficient to overtake her before she had reached the top of her climb. I said nothing, but she heard my footsteps behind her and halted. In the vague light from the lamp on the landing below I could just make her out. She was covered with a long coat of some dark material, and as Hobbs had said, it was wet through, for water dripped loudly from it onto the uncarpeted portion of one of the steps.

"Who's there?"

It was Gray's voice. She had not rushed naked into the storm, then. But how had Hobbs known of her absence? And how could she have visited her room, dressed in the heavy garments she was now wearing, then left the house while I stood against the door of my own chamber, struggling to regain composure after the shock of seeing her madness in the library?

"I've been looking everywhere for you," I said, lamely.

"What did you want? But I really haven't time now. Tomorrow. I'm wet to the skin, I must go and change. It was the dogs. I had to pen them."

"I was afraid . . ." I began and paused. How could I say anything of what she had so recently been to this woman who now seemed sane enough?

"Of what? Isn't everything all right?"

"Yes . . . yes, I guess so. I——"

"Then you'd better turn in. And I really must get out of these wet things."

"Yes," said I.

She turned from me, then back again.

"Good night," she said, gently. "I'm really very sorry. Please forgive me. We'll talk tomorrow."

"Yes," I said again. "Good night—Gray."

She was gone. I descended a few steps to the level of my own apartment and took my way along the hall toward it, my brain whirling again with the mystery of the woman's movements. I could not understand how she could so swiftly have regained control of herself, and I was beginning to think that it might not have been madness that had made her a vile thing before me in the library. What if, after all, she was not mad, but vicious?

So pondering, I opened my door and entered the room. Then I paused again. I remembered having left my door ajar, purposely, so that, in case of need, I could retreat into it swiftly and noiselessly. And I remembered having left my light burning. But the door had been fast shut and the single light had been turned off. The room, as I entered it, was in total darkness. Someone had been in there during my absence. I lighted the lamp again and stood beside it, listening and trying to decide on a course of action. I *might* have latched the door, or the currents of air in the rooms and passages, consequent upon the gale outside, might have sucked it shut. But I did not think so. Certainly I could not have been mistaken about the lamp, nor could that have turned out of itself. I concluded that whoever the visitor had been, it must have been the person who had been there last night and whose lips had lain against my throat.

There seemed nothing to be gained by leaving the apartment and going again a-prowl. I would undress and lie in bed, waiting for something to happen. I wondered whether I should be able to lie still in bed without falling asleep. I thought that I really needed a night's sound rest in order to clear my brain and allow me to see better, tomorrow, what I ought to do. For after Gray's revelation I had no wish to continue the pretense of making a search into the origins of New England literature, whether they might be Elizabethan or any other.

I had removed my shoes, my scarf and collar, and my shirt. Then it occurred to me that the nocturnal visitor might very well return. I did not wish to awaken in the morning with evidence of another unexplained kiss upon my throat. And if I undressed I doubted my ability to keep awake. Better to sit, fully dressed, in one of the comfortable chairs there. Then, if sleep did overcome me, at least it would not be sleep of a very sound quality. Moreover—and this had been taking shape in my brain, though not more than half consciously, during the past hour—Gray's tale of her father's mode of killing his wife and of his attempt against his sister Barbara had been so like the old legends of vampires, of which I had read many in my youth, that the kiss now carried a new and terrible implication. Had it been a woman, after all, who had kissed my throat? Or had it been Gray's father . . . the male vampire . . . the werewolf . . . the Undead . . . ?

For a long time I sat still in the chair I had chosen. So much had happened during the past twenty-four hours, and so many changes had taken place in my consciousness, that my life as I had known it up to yesterday seemed strange and remote. How long had it been since I had seen Muriel and heard her voice? It was only by an effort that I recalled having deliberately put her out of mind. I had done that when Gray came into it. And now Gray herself had become impossible. In the choppy seas of emotion that tossed my soul that night, I could steer no straight course. There was no beacon anywhere. I felt small and ineffectual and was afraid deep within myself. Tomorrow I must take leave of Ormesby, let the mad Gray plead with me as she might. If I remained here, I doubted that I myself should long retain the thing called sanity.

Slowly I became oppressed by a feeling that I was being watched. I sat very still and rigid in my chair. I listened. Yes! Yes! There was no mistake about it. Water dripped somewhere near me, as it had dripped from Gray's wet coat on the bare steps outside. I arose and went into the bathroom. It was not there. The taps were all properly shut off and dry. The little room was tiled from floor to ceiling and the floor was itself of tile. There was no opening anywhere, save the one small window, and this, when I examined it, was fast shut and locked. No water of the late rain had entered around it. I returned into the chamber, determined to sit still no longer in a chair, waiting for the dawn. I was resolved to learn how beings could enter my room and look at and kiss me without having come through the door or a window.

I had resumed my shoes and shirt. I now went to the clothes closet, which contained the third door opening into my room. There was a lamp in there, which I now lighted. The closet was about seven feet long by two in depth. There was not one suspicious thing to be seen there. The walls had been painted a light gray. They were common plastered walls. Hooks for clothing ranged completely around them, from one side of the door to the other. These hooks were empty of clothing. I had hung nothing of my own there, since I possessed no other outer garments than those I stood in and my underthings and shirts were in a drawer of the walnut bureau across the room. I was on the point of turning away. Then I saw the little pool of water on the floor. A red gleam of the light made me think, for a moment, that it was blood!

So Gray had been here! She had not removed her wet clothing, but had entered this closet in some way. That way lay toward the wall on my right—which would have been the wall on my left had I been facing the closet door from within the room proper. Under the light of the lamp I could make out a tiny stream of water leading in that direction from the pool. Well, if she could come to me that way, then I could go by the same route to her. And I would. I wanted only matches, which were to be taken from a pocket of my coat. Gray was not mad, then. Gray was as sane as I, if she was ever sane; or else she was not sane, ever, but was veritably as mad as a wolf, even when she appeared to be most rational. There was no alternative.

And yet . . . it *might* have been Hobbs. Why not? I did not like the fellow's looks. Why should he not have come here, spying upon me, even though he could not have supposed I had anything about me of value great enough to motivate an attempt at robbery? But now that I had a clue to some of the mysterious doings in this house, I was in mood to follow it to a conclusion, let it lead me whither it would.

Matches in hand I approached the wall toward the north. And

it may be well here to explain that this clothes closet had been placed in the room comparatively recently. By that I mean, it had not been originally built into either the north or the south wall of the chamber, in one or the other of which it ought naturally to have been placed. But that wall dividing the room from the hall-way had been later doubled, so that the closet lay between them. I had already observed, without having given it any thought, that my door did not open directly from hall to chamber, but gave into a short passage of not quite three feet in length. But when I had come to the north wall of the closet, I found it to be as solid as any wall could be. Then in an instant, turning about as I did to examine my whereabouts, my elbow pressed against what I had assumed to be an area of solid masonry to the eastward, but which now gave way before the pressure. What had appeared to be plaster, to a hasty glance, turned out to be no more than a curtain of heavy canvas, painted or stained to resemble the walls about it. Beyond it was a narrow passage which led away from the closet for a distance of perhaps twelve feet, as nearly as I could estimate it by the light of burning matches. It then appeared to end. But I could not be sure that it did not turn abruptly to the right, though this could not have been, since such a turning must have brought me again into my own room. The passage before me was very narrow, being barely wide enough to permit me to traverse it without sidling. And at the end of it I saw that the turn was to be made to the left, not to the right; and when I had placed my hand against a second canvas curtain there, and had darted under it, I found myself inside a second closet, similar in all essentials to the first. There was an electric lamp within it, depending by a cord from the ceiling. I turned it on, then opened the door, cautiously and half expecting to surprise my spying visitor in the room beyond.

But the room was empty. It was, moreover, almost bare of furniture, save for a green old faded carpet on the floor and for a large portrait hanging upon the wall directly before my face. That portrait seemed to be well worth examining, though I could not do so by any better light than the indirect one from within the closet. Even so, however, I saw plainly that it was the portrait of a smiling man, and I had no slightest doubt that it was the rep-

resentation of Gray's and Ormond's father. Certainly the fellow
was an Ormes. There were the same asymmetrical face, the same
curious yellow eyes, the same features, handsome and yet not
handsome, which had become somewhat blurred in Ormond's
puffy countenance, but remained clear-cut and distinct in the
younger Gray's. I cannot render a good description of the yellow
eyes. I suppose the man who painted them could not have put his
impression of them into clear wording. But he had caught with
his brush, more surely than anyone could have done it in speech,
the very look that the creature's eyes must have held in life, since
it was the look I had more than once seen tonight in his crazy
daughter's. I had no long time to devote to my examination of this
madman, this fiend who tore out the throats of helpless women
and sucked their gushing blood and fed upon their living flesh.
Just to the right of the portrait was a narrow door. I was about
to open it, thinking to find it leading into another closet, when
something about the eyes of the portrait caused me to pause.
They had followed every movement I had made in the room. So
much I had previously seen, noting it with the slight shudder one
feels upon making such a discovery in a portrait. But where they
had been yellow now they were red! I looked again. There was
no doubt of it. The light was not of the best, cut partially off, as it
was, by reason that the closet door would not fully open back to
the wall. Nevertheless it was quite sufficient for me to see that the
color of the eyes in that portrait had changed—unless I had been
mistaken in thinking them yellow upon first seeing them. And I
did not think I had been mistaken. But that was by no means all!
As I stared fixedly at those red and reddening eyes, I grew conscious that they were alive! They moved, at least, and they stared
down upon me with a malignity that surely was more, or less,
than human. I felt my blood growing cold beneath it. My impulse
was to turn back along the way I had come, seeking the safety of
my own room, which would at least hold me concealed from that
vindictive hate. Unless . . . unless it had been this stare that I had
felt upon me as I sat in the chair in my room . . .

  Yet to my own credit be it said, I did not give way to that impulse. I struggled with my terror and overcame it to the extent of
dashing to the narrow door I have mentioned and wrenching it

open. I had come so far; I was not going to be turned back until I had explored this secret means of communication to its end. At my feet was a flight of winding metal stairs. The blackness down there was absolute. I lighted another match and peered down into it. Need I say that I hesitated? that I dreaded going into that yawning silent darkness? Yet the spirit of the chase was in my blood. I had set out to learn the secret of how the person who had kissed my throat had gained access to me, and I had learned it. That mystery had been dispelled. Now it appeared that I might be upon the heels of something more. I went down the winding stairs—they were of wrought iron, and the brick walls had been built around them—until I came to the bottom. There was another door there. It also was very narrow, of unpainted pine boards, and it hung upon hinges that allowed it to swing in either direction past its frame. It was unfastened; indeed, there was no catch anywhere wherewith to fasten it. Passing through it my match went out, and I had some difficulty in striking another. At last I had a light. Then I knew that I had solved the mystery of the disappearance of the Lady in Mauve.

For I had entered the library and I was in a passage that ran straight toward the fireplace in the middle of the north wall of that great room. On my right, as I stood there, were the fixed bookshelves, which were not here so deep as to reach quite back to the wall, as they appeared to do from the front. And so the Lady had been, after all, a mortal woman, and she had entered this passage through the panel which I now plainly made out before me. It opened to my pressure on a handle of wrought iron, sliding quite noiselessly toward the fireplace for a distance of what I judged to be just one foot. I stepped into the opening, intent on learning how the panel could be operated from the other side. Then I started swiftly back, dragging the door to behind me with all the force of which I was capable.

A lamp in the library had been lighted just before my face. And I had seen the most horrible sight I had ever looked upon. Gray Ormes stood there, facing the panel, distant from it not above five feet. She was entirely naked. Her hair was unbound and it was tumbled wildly over her face and shoulders and matted heavily against her breasts. From head to foot she glistened filthily with sweat or with water, I could not tell which. Her eyes were not human. Her face was no longer anything but the face of a brute. In that instant I had seen that her eyes were red with the unholy fire of a wolf's eyes—or of those of the portrait on the wall upstairs—and that her face was writhen and twisted out of all semblance to humanity. The wide and heavy mouth was covered with blood, which had flowed in thin streams from the corners of it, dripping into the already matted hair upon the breasts. And when I stepped into the opening, she flung her dripping arms out toward me and burst into such laughter as I pray that I shall never hear again this side the grave.

I turned and ran, though I have no memory of doing so. It was the second time that night I had run from this mad Thing. Somehow I gained past the portrait, the eyes of which bored into my back as I crossed that chamber. I darted through the closets and the passage and into my room. I was just in time! Sickness overwhelmed me almost before I could come to my bathroom.

For I knew that the woman I had looked upon was not bleeding from any wound of her own. She had been gorging herself on living flesh and blood!

VII

What a fine thing it would be if one could act as reason tells him he should have acted—reason in retrospect! I might have done so many brave things that night. I might have flung myself upon the madwoman, overpowered her, and carried her, in spite of struggling, to her own room, locking her within it. I might have aroused the servants to help me subdue her. I might even have telephoned for the police. I did none of those things. When my nausea had in some part abated, I went and lay down across my bed, waiting for something of calm to return to my nerves and something of courage to my heart. That action must be taken, and that without much delay, I knew well enough. But I was not yet ready for action. And today, looking backward, I am not at all sure that my inaction did not prove to be as wise, in the end, as anything I could have done immediately.

But an insane person was at large in the house. Someone had already suffered as her victim. Something must be done to curb her frenzy before another, perhaps a greater, crime should have been perpetrated. I arose from off my bed and went out into the hallway, where I stood, as I had so often stood that night, listening for a sound to inform me of what went on. The motion cleared my dazed head somewhat. Gradually I realized that someone in that house had been hurt, that I must investigate the matter at once, since I perhaps was the only inmate of the place, not counting Gray, who knew of it. Moreover, if someone had been killed, then I did not purpose to lend myself to any such hugger-mugger burial as had taken place in the case of that elder Ormes and the wife whom he had butchered with his teeth.

The light at the head of the staircase burned steadily. No sound disturbed the stillness of the house and of the night outside; stillness that had succeeded to the storm. I tiptoed to Agnes's door and bent my ear against it, assuring myself that I had heard her regular and quiet breathing. Then I went softly to that door which Ormes had indicated as opening into his aunt's chamber. Listening there, I could at first hear nothing. But then I caught a faint sobbing and moaning. Was the aunt weeping now, as Agnes had wept earlier that night? There was no doubt that I had heard a sound, but now I knew that it was not a sound of weeping. Behind the door a woman moaned in pain, or in mortal terror. I knocked loudly, careless of who might hear. There was no reply from within. I turned the handle of the door. It opened, and I saw that the chamber was in darkness. But now, from one corner of it, I plainly heard the gasping and groaning of a human being. I groped for the button of the electric switch, found it and pressed it. A lamp in the ceiling flung out its swift white light. And away in one corner of the sparsely furnished room, huddled upon a wretched pallet that seemed to have been made of dirty blankets over a heap of straw, was the blood-stained body of a woman. It was Alice Hobbs.

She was yet alive, though not conscious. Her throat had been severely torn, but the blood did not leap from the wounds as it must have done had an artery or one of the jugular veins been severed. I judged that her fainting condition had been induced by

shock and fright as much as by the ragged gashes in her throat.
For even with my first glance I had seen, though I was no physician, that her throat had been torn open as if by teeth, not cut by
any keen instrument.

This, then, was Gray's victim. She had pitched upon this poor
servant, who had been privy to so much of horror already in that
house of fear. Alice Hobbs, who had known of the manner in
which the elder Ormes had killed his wife and sought to kill his
sister, now lay before me, wounded and bleeding from an attack
by that man-wolf's crazed and blood-hungry daughter.

But I did not believe that her life was in any immediate danger.
And I do believe that I said a silent prayer of thankfulness that
Gray had not succeeded in murdering her. But where was Hobbs,
her husband? Why had he not known of this thing?

All this passed through my mind during the second or so that
I knelt at the woman's side, examining the superficial wound in
her neck and making sure that her half-naked body was not otherwise injured. It appeared not to be, save for some long jagged
scratches on her arms and shoulders.

Then I leaped to my feet and ran to Agnes's room. I knocked,
but I did not wait for her to awaken out of sleep and ask my business. I opened the door and entered. Alone as I was in the house,
save for Hobbs, with these mad and merely silly women, I knew
that I dared take more seeming liberties without reproof than if
there had been another man present. So I entered Agnes Ormes's
room and approached her bed, grasping her by a shoulder and
shaking her roughly out of sleep. She sat up in the bed, raising
her arms so that the filmy nightgown fell away from them and
from her throat, and she would have screamed had I not clapped
a hand swiftly across her mouth.

"It's I, Seaverns. Hush! You must get up and come with me to
the back room . . . yonder. Someone's been hurt. I don't think the
servants ought to know. Miss Gray——"

"Gray?" She was blinking rapidly and striving to grasp the
import of what I was telling her. "Gray hurt? Huh? No? Barbara
hurt? Call Gray at once!"

It appeared that, hate the girl as she might, even Agnes turned
to her in emergencies.

"Don't you understand? Gray's . . . it was Gray that hurt her. Get out of bed. Hurry! Don't take time to dress."

I left her and went back into the hall, waiting outside the door for her to join me. In a couple of seconds she did so, drawing a silk kimono over her shoulders as she came. But when we had entered the miserable room in which the sufferer lay and she had seen the bloody blankets and the torn flesh, I was sorry that I had not allowed this useless creature to sleep on, summoning another to my aid in her place.

"Oh, my God! Oh, my God!" she muttered, standing several feet away from the wounded woman and lifting up her huge white arms in what I suppose she assumed to be an effectively dramatic gesture.

"Come on, help me with her," I ordered. "We must get her out of here and into a decent bed. How'd she come to be here?"

"Gray," whimpered Agnes. "I'll go get Gray."

"Don't you understand?" I demanded, roughly, seizing her wrist and shaking her as I might have been tempted to shake a refractory child. "It was Gray who did this. Gray's crazy, insane, blood mad. Leave her out of it. We'll be lucky if we can keep her quiet till daylight. Then I'll fetch the authorities and have her taken away. But get busy, you! Fetch me some towels, bandages, disinfectants and clean water. Hurry! Or tell me where to find 'em."

She stared at me with foolish, puzzled, frightened eyes, in which, to my utter disgust a cunning light of feminine submission began to dawn. Then she nodded, seeming at last to comprehend, and I released her wrist. She raised her hand, let it fall downward along my arm, turned and ran out of the room. And at that moment, with the suddenness of eternity, a dog screamed beneath the window of the room and all hell broke loose among the rest of the savage pack. Gray had told me that she had kenneled them during the storm. Now they were abroad again.

I challenge any man, however steady and strong his nerves, to hear outside the house in which he is, at dead of night, the brutal noise of fighting or coursing dogs or wolves and not experience a shudder and a thrill of terror at the sound. It is not that

we are not accustomed to such a noise. On the contrary, we are so
well accustomed to it—we know it so very deep within us—that
the emotion cannot be repressed. Thousands of generations of
our ancestors heard it nightly, cowering the closer to their fires
and huddling the farther into their sheltering caverns. Fear of
the wolf is bred into the very fibres of our being. We have not
been long enough away from him to have outgrown the terror
of his voice. And those dogs of Ormesby, hunting in pack, were
scarcely to be distinguished from wolves.

Suddenly the man Hobbs stood in the doorway, in his trousers
and with his night-shirt tucked loosely and hastily into them. He
said nothing, but stood staring at the unconscious woman. Then
he shifted his narrow eyes and met mine for a moment. Not a
muscle moved in his face.

"Do something!" I ordered. "Call a doctor. Fetch water and
bandages. She's been hurt."

"Yes!"

He turned and vanished beyond the frame of the door. For all
the astonishment betrayed by his manner and tone, this sort of
thing might have happened many times at Ormesby during the
course of his service there. The noise of the dogs outside came
now from a point behind the house and farther away from it. I
speculated on whether one of their number had been killed and
torn to pieces by the others, with the pack now snarling and fighting over the bloody remnants of his carcass. A groan, louder than
the rest, drew my attention back to the sufferer on that wretched
bed. I knelt beside her, straightening her arms and smoothing the
long hair from her pallid face. Presently she opened her eyes, staring at me with no sign of recognition in them, but also without
sign of fear. She moved her jaw to speak. This hurt her, evidently,
for she made a quick grimace and clutched involuntarily at her
throat. I slipped one hand beneath her head, striving with the
other to form a pillow of the tumbled blankets. And then she
spoke.

"Gray's . . ." she began, apparently unable to proceed at once.

I soothed her. Until some of the others came with bandages
and ointment, I did not know what I ought to do. I could have
lifted her and carried her to her own bed, but since she was not

suffering great pain, I wanted witnesses to my actions. Too many unexplained things had happened, and continued to happen, in that house.

"She's not here," I said. "Don't be afraid. We won't let her hurt you again."

Mumbling such comforts, I supported the woman's head and stroked her brows, thinking that she, too, must have been abroad that night, else Hobbs could have saved her from this.

Hobbs came back, almost before I supposed he had had time to gather the things he brought. Quietly and efficiently he knelt beside me, then brushed me unceremoniously aside as he prepared to bathe the torn throat and give it a first-aid treatment. He had bottles of disinfectant, some of which he poured on cotton and swabbed with this the deeper gashes. Apparently my surmise had been correct: none of the wounds was of a serious nature, for the bleeding had already ceased of itself. Then he straightened.

"Help me carry her to our room," he ordered. "We'll bathe her throat again and dress it when she's out of this."

Obediently I took hold of her by the shoulders, while Hobbs lifted the feet. He nodded toward the door and I backed out of it and started along the hallway toward the front of the house.

"Not that way!" he barked.

I had not liked Hobbs's face; his expression of crafty secretiveness and his nasal twang had alike made me distrust the fellow. But if a man must be a servant, then give me that servant who can, upon occasion, exercise the authority of a man who knows what ought to be done and how to do it. I began thinking that Hobbs might prove to be the Admirable Crichton of the difficult situation that was enfolding all of us.

"Where's your room?" I asked.

"Quite at the back—over the kitchen."

"Where is Miss Barbara's room?"

"Just opposite your own."

"Why, then, did Ormes tell me it lay toward the rear of the house?"

"I'm sure I don't know," said Hobbs, drily.

"Who uses the room where I found your wife?"

"No one. It's—it's unoccupied."

He was lying, and I knew it. Someone occupied the room we
had quitted. The filthy pallet in the corner was used. It came to
me that it was used by Gray during her frenzies. If Ormes had
wanted me to keep away from that room, how could he have
supposed that I should remain long in ignorance of his sister's
madness? I concluded that he had been ashamed to speak of it,
leaving me to learn for myself such secrets as I might.

But we had come to Hobbs's door and flung it open. I saw that
the room we were entering was worthy of civilized occupancy.
It was unquestionably a servant's room, however, for the menial
touch was everywhere. The deep bed under a window had been
slept in that very night. We laid the patient upon it and I turned
away toward another window, listening to the still-fighting dogs,
though the noise was fainter now and came from a point well up
the mountain side to the north. Hobbs again busied himself with
the woman's hurts, while I waited by the window, momentarily
expecting him to ask or order me to help him in some particular.
At last I heard someone approaching along the corridor.

It was Agnes Ormes. She had accoutred herself in a nurse's
white apron and cap, and she now affected an air of quiet impor-
tance that did not blind me to her utter lack of any knowledge of
what to do. She came into the room and moved about it, picking
up articles and laying them in different places, making a pretense of bustle while accomplishing nothing. I was thoroughly
disgusted. She went to the bed and bent over the sufferer, and I
heard her mutter something like "down in a minute" to Hobbs.

"I'm going to call a doctor," I announced. "Can you give me a
name and telephone number?"

"You'd better call Doctor Barnes," Agnes said, first looking at
me with hostility in her eyes, then allowing her face to relax in
such a smile as was a recurrence of her previous attitude of submission. "Tiltown 77."

I nodded and left the room. It seemed to me that I must call
Ormes himself on the telephone as soon as I had reason to think
he might have reached his office. I did not know where he lived
in town, and I did not want to ask that information of his wife.
It was not that I thought his help necessary for Alice Hobbs, but
that action must be immediately taken with regard to Gray. Inter-

mittent though her fits of insanity might be, it seemed to me that they were becoming far too dangerous to permit of her being left at large. And I could scarcely order her into custody of the police or other authorities without her brother's consent. I would as soon have depended upon a child's judgment as upon that of Agnes Ormes.

It was nearly four o'clock. Dawn was in the eastern sky, though the house itself, hidden behind the surrounding hills, lay yet in a pool of deep darkness. The moon had set. I went to the telephone in the hall downstairs and called Doctor Barnes, telling him that Mrs. Hobbs had been bitten by one of the dogs. He responded sleepily, mumbled something about this being the second time that someone at Ormesby had been mauled by one of the brutes, and said he would drive up as soon as possible. Then I went into the dining room and poured myself a stiff drink of whiskey.

I was turning over in mind the possibility that it might already be too late to call Ormond Ormes for advice in the matter of his sister's confinement. She had not been seen about the house since I had encountered her, naked and bloodstained, in the library. What if she had rushed again out into the storm, had released the pack, and had been dragged down? It seemed to me that I must determine this matter before calling my employer.

I was still in the dining-room when Hobbs entered. Seeing me, he made as if to pass through and into the kitchen. But I had guessed his purpose there. His nerves were probably as much in need of sedatives as mine were.

"Come here, Hobbs," I said to him. "Take a drink, man. You need it, by the look of you."

He poured a drink, his hand shaking slightly, though he controlled his facial muscles as well as he had been able to control them in the room upstairs.

"How's your wife?"

"Better, sir, I hope. She—she can't stand the sight of suffering, sir."

"The sight of it? But it's she who——"

"I mean, sir, the sight of—of illness in others."

Suddenly I understood that he referred to Gray's malady.

"Then she ought not to live in such a house as this," I said, sharply. "But why did she leave your room? To help ... well, to help anyone?"

"She says she thought she heard Miss Barbara call. I was asleep, sir."

"Barbara, eh? I wonder ... But never mind now. I'm going to telephone Mr. Ormes, Hobbs, as soon as it's possible. Meanwhile there's a woman who may be inside this house, but I've reason to think she may be outside. You heard the dogs. You helped to pen them, didn't you?"

He nodded.

"Well, what do you think?"

"I'm afraid, sir, you may be right."

His answer made no sense, strictly speaking, yet I understood him.

"Take another drink," I directed, "and give me one."

He did so. Not looking at me, he drank. I swallowed my portion, then set the glass down on the sideboard. At once he removed it, snatching up a napkin to wipe from the polished board such drops of liquor as might have been clinging to the bottom of the glass. It was apparent that he had laid aside his authority and resumed his servant's coat. But I had somehow gained a feeling that, for all his evil squint, I could trust Hobbs rather further than many a man can be trusted; and I did not want him to be too servile. It would render difficult such questions as I meant later to put to him and such advice as I might wish to ask.

"Do you suppose, Hobbs," I said, trying to catch his eyes, "that the ... damned dogs out there were howling and fighting over ... over anything ... human?"

"I don't know, sir," he replied, after staring at me for a second. "I—I hope they weren't, God knows!"

"Then I'll go out and find out about it," said I. "But those brutes will tear me to pieces if they can. Have you a good whip and a gun?"

"Yes, sir. I'll fetch them to you, sir. You'll need a torch, too."

He went swiftly out of the room.

VIII

Before going outside, however, I intended retracing my way through the secret passages I had discovered, convinced that I ought to explore farther that one which ran back of the great bookcases in the library. It had appeared to end against the stone wall forming part of the chimney, but I had already discovered that these apparent endings resulted, after a turn at right angles, in a continuation of the mysterious way. I did not think the builder of it had wanted merely to construct a means of going unobserved from the library to the bedroom which now chanced to be occupied by myself.

Hobbs, the efficient one, returned to me after a minute or two. He carried a flashlight, a revolver of thirty-two calibre, and a dog whip. I made sure that the revolver was fully loaded.

"I've telephoned for Doctor Barnes," I told him. "Perhaps you'd better complete your dressing. I don't think there'll be any sleep for anyone in this house the rest of the night. Also, I've told the doctor that your wife was hurt by one of the dogs. Maybe you'd better post her, so she'll be able to confirm that story."

"Yes, sir. I'll go to her at once, sir."

"Now I'm going out. If you hear firing, you'd better look around for me. Those dogs may get me treed, and there are only six bullets in this thing. I'm sure to waste five of 'em. I'm not a dead shot."

"Yes, sir. Very well, sir."

I left the fellow standing there. He had seemed to be human enough while working with me over the wounded woman upstairs. Later, when drinking with me to steady our nerves, he had shown an ability to assume equality in rank. Now he had relapsed into the automaton, seeing nothing and everything, hearing naught save all matters and things he might later be called upon to remember, and speaking nothing not set down in the book from which he had learned his servant's etiquette.

I went back to my own room, since I did not possess the secret of opening the panel from the library side. Passing Agnes's door, I saw that it was fast closed. I heard someone moving within the room, concluding that Agnes was probably trying, in her futile way, to find accessories to her nurse's uniform. She was the kind to suppose that nothing could be done without the proper dress. Then I heard voices in the room farther back, that opposite my own, from which I judged that Barbara was awake and being put in possession of the events of the night, probably by Gray. I could do nothing to help, so I did not disturb them. Doctor Barnes ought to be arriving very shortly. Through the windows of my own room I saw that the mountain tops were burning with liquid gold.

It was but the work of a minute or two to follow the passages to the point where the panel gave into the library. I resolutely endeavored to keep my eyes from those of the portrait, as I passed it, but I was obliged to glance into them, nevertheless; and in the beam of my torch I fancied they were not less malevolent than when I had first discovered them following me about the room. But I tore my gaze away and descended the winding stairs. I came to the chimney and, as I had supposed would be the case, found there a turn to the right. Moreover, there were more iron steps before me, and I say that they wound about the great chimney and led downward into the earth. Was the mad woman I sought crouching somewhere below me?

Holding the flashlight in my left hand and the whip ready in my right, I descended the flight, which wound to my right as I went. When I had counted twenty-one steps, I had come to a point directly under the topmost tread. But the stairs continued downward around the chimney. I waited, listening, but heard nothing. Cautiously I advanced my foot and began this further descent.

The foundations of the big chimney must have been sunk very deep into the detritus on which this house was built, or so I was thinking at the moment. I had descended a total of thirty-eight steps. There were no more. I found myself in a little space of perhaps five feet by ten, with a cement ceiling about five feet from the floor. The room, or area, had been dug out of the clay or gravel composing the surrounding earth, and it had been walled on all sides with cut granite. And into the rounded wall of masonry which made up the foundation of the chimney, I saw that through the angle formed by the ceiling and one of the walls of this room plunged a great pipe of wrought iron, at least two feet in diameter, cutting diagonally across and into the masonry of the well. That well might have been a huge cistern. I reasoned that it must once have been a cistern, constructed for the retention of rain water. The iron pipe must have been the conduit which drained water from the roofs into the well. Later, with the erection of the chimney above it, consequent upon construction of the library, use of the cistern had been discontinued—probably—and its walls utilized for the chimney's foundations. It subsequently developed that my surmise was a good one. But why had the staircase been twisted about the well? What was the purpose of this little room at the bottom? Why should expensive iron steps have been installed to let members of the household reach so insignificant a room as I now stood in? I threw the light of my torch over all surfaces without discovering anything to serve me as a clew for the answering of those questions. Yet I was convinced that the answer had a very definite bearing on more than one of the mysterious happenings in the house above.

It was plain that the woman I sought was not here. I must go outside to find her, after all.

But she had been here!

Just as I was about to begin my ascent of the stairs, I saw on the wall to my left, that is, on a wall of the well, a mark which caused me to train the beam of my flashlight directly upon it. It stood at a height of about five feet from the ground. It was a mere smudge on the gray stone. Perhaps, after all, it was nothing.

But when I had examined it with more care, I made out that it was the mark of a human mouth. And that mouth had been wet with blood when the lips had been crushed against this wall!

All the more, now, I wanted to find Gray Ormes. In the first place, the scream I had heard just before the dogs raised their hellish clamor outside had come to my ears as the cry of a beast in pain; but it might very well have sprung in that bestial manner from some tortured human throat. If it had, then I did not suppose that the insane creature I hunted was still a living being. It might very well have been her scream. Yet, on the other hand, if it had been a beast's cry, she must have set the ferocious dogs on to the attack of one of their own number, or of some other helpless animal. Even (it was possible) to the dragging down of another human being. In any event, I told myself, the woman was crazy and at large; and she must be found and confined before she could do more evil.

I wondered, for an instant, whether Doctor Barnes, when he arrived, could be hoodwinked into supposing that the ragged wounds on Alice Hobbs's neck had been made by the clean, sharp teeth of a dog. But as I remember back upon the events of that night and of the emotions which swayed my actions, I think that my predominant reason for wanting to find Gray before harm came to her and before anyone else could find her was one of pity. It had been only last evening, before she came to me in the library, that I was revolving dreams of love for her. The madness of which she was victim was an inherited madness, for which she could in no least wise be blamed. Surely, for all my loathing of her deeds and for all the horror with which the sight of her had inspired me, standing as she had before that panel and reaching out her dripping arms to embrace me, surely the tenderness I had yesterday felt could excuse my present wish to shield her, even from herself.

I climbed to the passage leading away from the chimney and came to the panel between the passage and the library. Pulling it aside, by means of the handle, I stepped through it, carefully playing the beam of my torch ahead of me, since the interior of the house was only beginning to be lightened by the day outside. There appeared to be no one in the room. Then I turned to examine the panel itself, striving to learn the secret of opening it from the side on which I now stood. I spent some minutes at the task. The bookshelves slid sidewise with the panel—so much was plain. They had been very carefully cut and fitted, so as to move in grooves in the shelves to the right—I mean, of course, the permanent shelves to the right. It was evident, however, that the panel itself could not have been moved to the right had the shelves it carried on its face been loaded with books. That accounted for the fact that they held only a few books at the present time, and

those volumes had been thrown down onto their sides by movement of the sliding shelves. As I have previously said, the opening
was just a foot in width. But I could not discover the lever or other
agency by which the thing could be moved, once it was closed,
and I was losing valuable time from my search If Gray had been
killed by those dogs, I wanted to find her body—or what should
be left of it—before strangers arrived on the scene. I was about to
turn away, toward the door through which one might gain into
the dining room. A tiny sound held me.

It was a slight swishing, as of silken garments. My Lady in
Mauve? But I could see no one. Then I thrust my head through
the opening in the shelves and threw the beam of my flashlight
along the passage.

The Lady in Mauve stood before me, just at the head of the
iron steps!

Straight into the glare of my torch she looked. Her eyes did
not blink. Not a muscle (if ghosts have muscles!) moved in that
lovely face.

Suddenly, from my nerveless fingers, the torch fell with a thud
to the floor. The light disappeared. I remained in semi-darkness.
I bent swiftly, groping over the floor for the flashlight. I spent several seconds finding it. And when I had secured it, and had again
spread its light along the passage, the Lady had disappeared.

Had she passed me? For she had seemed to be coming toward
the little unpainted pine door when stopped by the light I had
caught her in. Or had she gone down the stairs?

I would follow her! Somehow, I was not afraid of this beautiful creature. I ran into the passage and along it. At the top of the
stairs I paused. Fear came upon me for a single moment. But I
mastered it. Slowly, deliberately, I went down the stairs until I had
come, at last, to the foot of them.

The little room down there was absolutely empty.

Moreover, now I thought of it, the little room had been empty
during the time of my first visit to it. *Yet a few minutes later, while
I still examined the panel, upstairs, the Lady in Mauve had come to the
passage. And she could only have come there from this little room.*

But though I carefully examined every square inch of the
masonry about me, some of which had been coated with cement,

some of which was of gray granite, and some of which was brick-work, I could find no slightest evidence of an opening anywhere. I had concluded, upon finding the passage back of the library, that the Lady in Mauve had been a flesh-and-blood woman, after all. Had that conclusion been too hastily made? Might not a ghost have made use of the opening I had lately been examining?

Thinking of such things, I slowly climbed back to the top of the stairs. It was no less imperative that I go outside and search for Gray Ormes. I must leave the mystery of how the Lady had come up those stairs behind me until a later time. Therefore I left the library, went to the front door of the house and let myself out, carefully springing the lock so that I should be able to enter again without ringing the bell.

The black darkness about the house was now much diluted by light from over the eastern peaks. Shadows under the trees were still very heavy. But after a few moments my eyes had become sufficiently accustomed to their surroundings to make out objects with fair distinctness to a distance of forty or fifty feet. I heard nothing of the pack. Very quietly I slipped away from the door and took my way around a corner of the house leading towards that wing containing the library. I carried the whip in my left hand, having made sure that the little revolver was in a handy pocket. But if the dogs at Ormesby were depended upon to keep away prowling men, they might as well have been dispensed with, or so I thought at the moment. I continued without molestation around the long wing and came to a stand well to the rear of the place. Back of me rose the trees, becoming more abundant as they moved uphill from the grounds. And then, far away, and coming rapidly toward me, I heard the barking and baying of the entire wolfish pack.

I looked swiftly about for some place of safety. I did not want to retreat into the house, nor did I wish to climb into a tree and sit there helplessly. The only other thing offering shelter was the garage, and I ran for it. I had not more than two hundred feet to go, but before I had covered the distance the leading dogs had gained almost upon me. How they had learned of my presence in the grounds I do not know; probably their sense of smell had told them that a stranger was abroad, or their preternaturally keen sense of hearing had informed them. Whatever the means, my estimate of their watchfulness was vastly augmented during the few seconds I needed to run to the garage door, fling it back on its rails and enter, barely in time to escape the rush of three big brutes which hurled their bodies against the door even as I was closing it. I was safe enough, but I might just as well have remained within the house. In the house I had at least learned something —I had explored the secret passage from end to end. Now I could only sit quiet and wait for Hobbs to call the dogs away, unless I fired my revolver and brought him sooner than he might otherwise be expected to come looking for me. And I did not want to do that. Since I had found no traces of Gray's body, though, it must be admitted, I had not searched either very far or very diligently for it, it might be that she had not been harmed. If that were the case, then she would probably hear the shot and come herself to investigate. I dreaded seeing her again, even though she might be quite sane now. I had loved the girl too recently to be yet wholly healed of the hurt her madness had given. Meanwhile I could amuse myself by an examination of the cars in the place. Yesterday, when I had been in there, I had been too preoccupied to see more than the coupé I had received permission to use.

There were three cars. A large, expensive sport roadster I assumed to belong to Agnes, since she had told me of possessing a new motor, which she was not pleased with. There was the coupé I had yesterday driven. And there was a small sedan of cheap make which I took, from its somewhat battered and disreputable appearance, to be devoted to use of the servants. There was a large work bench running the length of the building at one side. This was covered with tools, pots of grease, worn-out inner tubes, all the odds and ends that accumulate about such places. I was in no wise interested in the articles I was seeing by aid of my flashlight. But my mind was busy with the problem of what was to be done with Gray. It was not my problem to solve, and yet I worried over it as much as if it had been. If she were sane today, how could I face her, how could anyone face her, and demand that she leave Ormesby for confinement in some institution where, in her next outbreak of frenzy, she could do no one any harm? It would be like striking her across the face. I didn't see how it was to be accomplished, by myself or by another. And I continued for several minutes to gaze carefully at this small tool broken and at that gearing, hardly conscious of what I was seeing. It was in this way, however, that I came, quite by accident, upon the blood-stained stockings.

I thought at the first that they were dirty rags which had been used for wiping one of the cars. But they were tan silk stockings, a woman's, of sheerest weave, and I noticed—by the merest accident, as I said—that they bore blood stains. More than that, the blood upon them was fresh. It had not yet lost its bright red color. Someone had thrown those stockings upon the bench within the period of but fifteen or twenty minutes before I entered the place.

But where had that person gone? If it were a woman, where had she gone after leaving her stockings here? How came they to be blood-stained? More than that, how came one of them to be soaked in blood to the knee? The blood was fresh. I did not think, upon reflection, that a man had left them there. I was thinking of Gray Ormes. She had been quite naked when I last saw her, but of course she had had ample time in which to resume her clothing. Still, she had not worn stockings during our meeting the previous evening. If she had dressed, then, it must have been in other clothes than those she had discarded in the library. Her frenzy might have passed. It could not, then, have been her scream I had heard among the dogs. But whose blood was I now looking at as I dangled one of the silken things from a finger?

One thing seemed self-evident now. If this was a further trace of Gray's work, then, be it as difficult as it might be, she must be taken away from Ormsby and confined somewhere in safety. These fits of fury were recurring too frequently. Surely she must have been placed in an asylum before this if they had attacked her so often in the past. No, I could not help thinking that she might have become permanently deranged. I must get back into the house, somehow, obtain Ormond's address from Hobbs, perhaps, and call him on the telephone. After that I ought to be leaving the place, though I did not resolve to leave before Ormes's arrival.

A small sound disturbed me. The dogs outside had withdrawn

and it was not a sound made by one of them. I do not know why it attracted my attention, save that, with the ear for mechanical maladjustment which seems to have become the normal heritage of my generation of Americans, I supposed that one of the cars leaked oil. I wondered which one it was, idly thinking that I must mention the matter to Hobbs, so that he could remedy it or have it looked after by a professional mechanic. Moreover, tense as I was from discovery of the stockings, and weary with my night's adventures, I caught at small happenings and fixed my attention upon them to save my nerves from snapping. I listened. There was no doubt of it. Oil, or some other liquid, dripped onto the concrete floor in the neighborhood of one of the cars. So then I stooped far enough forward to follow with my eyes the beam of the torch; and under the coupé I saw what it was. Something dark dripped from the body of that machine.

But it was not oil. Even with my first glance at it, I knew it was not oil. It was blood.

So knowing, I surmised that I had come upon the object of my search. I steeled myself to look through the window of the car door. Gray would be there, probably she had killed herself. Perhaps, regaining sanity and remembering something of what she had done, she had fled here and slain herself to escape the horror of living in her own body. Slowly I approached the car. I hated to look. Yet it must be done. And now I would do it.

The corpse in the car, however, was not Gray's. It was that of Agnes Ormes.

But I had left Agnes in her own room, as I passed it, not half an hour since. I had plainly heard some person moving within that room. It might have been someone else, but I had seemed to recognize the sounds as having been made by the ineffectual Mrs. Ormes. We habitually recognize sound in this way, though, when put to it, we are at a loss to explain why we have so recognized it. Also, I had heard voices in Barbara's room. Had Agnes come here while I explored the little room at the foot of the winding iron stairs? Had she been here longer than that? I could not answer those questions. But the fact that I was looking upon her body appeared to prove that Gray had not returned to the house.

Agnes was quite dead. Her throat had been cut, deeply and

with a very sharp instrument, for the head was all but severed.
And it was not her stockings I had found on the bench. Agnes
had come or had been brought here wearing the clothing she had
worn when I last looked upon her in her life. That had been a
nurse's white apron and cap, with black stockings and with black
shoes. I very well remembered the stockings. When she had risen
from her bed to go with me to Mrs. Hobbs's aid as she lay in the
miserable little room, I had seen her legs from ankle to calf under
her thin dressing gown, and I had then noticed, idly and without
giving the small matter any attention, for I was not interested in
Mrs. Ormes's body, that her calves were more hairy than a woman's usually are. Therefore, when I later saw her in the Hobbses'
room, my eyes had wandered of themselves to rest upon her
lower legs, and the black silk stockings had then caught my attention, perhaps because one sees them so seldom nowadays.

But the most horrifying thing was the discovery, which I immediately made, that the woman's throat had been first slashed
with a sharp knife, probably a razor, and then torn farther open as
if by the insertion of fingers into the gaping wound. Also, it had
been gnawed!

There was no doubt of it. I had seen flesh gnawed by dogs,
and I had recently seen the throat of Alice Hobbs. Gray had been
here. Gray must be still abroad.

There was no blood on the outside of the car, save a great
splotch of it across the nickeled handle of the door. But now,
looking closely, I saw that drops of it led to the bench where I
had found the stockings. The murderess had wiped her hands
on the silken things. Probably they had been already lying there.
They need not have been Gray's; at least, they need not recently
have been upon her legs. The interior of the car was splashed and
soaked with blood, as, naturally, it must have been. I judged that
Agnes had been killed after entering the car. Perhaps she had intended driving to the village for something, maybe for something
needed by the patient upstairs. Perhaps she intended driving the
coupé because she did not like driving her own new machine. A
great pool of blood lay on the rubber mat beneath her feet, and it
was from this pool that the dripping came. There were the marks
of bloody hands on the victim's face and on one shoulder and on

one wrist. There were other bloody finger and palm prints here and there over the white nurse's uniform. I thought that no further evidence was needed to direct the searchers for the woman's murderer. I myself, though I am no criminologist, saw plainly that those marks had been made there by a female hand.

I opened the door of the garage and looked out. The dogs had gone away and left me alone, apparently having made up their canine minds that they had no chance of getting at my legs and throat. And that, too, was a strange thing, when I considered it. Surely the brutes must have smelled the fresh blood spilled inside that little building. Why had they not lingered in the close vicinity of it? Why had they not tried frantically to force a way within it? It could only have been that Gray had been outside and had called them away. I did not think that they would have obeyed Hobbs, considering the conditions.

But now they were not in sight and I could hear nothing of them. Nevertheless, knowing how swiftly they could cover distance about these grounds, I paused for some seconds, carefully taking note of every accident of the ground over which I must run to gain the front door of the house. It was broad day, now. The sunlight had crept over the peaks and down the sides of them, so that the level on which Ormsby stood was bathed in its early splendor. I gathered myself to leap out, drag the door shut behind me, then dart for the house.

In that moment a car left the screening of a clump of trees between the house and the end of the Ormsby drive, swept up the drive as if its occupants were in great haste, and was brought to a stop before the door, a stop made so suddenly that all four wheels were locked by the brakes and dragged screeching along the gravel. Doctor Barnes, I thought, must be in more haste now than his sleepy response to my call would have allowed anyone to suppose he would be. Maybe I ought to call out to him to come into the garage and be witness to the thing I had discovered. Mrs. Hobbs's condition did not necessitate his immediate presence. I was just opening my mouth to shout his name, seeing him emerge from the car on its left-hand side, it having been stopped with its rear toward me.

But I did not call out. The man who left that car on the left-hand side and walked swiftly behind it was not Doctor Barnes, though I had never seen the good doctor. It was Ormond Ormes. And he opened the door on the right-hand side and assisted a woman to alight. She was muffled in a coat the collar of which came well up over her face, while the rest of it covered her body to the knees. So I did not call out to Ormes, nor did I leave the garage at once, as I had fully meant to do.

My reason for staying where I was, with a recently murdered woman behind me, was purely a personal one. Some may even think it a foolish one. It is not for me to judge of that. I know only that the woman who had alighted from the motor car which Ormond Ormes had driven, and who was now entering his house with him, was the woman who had been, until recently, my wife.

I had loved Muriel too long and too well to be put out of my recognition of her because of the muffling coat that she was wearing.

IX

What was Muriel Piercy doing here with Ormond Ormes?

That she was his mistress was my immediate conclusion. Well, of course it was! In a flash it came to me that I had been hired for this preposterous task and brought here at Muriel's instigation. We had parted and she had divorced me, but I could believe she kept enough of the old feeling to have persuaded her lover to offer me this haven for a little while, during which I might save some money and get in position to face the world with renewed strength and courage. Yes, I undoubtedly owed my job to Muriel's beauty and to Ormes's admiration of it. But why had he brought her here? If she knew that she must encounter me at Ormesby, it was not like her to come. Ormes himself—why should he have risked such a scene as he must have known might very well ensue when he confronted me with her? Yet, whatever the reason of her being here, I could not think that it was a light one, nor that she could have lent herself to any wish on Ormes's part to humiliate her former husband. But I would return to the house, keep out of sight for an hour or two, and in some way learn the cause of this visit. Besides, I must return to the house in any case. Agnes's murder ought to be reported there without any more delay.

And yet ... and yet ... if Muriel was Ormes's mistress, how dared he bring her into his wife's home? Whatever might be the state of feeling between the man and Agnes, it was scarcely in her —I reasoned as if Agnes were still alive—it was scarcely in her very human nature to endure such an affront as she must consider this to be. Had they come, then, to announce to Agnes and to all the women of Ormesby that Ormond was abandoning them? That he was leaving with Muriel? But in that event, would he not have come alone? If I knew Muriel as I thought I knew her, she would not have accompanied him on any such errand, not because she lacked courage, but simply because she would not have been sufficiently brazen.

But what of the dead woman in the car? I thought of flight. Suppose I were to slip from the garage, keeping among the trees and out of sight of anyone who might be looking from the house, and walk to the village, where I could perhaps obtain some means of leaving the country.

Could I? How? I had sixty-eight cents in my pocket—less than that, since I had bought cigarettes last evening in Tiltown while waiting for time to keep my engagement with Gray in the library. Again, Hobbs knew that I had left the house ostensibly in search of his wife's attacker. He would testify that I had asked him to arm me. Suspicion of having committed this murder in the garage must naturally fall first of all on me. I already saw the headlines in the New York papers, and heard the gossip among those clubmen whom I had once called friends. I might, in time, establish my innocence. There were bloody finger and palm prints enough on Agnes's flesh and clothing to prove that I had not touched her after her death. But all this would require time. All this would require money. I knew something of the chances an innocent man takes when facing the police and courts without money or influence. And if I left the scene clandestinely the very fact of my flight would fasten upon me a guilt I might with difficulty disprove, the guilt of having been, in some measure, accessory to this crime.

All this spun through my head while I stood peering out through a slit in the door of that garage, unable to make up my mind whether to run boldly to the front door of the house and boldly enter it, or to find my way in furtively and unseen by any eyes, save perhaps those of the man Hobbs.

It was the latter course that I finally decided upon. And what decided me was the realization that, if Muriel did not know of my presence at Ormsby, an open entry must be even more embarrassing to her than to myself. The dogs had retired to some distant part of the grounds, as I said previously. I slid back the door, slipped through it, dragged it shut, then scurried for the entrance to the kitchen of the house. The door was unfastened. Hobbs was in there, bustling about, preparing to cook breakfast for the household. I threw him a glance, shaking my head. Then I strode into the short passage leading to the dining room. Were Ormes and his guest there? It occurred to me that he would not yet have taken her there, seeing that the meal was still far from being ready to serve. Perhaps they were in the library. There were other rooms, but they were seldom used. I entered the dining-room, crossed it, and advanced toward the front door. As I did so, Hobbs came into the room behind me.

I was about to warn him to keep my presence from knowledge of the others, but an intuition warned me not to do so. It is always best, in such a position as I occupied, to let your adversary act first, until he has done something to give you the advantage. Besides, Hobbs was not my servant, though I felt him to be quite willing to act under my orders in the matter of capturing the family maniac. But I would question him.

"I see that Mr. Ormes has come home, Hobbs. Is he in the library?"

"Yes, sir."

"There's a lady with him, isn't there?"

"I can't say, sir."

"Probably I was mistaken," I said. "It's of no consequence, of course. Has Doctor Barnes arrived?"

"No, sir. Not yet, sir."

"That's rather queer, isn't it?"

"Well, yes, you might say so, sir."

I made as if to turn away. His eyes begged me.

"No," I said, understanding him. "I didn't see anything. Are you sure she isn't now in the house?"

"Quite sure, yes, sir."

"Well, I looked everywhere for her, outside. It's mighty strange."

Was I wrong not to inform him of the fact of Agnes's murder? I could not decide that without taking further thought.

"I fancied I heard Miss Ormes's voice in Miss Barbara's room when I passed there a little while back," I said, trying to gain time and think what was best to do.

"Hardly, sir. I was there just a few minutes ago."

"Ah! But where is Mrs. Ormes, Hobbs?"

"Gone to the village, I believe, sir. I can't say why, since none of the shops will be open so early."

I left Hobbs and went swiftly up the stairs and into my own chamber. Barbara's door was still fast shut when I came opposite to it. I had heard no sound of voice or movement. I wondered why the doctor had not yet come.

When ought I to break in upon this family's intrigues with the announcement of my discovery of murder in the garage? But I had a means of learning something of what went on down there in the library. It would be eavesdropping, of course. Do you think I hesitated because of that?

Flinging the torch and dog whip onto my bed, I slipped through the closets and passages and down the winding stairs that led to the little narrow door opening into the library. I heard voices as soon as I had passed the swinging door, but they came from the far end of the long room and I could not distinguish the words, though I recognized Ormes's voice and Muriel's clear tones. Then I opened the panel. The words were now much more plainly to be heard, though occasionally I lost a line or so. She appeared to be remonstrating with him.

"I don't see why you insist on it," she was saying. "I simply can't do it, and I won't!"

He replied with something I could not catch. I peeped cautiously around the edge of the panel to see them seated in the same chairs Gray and I had occupied the evening before. Muriel still wore her coat, though she had unbuttoned it and thrown it back from her face and breast. Ormes's overcoat and hat lay on another chair. They had been driving by night and in rain, I reflected, which accounted for the wraps in June.

"No," said Muriel again, and even more emphatically. "I've come so far. I will see her and tell her what you want me to. I'll explain why I am entitled to this money and why I must have it at once. And if it's necessary, I'll go to the lengths we agreed on to force her to give it to me. But I won't be a party to what you propose. And I won't . . . well, I've told you that before, I'd rather not go into it again."

He leaped from his chair, flinging up his hands in a gesture of chagrin and helplessness, turning toward me as he did so. I skipped swiftly back into the passage. I believed he had not seen me.

"At least wait until after you've had a talk with Agnes," he said, louder than he had yet spoken. "Will you stay here? We'll have some breakfast, shortly. I'll go now and see if my wife's awake. Will you wait? Do you want anything?"

I did not hear her reply, which consisted of a good deal more than a simple negative or affirmative.

"I'll have my man bring some coffee to you here," he said.

Judging that he was about to leave the room, and that, since he would then have his back to me while she would naturally be looking at him, it was safe to do so, I again stepped close behind the panel and peeped around it. Ormes walked to where his coat and hat were lying on a chair near the fireplace. He took them up. Muriel had also risen and, as I had thought she would be, stood facing him. He strode toward the door, having to pass close by her on his way. Then, without warning of any kind, so far as I could see, he dropped hat and coat and sprang upon her. In an instant he had flung his arms about her, had bent her head back, and was kissing her face and neck, striving to reach her lips. She struggled. It was a real struggle and no pretense. It was evident that she did not want to be kissed. I was out from behind the panel and advancing toward the group before I remembered my wish to remain concealed until I could learn the cause of this outrageous visit.

But my interference was not required. Muriel summoned her strength and pushed him violently from her, so that he staggered and almost fell. I darted back to my panel and got behind it. I remembered very well Muriel's ability to look out for herself. Ormes, swaying slightly before her, though I did not suppose him to be intoxicated, grinned sheepishly and adjusted his rumpled hair and necktie. Then he shrugged, picked up his hat and coat, bowed mockingly in her direction, and left the room. She had not appeared to be frightened nor greatly surprised at his attack. She also remained standing after he had gone, putting back loosened strands of her brown hair and then calmly proceeding to powder her nose with a puff she carried in the tiny bag dangling from her wrist. From my place of concealment I concluded that they probably had kissed before, but that she objected to doing it under this roof.

I suppose that the senseless bitterness within me at that moment was a very human bitterness. It was none the less inexcusable for all of that. If we are to overlook and forgive all that is human within us, we shall be condoning our deepest crimes and our most egregious follies. The woman was no longer my wife. I had no slightest right to interfere in any love affair she might be having with Ormond Ormes, or with any other man. And I could not rid myself of a notion that she had put forth her feminine hand, in the only way most women can, to help me by making Ormes give me a job and pay me for doing it. Nevertheless, for all that, she may not have known that my work had brought me to Ormesby. I had just been witness, moreover, to such a scene as convinced me that she was not yet utterly shameless. She would not permit embraces within the walls of his wife's home. All that passed through my mind, and I used it as an argument against the emotion of jealousy that urged me to confront Muriel where she awaited this Ormond Ormes, demanding that she leave the house with me, shaming her for having come here, persuading her, with such passion as I knew in that moment that I could summon, to come with me again for old sake's sake.

Ah, that, then, was the fundamental reason for my bitterness! I had not succeeded in putting Muriel entirely out of my heart, as I had put her more and more from my thoughts of late. We had parted. I had suffered pique. I had good reason to suppose that she was earning her living as such women commonly earn it. Oh yes, and I had been temporarily glad, as any married man might have been, of my unaccustomed freedom. I had said to myself that I was well quit of her. Hereafter, traveling alone, I should go farther, whether "down to Gehenna or up to the Throne." And I had all but given my heart to Gray. Yet now, seeing the love of my youth before me, seeing her in another man's arms, seeing her under his roof, undoubtedly his accomplice in some more or less shady intrigue, and perhaps his mistress to boot, I knew that I still wanted her again as I had always wanted her. I knew now why I had not succeeded of late in arousing to any emotion strong enough to drive me to accomplishment. I grew aware, at long last, that without knowing it my life had come very near such aimless drifting as must have brought me, in the end, upon the rocks.

But I could not stand there musing upon such things. Ormes, if he had gone to his wife's room, must very soon discover that she was not within it. A search would be made about the house. It would extend into the grounds. Probably someone would go to the garage to learn whether she had left Ormesby in her car. The body would be discovered. The authorities must then be noti-fied. There would be strangers, crowds, horrible, curious, gaping mobs of men and women, prying in and about the house. It was not unlikely that we should all be arrested and held for question-ing. And all the while the real murderer was still at large, running naked and wild, so far as I could say, over the countryside.

But my God! What a nest of murderers, maniacs and villains I had stumbled into! And Muriel had stumbled into! The thought of her being here and in as imminent danger as I, danger of arrest, humiliation and shame! It was that thought, I suppose, more than any other, which decided me to show myself at once to Muriel, offering my aid, such as it was, to effect our escape to-gether. I forgot that she had been journeying by night in Ormes's company. I forgot that she had come to his country house with him, the very house which sheltered his lawful wife and his sister, for the purpose of forcing someone within it, probably either that wife or that sister, to comply with some demand involving the payment of money. And I forgot the possibility that she had come here, knowing that she might very well encounter me and cynically indifferent to such humiliation as she must thus impose upon the man she had once professed to love. I remembered only that she probably stood in some danger and that I must endeavor to help her out of it. Even today I am not wholly ashamed that I recalled no more than that. Yes, I would go out to her at once.

But a sound delayed me. I have taken some time in the telling of all that passed through my mind, but Ormes had really been gone only a few seconds. He could scarcely have visited his wife's room. If he had met Hobbs he may have learned of her absence from the servant. Perhaps it was that. Or he may have learned of Gray's madness and of her doings of the night, and that may have affected his plans. Whatever the reason for his swift return, he was already at the door. I had heard the sound of his footsteps along the passage. In one moment he would enter the library. No doubt he would invite her to have breakfast, provided, of course, that no news of Gray had yet reached his ears. And I suppose that Hobbs would not eagerly seek an opportunity to speak of the matter. Indeed I had a feeling that Hobbs was going to leave that duty entirely up to me. I proposed, therefore, to leave at once along the way of the secret passages, gain to my own room, then descend the front stairs boldly and march to the breakfast I had a perfect right to expect awaited me. I slipped back into the space behind the bookcases and drew the panel into place. Yet for just a second I hesitated. The two in the library seemed to be approaching that very panel. The floor was of parquetry, as I have said, and I heard their feet moving rapidly across it. Also, now, I heard the nearing murmur of Ormond's voice as he explained to her, perhaps, some alteration in plan. And now they were just before the panel.

Why was he taking her upstairs that way? It could not be for the purpose of keeping her presence here a secret. Hobbs knew of it, for all that he had lied about his knowledge. Others must shortly learn of it. Ormes had said that he intended apprising Agnes of it. The way was a shorter way than that up the front stairs, but the saving in distance hardly compensated for the persuasions he must be using to get her to accompany him through so suggestive a series of doors and passages. It did not occur to me that Muriel might have been here before, and that she might be as familiar with Ormsby as I had tried to make myself. As it turned out, however, this was not the case, and the murmuring of Ormond's voice, as he approached my place of concealment, was made up of the words he was using to lull suspicion in her that he might be intending treachery.

I had no wish to be surprised eavesdropping. I ran noiselessly along the passage and turned down the stairs, descending several of them so as to be well out of sight when Muriel and Ormes should have come through the opening. But then I saw that, standing as I did in deep shadow, I could risk going back to the corner and laying an eye to it, and I did so. I shall not claim that the thought, as I stood there, of the Lady in Mauve possibly coming up those stairs behind me did not make me shiver!

I saw Muriel enter, turning to look expectantly at her companion. Was she afraid of him? I could not know. But many a woman has come to grief, even when she entertained no fear of a man who meditated treason in such a place of concealment. I gripped the butt of my revolver and told myself that if he tried again to put his fat hands upon her, as he had done in the library, I would drive him away from her at the point of the gun, regardless of its being his house and regardless of all consequences. And let her, after that, refuse to go away with me if she would. Yet whether she might so refuse, I did not much think. As a matter of fact, I suppose I lived those moments emotionally only and did not think at all.

Ormes entered the passage close behind Muriel, turning back to draw the panel shut behind himself. I heard no sound, save the very slight scraping of wood on wood. But Muriel must have heard something, for she started and clutched at Ormes's arm, and her own arm raised quickly and pointed toward the narrow door before her. A moment later that door swung open and Gray stood framed within the space it had occupied.

I think that I must have been far more surprised at this appearance than either of the others. I had every reason to suppose that Gray was still running naked and bloody somewhere in the woods or on the hills outside. I could scarcely believe my eyes when they told me that she was decently clothed in a suit of dark and slender blue, her hair coifed after the manner she habitually affected when sane, her face calm and composed. Not a trace of violence remained upon her person. This was the Gray I had waited for in the library last evening, the girl I had thought to love.

She looked long and levelly into the eyes of the two before her. Then she drew slightly back toward the winding stairs, beckoning with her upraised hand for them to follow her. They did so, after what seemed to be a second's hesitation. And I, more puzzled than I had yet been over any happening at Ormesby, started out from my hiding place, resolved to follow the trio. Not one of the three, with the women thus meeting so far as I knew for the first time in their lives, had spoken a single word.

X

Gray's appearance in any guise would have been surprising enough. That she had received her brother and my former wife as she had, decently clothed and without the slightest sign of astonishment at finding them in the passage—all this, I confess, puzzled me more than anything I had so far encountered. It quite drove out of mind all shame I might otherwise have felt at acting the spy and eavesdropper as I did. And yet—let me be honest! —I do not suppose that I can lay my lack of manners to the rare quandary I was in. There had been a time, true enough, when I should have thought such a course dishonorable. Now it was no more than a measure of self-defense. I stood alone. I had no single friend on whom I could absolutely rely. I must gain knowledge in such ways as offered. And I hope that I shall not be put down as a man too deeply sunk in the mud of cynicism, but it seems to be a fact that an indigent man has no more call to be honorable than an indigent woman has. Moreover, there were reasons guiding me that stood quite outside my selfishness. Crime had been done in that house, and, for all I knew, more crimes were being plotted. A woman who had been my wife was there, whether aware of my presence or not, and I believed that the man in whose company she had come meditated evil toward her no less than toward others. To be brief, and whether it was excusable or not, I followed Gray, Muriel, and Ormes through the narrow door and up the winding stairs.

Keeping well behind them, I yet followed closely enough to know, by the noise of their passage, what direction they took. Thus I found that they did not go by the secret way into my room, but through the room in which hung the portrait of the man I had taken to be Gray's and Ormond's father, and out into the wide hallway. I peeped around the edge of the door and watched the three of them traverse the hall and enter Ormond's chamber. I had not yet been in that room. I supposed they chose it now for a conference, probably because it had not been occupied last night and lent a greater degree of security than would any of the rooms downstairs. They entered and closed the door behind them. Then I, too, went out into the hallway, wondering how, without risking my ear at the keyhole, I was to overhear the talk that would ensue within that apartment of Ormond Ormes.

The three had passed Barbara's door without so much as a glance at it. It had been closed. But just as I came opposite it, it opened and a man with a beard came out. He carried a physician's satchel. I halted and introduced myself.

"Doctor Barnes? I am Seaverns, who telephoned you."

"Glad know yuh, Mist' Seaverns," mumbled the man of medicine.

"How is your patient?"

"Mrs. Hobbs? She 'pears to be O.K. No fever. Superficial abrasions. Shock, mostly. But what 'bout that dog? Rabies? D'you know which dog 'twas?"

"I haven't the slightest notion," I replied. "Doesn't she know?"

"No. Says she went out for a stroll in the dawn and the whole pack jumped on her. Damn' fool thing to do! Why do they keep such brutes here? Ought to get rid of 'em. Danger to life and limb. Well, I'll wire for vaccine. Ought to be here this evening. Can't take chances with rabies."

Hobbs must have coached his wife very carefully in what she was to tell the doctor. A stroll in the dawn indeed!

"Is there anything in particular to be done for her?"

"No. I'll be back this evening. Prob'ly 'bout seven. Meanwhile

—where the deuce are all the women of this place? Just looked in on Barbara. Old patient, you know. Where's all the others?"

"I'm sure I don't know, doctor. I'm myself looking for Mrs. Ormes. Everyone seems to have gone out."

"Oh, well. Never mind. Damn fool fam'ly! I'll be back. See you later."

He went away down the stairs. Going to the head of them, I heard him open the front door and let himself out. Just after he had closed it, Hobbs, a few seconds too late, came from the dining room. A moment later I heard the sound of a motor being started outside. Apparently Doctor Barnes had no suspicion that it had not been a dog whose teeth had torn his patient's throat. Stepping as close to Ormond's door as I dared, I could hear only a confused murmur of voices from the other side of it. But I did not wish to be caught there, in event of any of the three opening that door suddenly. I strolled back to Barbara's door. It had been left ajar by the departing doctor. I pushed it farther open. She sat before me in a chair by a window. And yes! It was my Lady in Mauve.

And though she was not a ghost, yet she certainly had ghost-like ways.

"Excuse me, Miss Ormes. I didn't knock because I was afraid of disturbing you. How do you feel? Better, I hope?"

"Pretty well, thank you," she murmured.

I edged over the threshold. There was no reason for my entering that room, save that my nervous state demanded that I be either doing something or talking with someone.

"Is there anything I can do for you?" I asked. "Have they brought you any breakfast?"

"Thank you, no. Hobbs will prepare something for me, later. I've no appetite this morning."

I searched for something to say. I didn't want to leave immediately, now that I had gained an entrance here. Presently she continued:

"I'm very glad you came, Mr. Seaverns. I'd like to talk to you." And she smiled at me, the smile baring her perfectly white and even teeth, teeth that well-nigh gleamed, I thought, though she sat partly in shadow.

I also smiled and spread out my hands, indicating that I was at her service. She pointed toward a chair. I got it, placed it near her own, then went and closed the door.

"Is it about a certain . . . accident?" I asked, seating myself and leaning near to her, so that she need not speak loudly.

"Yes."

"Ought we to talk now? Are you strong enough? Perhaps later . . ."

"Why not now?"

"I may tell you," I said, thinking that she might be worrying over Gray's state, "that everyone who ought to be here is . . . well, sane and in his or her right mind. Gray is now with her brother. They're talking in his room."

"Ormond here? You're sure?"

"Yes. He arrived a few minutes since." I did not think I ought to tell her, at least, immediately, of Muriel's arrival in Ormond's company. "They're having a family powwow, I take it."

"But he— How dared he come without letting me know?" She might have been speaking quite to herself. "I— When did he come?" she demanded, abruptly dropping her absent air.

"As I said, a few minutes since. Perhaps half an hour."

"Ah! Well. No more of that now. But she——"

"Make your mind easy, Miss Barbara. I've seen her. She's clothed and in her right mind."

"Of whom are you speaking, Mr. Seaverns?"

"Of Gray, Miss Barbara."

"Gray?"

I must have stared a bit, I suppose. Of whom else could she have supposed me to be speaking? Agnes Ormes had not played the wolf-woman last night. And there remained only Alice Hobbs.

"Yes," I replied, at last.

"But I'm not. I don't mean Gray. Of course Gray is in her right mind. If only she'd go out of it, now and then . . ." Her voice trailed away. Almost I thought she would forget again that I sat before her. But she checked herself. "No, I meant the . . . other—"

"As for Mrs. Ormes," I interrupted, "I can't tell you where she is. She isn't in the house, I'm afraid."

"Nor do I mean Agnes. I mean Grayce."

"Grayce? Who, then, is Grayce?"

"Why, she's ... Oh, but don't you really know? I thought you were with her last night. It was Grayce who——"

She said something additional, which I did not catch. For a great light had flashed upon me. Mrs. Hobbs had said "Grayce," last night, and not "Gray's," as I had thought. Grayce must be Gray's twin sister! It was Grayce who went mad and attacked people. It was Grayce who sometimes used the little room near the back of the house, containing the filthy pallet. It was Grayce for whom they were all concerned this morning. That is why I had missed my appointment with Gray. Grayce had come to me in the library and I had left her before time for my meeting with Gray. It was Gray who had penned up the dogs, and it was Grayce who had released them again. It was Grayce who had attacked Alice Hobbs. It was Grayce who had killed Agnes Ormes. Gray's calm appearance of a few minutes since, her presence now in conference with her brother and my wife—these things and the possibility of them began to be explained.

"I must confess," I said, "that I knew nothing of Grayce's existence. I thought Gray was the only sister Ormond had. He never mentioned any other, unless ..." But I did not finish that sentence. I was wondering whether he had mentioned Grayce after that luncheon at the club. "But as for Grayce," I resumed, "I went out this morning, looking for her, that is, I was looking for the person who had attacked poor Alice Hobbs. I didn't find her. So far as I know, she's somewhere outside still."

"It will probably be all right," said Barbara, "so long as the dogs are quiet. She's probably asleep somewhere. It's happened this way before. Our little Grayce hasn't the strength of mind to—The danger is, she may awake and leave our grounds. She must be found, Mr. Seaverns; she *must* be found and brought back here. It used to be that she would obey me. But lately she acts as though she knew more than her teacher; that is, I appear to have lost a great deal of my old influence over her. I was trying to calm her last night when she——"

"But if you were with her, how came the servant to be——?"

"As I was about to tell you, she broke away from me. I couldn't find her. Of course I didn't look very thoroughly. It's happened this way before, you see. After a while I took for granted she'd gone outside. So I came back to my bed."

Again I stared at this woman. What? She had left a mad girl to go roaming naked into the night and had made no attempt, either to find her or to have someone else do it? Why hadn't she at least called Hobbs to help her look? Something of what I was thinking must have appeared in my eyes.

"You are wondering why I did that?"

"Well, naturally, I . . ."

"Because—but you couldn't possibly understand, Mr. Seaverns. There's a bad taint of insanity in this family. I'm used to it, I've seen it in Grayce, of course, for years, and before that . . . but never mind! As I say, you wouldn't be able to understand."

I nodded, somewhat grimly, I suppose. I fancied I understood better than she thought. At the same time I did not understand how she could have so callously left her niece last night. Merely being "used" to Grayce's frenzies could not have made any normal person indifferent to them, or to what might befall the girl when subject to them.

However, I did not wish to push this apparently frail little person too far. I had been told that her nerves could not stand fright or irritation. I concluded, though, that this amazing attitude of Barbara's must be further investigated when I should have more time for it. Besides, Hobbs had said that he had heard his wife say she fancied herself called by Barbara. That is why the servant had left her bed and room. Perhaps, after all, more had happened than I believed had happened. I had been long enough at Ormesby to have learned that nothing there could be accounted for readily and by the obvious explanation.

"You mustn't fret, Miss Ormes," I said, with what courtesy I could summon, considering the feeling I was at that moment entertaining. "I'll go out and look again for your niece. Do you think her brother, or her sister, could help?"

"Oh, yes. That is, Ormond can. But Gray . . . she's always hated Gray. No, Gray mustn't go."

"Thank you for this information," I said. "I was pretty much in the dark before. Now I begin to see my way."

"I wonder whether you do. What do you know about . . . about my nephew Ormond?"

"Not very much, I'm afraid."

"Then I'm going to tell you things you don't know, things you'll be shocked to hear, but things you ought to know. At least, since Ormond has come back here without my . . . that is, without letting me know. . . . But you'll understand better when I've told you. I need a friend, Mr. Seaverns."

I murmured that I'd be glad to help her in any way I could.

"I'm . . . I'm beginning to be afraid here," she went on. "Gray holds the upper hand, nearly always, but Gray can't be everywhere. She was asleep, last night, and in the storm she couldn't have heard anything, anyway."

"I was awake," I interposed. "But I didn't hear anything; that is, I didn't hear anyone call for aid. I just happened to hear groaning . . . afterwards."

"So you see! Yes, you ought to know. I shall need you. Ormond would probably want to kill me for telling you, but I'm . . . afraid! Ormond himself . . . of late . . ."

She broke off, hesitating, as I thought, for words in which to proceed. I caught at her hinted meaning.

"But good Lord! Do you mean that he, too, is . . . is going . . . ?"

"I'm afraid of it!" And yet, strangely, enough, her eyes *danced* as she said that! "He brought you here to write that . . . that history. But the time expired more than a year ago."

"What?"

"Yes. Gray reasoned with him. I did, too . . . in a way. He wouldn't listen. He said he knew the very man to do it, and he argued that the will could be set aside as soon as the book should be completed. That, and other queer things he's done. There was the marriage with Agnes."

"Do you care to tell me about that? I've thought it might explain a lot of things."

"Oh, it would, if you knew enough!" She smiled swiftly, then her face resumed its sober look. "It was ten years ago. He suddenly decided that he ought to marry her. I don't believe she'd had any idea of forcing him to, but he claimed that he'd . . . well, that he'd wronged her, Mr. Seaverns. At least, that his fa— at least, that she'd been wronged. So he married her. Then, afterwards, he gave her money."

"Much of it?"

"A hundred thousand dollars. In Government bonds. Lately he's wanted her to return them to him. Of course she's refused. She's quite normal, you see."

"You mean . . . But I see you *don't* mean her being normal consists in clinging to the bonds. But why does she continue living here? Why doesn't she go to town?"

"I really don't know. She's seen enough to know that there are secrets at Ormesby. She's . . . she's not above using them. Besides, she probably had good reason for *not* wanting to marry Ormond. Since then, she's done everything to get matters into her own hands."

"I see."

"I wonder whether you do. But that's all I had to say, Mr. Seaverns. I don't know why you should be disturbed with our . . . our troubles." She smiled, slyly, again. "But you're here in the house, and you've probably seen some . . . some strange things. At least, you'd think them strange. There are things you don't know and haven't seen . . . but I can't tell you."

"Yet if I'm to stand your friend, and the friend of Ormond and Gray, maybe I ought to know a little of them, at least."

"I think not. You're not . . . well, you're not yet prepared, you see."

I did not press her to tell me of them. I supposed that I already knew enough of what she had in mind to guess at the rest. Yet it came to me that this woman might be of use to me in the work I should have to do among this crazy household. It might be well to give her an idea of the extent of my knowledge of the family's history; she would be the less inclined, in future, to hide further information from my understanding. In a few words I told her something of what Grayce had revealed to me. Her eyes widened in a stare of amazement. I saw her cheek grow pale, and for a moment I feared that I had taxed her beyond her strength. I wanted to reassure her.

"The secret is safe with me," I said. "Why should I ever tell it to anyone? No one was to blame for anything that was done, no responsible person, that is. And as for the manner of the disposal of the bodies, I can understand Ormond's desire, and yours, too, I take it, as well as Gray's, to avoid scandal and the shame of letting the public know. I don't blame anyone for the things that were done. Only . . . it might be of value to know where they were buried."

"So Grayce, the little fool, wasted her time by telling you all that? I thought she was with you for a very different reason." She seemed to be looking quite through and beyond my face. Then her manner changed. "Why should you know that?" she demanded.

"I haven't any valid reason to give you." What had she meant about Grayce wasting her time? "I merely thought that with Grayce liable to . . . and Ormond, too, you say . . . it leaves only Gray, so long as you're not very well. It leaves only Gray and myself to look after things. If I'm to help, I ought to know what to reveal and what to keep under cover."

"Yes. Yes, I see that. Perhaps you're right . . . in a way. Well, I'm going to trust you. Perhaps I'm wrong to do it, but I'm going to. You've become a part of all this. I've a notion that you can't leave . . . now." Grayce's very words! "Listen: Back of the shelves in the library——"

"I know about the passage," I interrupted. "I've explored it. I've been down the iron stairs from top to bottom."

"You've certainly learned a lot in the short while you've been here! So it was you this morning with the flashlight! I couldn't see your face. But did Grayce show you the crypt?"

"The what?"

"The crypt. The little room at the bottom of——"

"No, I found it myself. I asked 'What' as I did because I was thinking of a . . . well, of a tomb, you know."

"Which is exactly what it is. That's why we call it the crypt."

"You mean . . . ?"

"In the well, yes. Through the pipe, you see. Both bodies are there."

I shuddered. This family had not so much as decently interred the bones of Ormond's and Gray's father and mother! And of Barbara's own brother! The two corpses had been slid down the great pipe of wrought iron which I had noted, feeling, even as I looked upon it, that it in some way bore upon much of the mystery surrounding all the persons and all the doings in the house of the Ormeses.

"But the top opening of the pipe?" I asked. "Where is that?"

For answer she rose from her chair, crossed the room, flung open a door to the closet in which I had supposed she hung her clothing. I saw that the closet was quite devoid of everything used or worn. And I also saw, projecting from the wall at the back of the little space, such a black and gaping mouth as might have been thought, in older times, to lead to the Pit itself. Down that horrible hole had gone those bodies, then! And this frail woman, this nerve-shattered Barbara with the angel's face and the gentle, modest manners had lived and slept in this room for days, months, years, and all the while with knowledge that she stood, as it were, at the open door of a tomb! What if one or both of the cadavers had lodged in the pipe, had not slipped all the way through? Did I even then shudder involuntarily at catching with my nostrils a faint, sickening odor of decayed humanity? It may have been fancy, and no doubt it was. But I could be sure that Barbara bent slightly downward toward the mouth of the pipe and drank a long breath from it, contentedly and somewhat greedily, as though she had once luxuriated in the smell of horror that must have been exhaled there.

Moreover—*had she herself gained to the crypt behind me by sliding down that pipe?*

Abruptly she turned away from the place and closed the door, seeing to it that the old-fashioned thumb latch fell properly into place.

"Now you know that also," she said, smiling a hard, grim, dry little smile, and dusting her fingers daintily, as though she had been handling something smutty.

I was profoundly shaken. I had been shown no more than the end of a large pipe of wrought iron. Yet the associations it had, and, more than all else, the satisfaction this strange woman appeared to derive from having that open pipe in her own room— these, I confess, shook me deeply and as I had not yet been shaken by any happening or by the discovery of any previous happening at Ormesby. How very little, after all, do we commonly realize that we, ordinary human beings, clothed, sane and respectable, have within our natures the very hungers of the beast. We read of some brutal murder, some peculiarly atrocious handling of the insensate corpse. We shiver vaguely and give thanks that such things are not done by the people we know and love and respect. And then, when the murderer is caught, he, or she, turns out to be the same sort of decent, respectable, ordinary person we have claimed for our neighbors and for our friends. And we shudder again, deeper within our souls, this time. How could such a person have done the nameless thing that has been done? How could he, or she, have looked upon so horrid a deed and still lived, knowing that his own hands have wrought this ruin, that his own fingers have dabbled with this carrion, that his own soul has triumphed in this shameless union with incestuous, reeking death?

Hardly aware of what I was saying, I began to tell Barbara of the visitation I had had on my first night at Ormesby, proof of which lay in the mark which was still to be seen below the collar of my shirt.

"You were ... kissed?" she asked, absently, and with a curiously flat and brittle quality in her tone.

"Call it kissing. I suppose a vampire would call it that," I replied.

She nodded, slowly, agreeing with what I had said, yet not appearing to be troubled by that at which I plainly hinted.

"I've been thinking," said I, after a pause, "that even if Grayce were confined in a sanatorium, she might continue telling things. It might be far more dangerous to do that than it is to keep her here."

I was watching her carefully. She sat staring straight ahead of her, but her eyes had within them a reddish gleam as she looked, and they were fixed upon that very spot on my throat, hidden though it was by the collar of my shirt, whence the mark of the sucking mouth had not yet faded.

"Yes," she said, not bringing her eyes back to meet my own, "that's what I fear, too. It hasn't been discussed. Gray and Ormond would both die before they'd consent to anything like that."

"But I've been thinking, Miss Barbara.... What of the water

in that old cistern? For that's what it must have been before the chimney was built over it."

"That's what it was, yes. The cistern leaks. That's why my brother built over it. Something happened at the bottom, years ago. Water won't stay in it. A fissure in the granite, I suppose."

"But who did all this? I mean, who put the bodies down there? Ormond?"

"Yes. But I helped. And Hobbs."

"He did? Hobbs knows that much? But what of him? Can he be perfectly trusted?"

"I don't know. I'm rather desperate, Mr. Seaverns!"

She sat suddenly upright in her chair, terror showing plainly in her beautiful face. I put out my hand as if to push her shoulder gently, so that she might lie back against her pillow. She moved away from the thrust of my hand, so that only the tips of one or two of my fingers touched the thin silk covering her shoulder. Yet that slightest of touches, even through the silk, was enough to inform me that her flesh was as cold as marble.

"You're cold!" I cried.

"Not at all. I'm rather too warm. I was cold all night, but since breakfast I——"

"But you've not eaten any breakfast," I interrupted.

For a moment she looked mockingly and insolently into my eyes, smiling in that grim little way she had. Then she began again to speak of Hobbs.

"We used to think we could trust him," she resumed. "My brother tried to kill him ... once ... when he was ... was crazy. Ormond interfered, at some risk to himself, and saved the man's life. He swore to Ormond that he'd always be his servant. But I don't know. ... Of late he's different ... since Agnes came. She nags him and his wife so. I *wish* she'd leave!"

And I wished I could ease Barbara's mind by telling her that Agnes would never nag Hobbs and his wife again. But I dared not do it. Already she was at the limit of her full strength. I feared that further trouble, particularly such trouble as my news of Agnes's murder, would throw her into a fever.

"I must go now," I said. "I'll get Ormond and we'll go find Grayce. You must try to sleep."

"Yes, I ought to rest. But—"

"I'll send Gray to you."

Rising, I moved my chair back against the wall, where I had found it. Then I laid my hand on the knob of the door. There I hesitated. Something else had come into my mind, and I wanted to ask about it, yet hesitated, both out of shame and because I half feared that the implications contained in my question might agitate this woman too much. Curiosity won the day, however. I had a battle to wage, not only against the curious public, but also against Ormes himself. I needed all the information I could get.

"There's one thing more, Miss Barbara. Has your nephew ever said anything to give you an opinion that he's interested in another woman? Anyone in New York?"

"Not directly. I did suspect that he was having an affair of some kind when he was here a couple of weeks ago. It was from something he said, though I forget what it might have been. I do remember that it made Agnes angry. But I don't know it to be a fact, and if it's true, I don't know who the woman is, nor anything about her."

"Barbara, dear! What's the matter? Are you ill?"

I turned swiftly. It was Gray. No, it was Grayce! She was sane. She was clean. She had bathed and dressed. She ran past me, without so much as a glance in my direction, and flung herself on one knee beside Barbara's chair. She mouthed tendernesses, solicitous questions, reassurances. I caught Barbara's eye over the girl's shoulder. She said to me, as plainly as if she had worded it, that she wished to be alone with Grayce, that I need fear no immediate recurrence of the girl's frenzy. I nodded in understanding. Then I slipped out of the door and across the hall to my own room.

I was not so sure that Barbara was right. It seemed to me that Grayce might become insane again at any moment. Had I not myself seen her change from tense control, last night, to vicious desire, and back again to something of sanity? I reasoned that these attacks would come upon her more and more frequently until her reason should have been thrown down for ever. Yet there was nothing I could have done to excuse my remaining in Barbara's room. It might have been that Grayce, sane now, had some remembrance of the things she had done last night, and wanted, undisturbed by the presence of a stranger, to sue her aunt for pardon. Besides, I ought to be rapping on Ormes's door and informing the plotters there of what had transpired in the garage.

And then, as to Barbara, I was, at the moment, too puzzled to think with any clearness. Barbara herself ... Was it possible that that lovely face covered the soul of a fiend? Why had she consented to live all these years with that open pipe debouching into the closet of her room? Why had she stared at my throat, her brown eyes red with hunger? Dimly and vaguely I remembered reading somewhere that a person who had been bitten by a vampire became himself a vampire, that he, in turn, must live on human blood, that he could not ever die and be at peace until his heart had been pierced by a stake. . . .

And what had Barbara meant by saying that she had been cold all night, but that now, since taking her breakfast . . . ? Was it possible that not Grayce but Barbara had . . . But no! That half-formed notion was too improbably horrible!

Something must be speedily done with regard to Agnes's body. If Grayce had killed the woman, was she even now babbling of the murder in her aunt's room? I wondered whether Hobbs knew of Grayce's return to the house. Thinking of Hobbs, I grew hungry. I stole out into the hall again, past Ormes's door, and down the broad stairs. Entering the dining-room, I saw that Gray was there.

She was seated at table, taking a cup of coffee. She was dressed, as I have said, in blue, and Grayce upstairs had been wearing brown. Even aside from these differences in clothing, however, I wondered how I could have been able to mistake the one sister for the other. There was a likeness, certainly, and a far greater one than the family likeness between Gray and Ormond, or between any of the children and the dead father's portrait with the wandering evil eyes. Yet where Gray was calm, poised, self-possessed, modest, and sheathed in dignity, Grayce was erratic and nervous, sinuous and sensuous, and with something repellent about her, even in her sober intervals, and with something wild. I had not been given the slightest reason to think that there were twin sisters of Ormond Ormes living in this house. Nevertheless I told myself that I should have suspected something like that from the very first. Undoubtedly it had been Grayce who had admitted us on the midnight of our arrival, for it was Grayce's deep voice which I had heard then and had heard but a few minutes since in Barbara's room. I thought that I ought to have known the difference by the voices alone. Yet I had not, and much of what was to follow can be now traced to that mistake.

Gray wished me a "Good morning" in pleasant fashion, though it seemed to me her eyes spoke of preoccupation.

"Should I apologize for missing our appointment last night?" she asked.

"It isn't necessary. I know that the dogs had to be kenneled. Yet they were loose this morning before daylight."

"I know they were."

"Of course," said I, "I know who loosed them. Now I must tell you something else."

At this point Hobbs entered, to bring me coffee and something to eat. I needed both. The secret I held, and which I was now resolved to divulge to Gray, had been a secret for several hours. I thought, however, I could afford to keep it until I had completed my meal. Gray, I noticed, was not eating. She had pushed her plate away and I saw that the food on it had not been touched. But she had called for a second cup of coffee.

"What is it?" she asked.

Hobbs came in again, bearing the girl's coffee. He paused, after serving it, to glance meaningly at me. I looked squarely into his eyes and nodded slightly. But Gray had seen the interchanged understanding and I felt her glance questioning me.

"It's about your sister," I explained. "She's upstairs with Barbara." Gray started up from the table. "No, don't be alarmed. She's quite all right—now."

"I have just left them together, Miss," Hobbs added.

"But ... with Barbara? She mustn't be ... there ... of all places!"

Nevertheless, Gray sank back into her chair. Her whole attitude expressed indecision. Her shoulders drooped and she toyed absently with knife and fork. Hobbs left the room. I ate my eggs as hastily as I well could without swallowing them whole. Even so, I fear that Gray must have thought my manners atrocious, if, indeed, she was thinking of me at all. But I wanted that food within myself before I told her of what was to be found in the garage.

"Tell me," Gray demanded, leaning far across the table toward me, "was she in there," nodding in the direction of the library, "with you, last night?"

Something, to this day I do not know what it was, prompted me to try an experiment.

"You mean ... Barbara?" I asked, supposing, of course, that she had meant Grayce.

"Of course," she replied.

"But ... Why, Good Lord!" I cried. I was rudely jarred.

"What is it, Mr. Seaverns?"

"Why, I ... that is ... well, I didn't suppose you actually did mean Barbara, you know,"

"Then whom ... ?"

"But ... why, she's ..."

"Ah, I see! You thought I meant my sister?"

"Naturally, yes."

Her eyes were vacant. She appeared to have forgotten my presence, I waited for what seemed to be several minutes, though it could not have been so long. I was thinking that Gray could not possibly be jealous of her beautiful aunt, but that ... At last I ventured to recall myself to her attention.

"Yes," I said, "it was Grayce. She ... I mistook her for you. I had just left her when I found you coming in out of the rain. That is, it was only shortly after I'd left her that I heard you entering. Then we talked on the stairs, you'll remember. Grayce told me ... well, a lot. Barbara has told me more. I want to have you know that I'm aware of so many of the secrets of Ormesby that you've all got to accept me as a friend of the family, whether you like me or not."

"Yes?" She eyed me haughtily. "That's as it may be, perhaps. But I don't want to quarrel with you. I suppose you mean, you want to help?"

"I do. In any way I can. I certainly wouldn't foist myself upon you if I didn't think I *could* be of service to you." She was staring quite through me. "To you in particular, Gray!" I cried.

She smiled then, wanly.

"Because I know a lot . . . more, even, than anyone else, at this moment."

"What do you mean?"

"Do you know," I asked, somewhat at a loss as to how to begin, "where your sister-in-law is?"

"Agnes? No, I suppose she went out for air. She was rather nervous and broken-up after Mrs. Hobbs's accident. I told her to go lie down and rest."

"Before I tell you what I mean to tell you regarding her, there's a question I must ask."

"Very well. I'll answer it if I can."

"I doubt," said I, leaning far across the table and staring into her eyes as she had lately done, "whether you can answer it. Indeed, I'm sure you can't. It will puzzle you as much as it's puzzled me, when you've heard it. The question is: what is your brother doing here with my wife?"

"Your what?"

There was no mistaking the genuineness of her astonishment. I felt that I could reasonably argue from it that Muriel herself was, as yet, unaware of my presence here.

"Muriel Piercy is my wife——"

"The woman upstairs now?"

"Yes."

"That isn't the name she uses."

"Isn't it? The fact doesn't astonish me. But what's she doing here?"

"If you really don't know . . ." Gray began, eyeing me coldly. I read the unspoken accusation in her eyes.

"No, I don't know. I haven't had anything to do with her coming here, whatever the reason is. We've been parted for some little time. I didn't know that she and Ormes were acquainted. I hardly think she knows I'm in the house. But I do know that she's here to help him demand money of someone——"

"I thought you wanted to know why she was here."

"Oh, I mean, for what reason aside from the one I've mentioned."

"Her relations with Ormond?"

"Yes."

"I know nothing about it."

"Then we'll drop that subject."

"But as to the demanding money . . . yes, it is to be demanded of Agnes. It's all wrong, I suppose. Maybe, legally, we haven't any right to do it. And yet the money isn't rightly Agnes's, but my brother's. He . . . he gave it to her when he wasn't——"

"Never mind," I said. "I know all about that."

"You do? But now he needs it. He's threatened with bankruptcy. She won't give up a penny. She has threatened . . . all of us. So Ormond is going to try a trick. Barbara suggested it to him." I made a particular note to remember that! "This woman, your wife, you say, is to represent herself as having been married to Ormond before Agnes was. She's to demand a hundred thousand dollars to keep her mouth shut about it. She's to swear—we're all to swear—that there was never a divorce. Whether it will frighten Agnes into paying . . . well, I don't know."

"It won't," I said, emphatically. "Couldn't any of you see that? She's not the woman to give up money, once she has her grip on it. But this is conspiracy. Can't you see that, either? If she wants to charge you all with conspiracy to defraud, she can have the entire bunch of you arrested and——"

"Oh, I suppose so! I know there's a risk. But what could we do?"

"As to that," I said, shrugging, "I can't answer. I suppose your brother could go bankrupt. Other men have."

"Maybe. Better that than rotting five or ten years in state's prison."

Nevertheless, I felt like a prig, saying such things to Gray, who must have known the truth of them as well as I. I had said them, not in reproof of the crime she contemplated, but as chiding her folly in running such a risk. I could not be sure, however, that she understood and believed in my motive; and, as I say, I felt somewhat like a hypocrite and a fool. Besides, I knew that no such effort against Agnes could now ever be made.

But the news that Barbara, my little Lady in Mauve, had been the inventor of such a trick——was no less disturbing than astonishing. And yet—a woman who could live with that pipe opening into her chamber—was it so astonishing, after all?

FINGERS OF FEAR

115

"Where," I asked, "does she keep the bonds? Here? Or in a safety vault?"

"I don't know. But I think they must be hidden here."

"There's one thing more, Gray. Your sister must be confined."

"No!"

"I tell you, yes! She's too dangerous to be allowed——"

"Pooh! She's wild, of course. Not dangerous."

I marveled. How in the world did Gray account for the condition of Mrs. Hobbs's throat? Did she actually believe, as we had led Doctor Barnes to believe, that a dog had done that mischief?

"I know what she's capable of," said Gray. "Her room is next to mine, on the third floor. Always I'm near enough to lock her in when one of these . . . attacks . . . comes on. Last night, I admit, I overlooked something. But I was very busy. I had agreed to meet you. The storm came up. There were the dogs——"

"I know all that. But the point is: you may very well overlook something else. I tell you she's more dangerous than a wild beast."

"And I say she's not!"

"Come!" I cried. "She hurt your servant last night."

"Grayce did?"

"Of course! My God, Gray, do you really think that——?"

"But how do you know?" she demanded.

"I know because I saw her, only a few minutes after she had done it. I saw her, naked as a wolf, with her mouth streaming blood and . . ."

"Oh!"

I paused, afraid that Gray might faint before me. She had risen to her feet and her face had gone the color of ashes.

"That can be hushed up," I went on, in a more gentle voice, however. "In fact, I don't think that Barnes or anyone else has the slightest suspicion that it wasn't a dog. By the way, the doctor will be returning here this evening for the purpose of giving Mrs. Hobbs an injection of vaccine. Rabies, you know. You see, he doesn't suspect. But suppose Grayce hurts someone else . . . and seriously . . . and even kills somebody?"

"Grayce?"

"Of course!"

"She won't! But we'll . . . we'll have to risk it."

"Why?"

"Why? Suppose, then, on your part, that we have her . . . confined, as you put it. Suppose she tells her guards and nurses certain things she can tell them. If you know as much about the secrets of this house as you say you do, well, what is your answer to that?"

"I see your point, of course. I admit it's a hard problem. But it must be solved in some way, and at once. Because, Gray, your sister has already . . ."

I paused, intentionally.

"Yes? What?"

"Killed someone."

Gray's eyes blazed at me. They were, for a moment, like veritable yellow flames. But by a tremendous effort she fought for and regained control of herself. I went round the table toward her. What I had further to say to her must be said in a tone which should not be heard beyond that room.

"It's true. I found her myself. In the garage. She's quite dead. Agnes!"

I put out a hand to support her, but she drew back, avoiding my touch. I turned and walked toward a window, to give her time to recover from this blow. Several minutes must have elapsed before she called me.

"Mr. Seaverns!"

"Yes?"

"It's . . . it's too bad that you went out there. I'm sorry about it. I had meant to . . . to remove the . . . body before . . . before anyone found it. I . . . I didn't have time."

"What are you talking about?"

"I mean that . . . I see I must tell you. It wasn't Grayce who killed Agnes."

"Then who——"

"No, it wasn't my sister, Mr. Seaverns. Nor was it . . . anyone else. I'll give myself up. I did it!"

Our eyes met. She stood there, gripping the back of the chair beside her, so that the knuckles of her hands showed white against the flesh surrounding them. I forced a smile.

"All right, Gray," I said. "I've already told you I'm not going to give away the secrets of Ormesby. We'll leave it at that, rather than argue now, when there's no time. But you must forgive me, my dear, when I say that I know you're lying!"

And then, without the slightest warning sign to me, she *did* faint.

XI

Never previously having seen a woman faint, I knew nothing of what to do for Gray, save to lay her on her back on the floor. Then I dashed into the kitchen, whence I summoned Hobbs to my aid. In a few minutes he brought her to and she was sitting in a chair, pale and with tumbled hair, but managing a wry smile at me in deprecation of the mid-Victorian weakness to which she had submitted. Her mother would not have been ashamed of such a failing, and her grandmother would have flopped to earth upon far less provocation than Gray had been given. I think, however, that her grandmother's mother would have been even more ashamed than Gray. But I digress.

Hobbs, the efficient one, poured her a drink of whiskey, which she took and swallowed without flinching. She was modern enough for that. Soon some color had flowed back into her cheeks.

"You may go now," she told the servant. "I'll be all right, thank you."

Left alone with her, I went close and laid a hand upon her arm.

"The thing you have always fought most bitterly against," I said, "is having any inkling of the family's weakness come to public attention."

"Yes," she replied, nodding, "it is. It's an obsession upon us, I suppose."

"Knowing that, I've no intention of betraying what I know. I haven't seen anything in the garage. I don't suspect anyone. If a way can be found of disposing of the body out there . . . Do you follow me?"

"Have you told Ormond?"

"No."

"He must be told at once."

"Very well. I'll tell him. I think you ought to go, if you're strong enough, up to your aunt's room. I left your sister there and . . ."

"Grayce there? Yes, I'll go up at once."

"Get her to go to bed and sleep, if you can. There's work to be done here today of which she ought not to have any knowledge, not only because it may disturb her but because we don't want her in position to tell."

"Yes."

"How do you feel now?"

"Better. I'm quite all right."

"There's one more thing I want to tell you. It's about myself. I didn't know that Muriel was coming here, but if I had, I . . . it wouldn't have made any difference. If you had joined me in the library last evening, I'd have made love to you. You knew that, didn't you?"

"Perhaps."

"The reason is, one reason is, Muriel isn't really my wife, any longer. We recently were divorced."

"Ah!"

"I think that informs you of everything you need to know about me at present. We'd better start."

She answered by rising and leading the way upstairs. Both of us paused outside her brother's door, but no sound of voices reached us. Gray glanced upward.

"She's gone to my room, I told her to use it."

Our fingers touched for a moment. Then, with a little smile for me, she turned away. I rapped on Ormond's door.

"Come!" he ordered, gruffly, not troubling to open the door for me.

I pushed it wide. He stood before the mirror of his dressing table, brushing his light hair. I had always thought him to be somewhat vain of his personal appearance, though why this should have been so I have no notion. I have remarked it, how-ever, in a good many homely men, and Ormond Ormes was far from being handsome. He saw me in the mirror and turned sharply. I could glean nothing from his face, which did not alter in expression, the expression of a man who is definitely annoyed and holds anger down with difficulty; but his nervous gestures betrayed a doubt of his own strength and position.

"You came home sooner than I expected you," I said, inanely enough, but lacking more appropriate words in which to make a beginning.

"Yes."

He had merely nodded into the mirror, not giving me any further explanation of his sudden return, considering, of course, that I was in no wise concerned with more of his affairs than the writing of a useless history. But I held the cards. I knew that I could at any moment startle him out of his pose of the superior fellow, powerful and at ease, and master here where I was servant. Yet I remembered his aunt's having told me of the insanity which had begun to have its way with him. I had to make him accept me as an equal, while myself remembering that he was a sick man.

"I have made absolutely no progress toward writing that history for you," I said, lighting a cigarette and tossing the match, in familiar fashion, into the fireplace.

"Well, why haven't you?"

"Why? I wonder whether you really want to know. Have you heard of what's happened here?"

"Eh? No. No, I haven't. Except . . . if you mean . . . I've heard that Alice Hobbs is ill."

"In a way, yes. The cause of her illness is my principal reason for neglecting your precious history . . . to give you an answer to your question."

"How do you mean?"

There was a tenseness under his exterior of forced calm that showed itself plainly. I saw that he was wondering how much I knew of affairs at Ormesby. I guessed that he shared the family's pride in keeping up appearances, what Gray had called their obsession. Yet he himself had risked having that pride brought down and the secrets of Ormesby made public property, and he had done that by bringing me into his house. Only a man blind, deaf and dumb could have failed to learn there the secrets he wanted to keep hidden. Moreover, he had brought me here upon a fool's errand, long after the reason for doing the writing of his history had gone out of existence. I thought that no more was needed to convince me of his failing mentality. Yet with all that, because I had seen him trying to kiss the woman who had once lain in my arms, and because I suspected that there had been kisses interchanged between the two, I hated him, standing there. Not five minutes since, I had let Gray Ormes see that in my eyes which, as I told her, I would have put into words had she met me in the library the previous evening, and I nursed no feeling of tenderness, at that moment, for Muriel. Yet I hated Ormond Ormes. Explain that on any better basis than the innate hoggishness of man, if you can.

"You haven't seen your wife, have you?" I asked, enjoying his uneasiness.

"No. No, I haven't. But come, Seaverns! What have you got in mind? What's it all about? Let's have it!"

"Have what?" I mocked. I do not excuse myself, but merely report the thing as it happened. "Suppose you begin by telling me a few things."

"Well, what do you want to know? Pardon me, but I've very little time to——"

"Oh, there's time enough. I want to know why you brought me here."

"Why, damn it! I——"

"You can save a good bit of time by chucking all the reasons you've already given me. I want the real one. More than that, I mean to have it, whether from you or from someone else. I know already how to get it. Can you guess how that is?"

"Just what do you mean?"

I was fast losing control of my calm. Jealousy was riding me hard. I had asked him the reason for my presence at Ormesby, but that, of course, was not the thing I really wanted to learn. I already had learned that. Underneath I was somewhat fatuously trying to pry into the secret of his relations with Muriel. I wanted to have him tell me what I should have hated to learn from him; or I wanted to hear from him a denial of what I suspected, he not yet knowing that she had been my wife.

"I mean this: Grayce was abroad last night. Naked and unashamed and raving. You know what that means?"

He nodded, slowly, his face going pale and his jaw sagging, while his frightened eyes stared hard into my own.

"Grayce attacked Alice Hobbs, of course. I know all about her illness. I take it that you know I know that much. Grayce did more than that, however."

He came close to me, grasped my wrist and clung to it.

"What? In God's name, what do you mean?"

I turned my head for an instant, glancing involuntarily toward Agnes's open doorway. He appeared to divine something of my thoughts.

"Do you know where my wife is?" he demanded.

"Yes," I replied, turning again toward him and looking hard at him through narrowed lids, "I know."

"Then . . . where is she?"

"First, who is the woman who came here with you?"

"What business is that of yours? A friend. We came here on business. It's not what you think."

"I know something of what the business is. It isn't that which puzzles me."

"Oh, you do?" he sneered. "You know a lot—don't you?"

"A hell of a lot more than you suppose, Ormes. You'd better be frank with me. I know everything that's hidden here, from the affairs of your father's attack on his wife and sister and your murder of him to——"

"Damn you!" he shrieked. "Close your face! It's a lie!"

His face was contorted with fury. The cold rage within me stood and calculated how much farther it could push him without pushing him into delirium. It told me that the borderline had almost been reached.

"Come!" I said, in a more gentle tone and with a less threatening manner. "I am not going to publish anything. If you must know it, I'm far too fond of Gray for that."

"Oh, so you *did* fall for her?"

"Not in the way you suppose, my friend. It's natural, however, that *you* would be thinking something of that nature. You're the kind of fellow to . . . But I've got to know about this new woman, Ormes. It vitally concerns . . . everything. I know why you brought her here. I'm fully aware of what she's to tell Agnes and the way you and Gray and Barbara are going to back her up. Oh, yes! But unless I know who she is, where you met her, and how long you've known her, and whether she's your mistress—until and unless I know all that I won't tell you where your wife is, and I'm the only person here who knows her whereabouts."

"Well! I don't know how you've learned all this. I'm sure Gray hasn't told you."

"Gray and I are very good friends, however."

"But she hasn't told you?"

"No."

"You must be either a professional detective or a fine amateur spy."

"Is there anything to be gained by insulting me?"

"Eh? Maybe. Maybe not. Well, then, assuming you've stumbled onto a few secrets, what's your game? Why do you question me about the woman you mention? What's she to you? She ain't my mistress, if that's what's bothering you? I've flirted with her a little—she's pretty enough, of course. But I saw early in the game that she was nothing but a gold digger. That's why I hired her to help me here."

Well, I had the denial I had been seeking. I was no more assured of the truth of it, however, than I had been before. If there is a more unreasonable passion than jealousy, and one less admirable, from any point of view, then I do not know what it is. Ormes's denial had, however, the virtue of forcing me to drop the subject. It was obvious that I could not, under any conditions, persuade him to deny his own denial.

"Very well," I said. "With that point cleared up, we——"

"Where's Agnes?" he demanded again.

"She's . . . dead!"

"What?"

"Yes. In the garage. In the coupé you told me to use. Her throat cut and . . . mangled."

"Good God!"

It was not from grief of his wife's death that the shock he took sent him reeling back against the dressing table, clutching at it for support. I did see, however, that he saw swiftly enough most of the complications in which that murder must involve himself and his family. The bonds he had wanted to force Agnes to surrender —they might become his own now, and without a struggle, provided the woman had not made a will and had it recorded. If she had done so, leaving her property to outsiders, then bankruptcy stared him in the face again. Besides, how was the fact of the murder itself to be kept from the public? How was Grayce's innocence to be established? How was the insanity that was eating out this family to be much longer hidden from prying eyes?

"I found the body," I told him, "more than two hours ago. I went out early this morning, looking for Grayce, who had not yet returned to the house after attacking her aunt. The dogs chased me into the garage. So I found it."

He staggered toward a chair and sank into it, burying his face in his hands. I waited for this first shock to pass. I felt no great sympathy for him, but I believed that he honestly dreaded the disgrace and the scandal about to fall upon him. I still think that he did. I am convinced that Gray's word "obsession" had been well chosen as a term in which to describe the Ormeses' fear of having their insanity made known. I do not know that they can be greatly blamed for that. It was a form of insanity more horrible——for surely there are degrees of it——than any other.

But I had not credited the fellow with recuperative power equal to that which he now displayed. While he yet sat in the chair, face buried in his hands, and before I had thought to break in upon his disordered state of mind with a reminder that some action must be taken without more delay, he had planned how to cast the shame and the blame of the crime upon myself. It is true that he had not planned well, but the fact of his having considered such a step showed me that he was not to be trusted unless I could defeat him utterly. Suddenly he lifted his head, staring with hate and fury into my eyes. Then he sprang to the door and slammed it shut, locking it and thrusting the key into his pocket.

"You can't get away from me!" he muttered. "You did this! Confess it, before I choke it out of you."

I stared at him in amazement. In a moment I saw how easily I had allowed myself to stumble thus into his trap. Of course he could accuse me, and of course the burden of proof of my innocence must rest upon myself. I should be presumed to be innocent in law. . . . I knew that pleasant fiction. But I should be arrested, nevertheless, and I'd probably be held without bail until that innocence had been established. If it ever was. Yet my discomfiture was not of more than a second's duration. I still held a weapon, a better one than the revolver in my pocket, and which also he probably did not suspect me to possess.

"Don't be a fool, Ormes!"

"I'm not a fool. You killed her. I can see it, now. Tell me why you did it."

"Come, I've no time to waste in playing up to you like that. You know I didn't kill your wife. Why should I have killed her? Do you think I'd have killed her to give you . . . Muriel?"

I saw that I had winged him. His clenched fists opened. He dropped his arms to his sides, and he stared at me again. I suppose he was wondering how I had become possessed of the woman's name. Also, though it did not so present itself to me at the moment, I suppose he was glad of this new reason I had offered for his listening to me. It might prove more bearable than the necessity of treating with me under threat of such knowledge as I had hinted at possessing.

"Come," I went on, "I know that she's here. I know about your conversation with her in the library. It was only by the grace of God that I didn't knock you down when you tried to kiss her in there. In view of all this, you'd better withdraw your charge, hadn't you?"

He mastered himself, I could plainly see the struggle that went on within him. But curiosity and the fear of what I knew forced him to conquer his anger and to bear with me.

"I hardly think you'll charge me again with that murder," I pursued, "even after matters are so arranged as to make it plausible that I might have done it. If you do, I'll be forced, purely in self-defense, to bring the authorities to look into the cistern under the fireplace. I——"

"What in hell are you——?"

"Well . . . isn't it true?"

He understood at last that I really knew far more than enough to bring disgrace upon him. I knew more than he could attribute to hearsay, or pass off with a gesture, or disprove with circumstantial evidence or the evidence of his forged British documents. He must have understood, also, that I had gained one or more of his women to my side, else I could not have learned some of the things I knew. He was beaten. I did not trust the man, villain as I now held him to be, but I felt that he was not so great a fool as to force me into revealing the secrets I possessed. He might be slipping into insanity, but insanity is rarely lacking in a low cunning, save when it is mastered by passion. I drew forth the little revolver from my pocket and pointed it straight at his heart.

"You see," I told him, "I've the whip hand. I could kill you where you stand and leave the house. I've a right to do it. No sentimental jury in this land of the free and easy would convict a man who shot down his wife's seducer."

"What?"

He sprang up and advanced upon me, heedless of the weapon in my hand.

"What the devil did you say?"

"You heard me well enough. I sha'n't repeat it. Muriel is my wife . . . legally."

"Seaverns, is this true?"

"Of course it is."

"I didn't know." He turned away toward a window. "I give you my word," he said, earnestly, after a few moments. "I didn't know that. I never met her until a few weeks ago. She never told me anything about you. She never mentioned that she was married. How could I know of it?"

I suppose that he had not fully grasped the fact of his wife's death. Probably his present earnestness was due, in some measure, to a desire to gain me to his side, so that I should not spoil the plan he had formed of forcing Agnes to give up to him the bonds he coveted. I had no wish to help him.

"Of course," I sneered, "you are a liar and a scoundrel."

"No, damn you!" he snarled, turning fully toward me and advancing once more across the room, nothing daunted by the menacing gun. "I'm not! I didn't know it. Not that it would have made the slightest difference to me if I had. Only . . . I'd not have been so dunderheaded as to bring you here."

I was wondering, meanwhile, what Muriel herself might have to say to my claim that she was still legally my wife. Moreover, I had confessed the fact of the divorce to Gray. But I had no time for any detailed reasoning upon such a subject as that. I had gained an important advantage over an enemy, and I must follow up that advantage. There would be ample time, later, for admissions, explanations, and perhaps apologies.

"So now," I said, "maybe you'll tell me the truth of why you brought me here."

"I did tell you, Seaverns. I really thought you'd get busy and write that history. I supposed you needed the money, too. We've always been friends."

"Didn't you know that the time set in your aunt's will had expired?"

He cringed before me as a whipped dog might have done! This chance blow had hurt him nearer than anything I had so far said. I could not help wondering at it. Did the man know that he was slipping into insanity? Was this the thing he most feared of all things in his life? Knowing of the taint in his blood and of the threat which it always held against him, he must have lived in such fear as made life a veritable hell on earth. On my word I felt something of pity for him as I watched him cringing before me, and before the renewed threat of that Thing within him. I hated doing it, but it seemed to me that one more job in a tender spot must clinch the fact of his subservience to me.

"Never mind," I said. "I know you're a liar, in spite of all you say. But maybe I can guess pretty well at your reason for lying. I've seen Grayce, both sane and crazy, and I've had a few words with Barbara and with Gray. I know what I know, Ormes. I'm not so thick-headed as you must have thought me. But let all that pass now. What are you going to do about the body in the garage?"

"I . . . don't know," he whimpered.

He was definitely beaten. Plainly he was in deathly fear of me now.

"I thought you'd not want it reported to the authorities," I told him. "So I said nothing to Doctor Barnes, when he was here, and so far I don't think that even Hobbs knows of it."

"Are you sure?"

"No, I'm not sure. He may have been out there since I left the place. I rather fancy, though, that he's been busy in the house."

"Then . . . then I've got to do something to prevent . . . But I must have time to think. Will you help me, Seaverns?"

"It depends. I'll help you if you play fair. What do you want me to do?"

"I—I don't know. Won't you leave me alone now? Leave me for a few minutes, at least. I must have time to think this out . . . alone."

It flashed upon me that he contemplated suicide. But if he did that, if he did that, we could call the police, attribute the murder to Ormes, then prove our contention by pointing to the crime against his own life. I am quite aware that many good people will condemn me for leaving him as I did, believing, as I did, that I should never again see his face alive. It is not a question, however, of right and wrong. I, and several women along with me, had become involved in such a tangled web of scandal and violence, that I was not in position to stand upon nice questions of proper conduct. If Ormes were to kill himself, it would offer a way out for all of us. I left the room hoping that my suspicion would prove to be true of the event. I had forgotten those bloody female fingerprints.

"Very well," I said, as he unlocked the door for me with the key which he had put into his pocket, "I'll go. But if you try any tricks, so help me God, I won't spare you, Ormes!"

"Damn it! I won't hurt you. I know when I'm licked."

"One thing more. Does Muriel know I'm here?"

"Of course not, unless you've told her. I've never so much as mentioned your name to her. She doesn't know I'm acquainted with you."

I returned the revolver to my pocket. I had ceased, some minutes since, to menace him with it.

There was one person I must see immediately and come to an understanding with. That person was Muriel. There would be no longer any chance of concealing my presence from her, even if I still wanted to do so, for Ormes—if he lived!—would say something as soon as the two of them met, were it no more than to question her as to her silence regarding her marriage. Therefore, as soon as Ormes's door had closed behind me, I took my way up the stairs toward Gray's room. Gray might be with Barbara, or with Grayce, or she might have joined Muriel. I must chance the last. And I did not think, for a reason I had, that it was much of a chance, at that.

The door of the room was open. I paused within the frame of it. Muriel lay, fully dressed, across the bed, resting, probably, after the fatigue of her night's journey from New York. Gray was not in sight. I rapped. The woman on the bed did not stir. She lay face down with her arms about her head. So then I entered the room and stood beside her, looking down upon her and silently swearing that she was even more desirable than Barbara's pale and fragile beauty. And I grew angry with myself that this should be so, because I knew, then, that the magic of her face and figure might very easily and swiftly have again its accustomed way with me. Not more than an hour had passed since I had been looking with much tenderness into the yellow eyes of Gray Ormes. Yet, standing beside that bed, looking down at the woman who had divorced me, leagued herself with my enemy, perhaps submitted to his intimate embraces, I said to myself that though I might kill her without pity, I could not leave her without regret. But then, in such extenuation as I may be allowed, I must say that the dangers and horrors surrounding me doubtless worked together to make of this woman whom I had known well and loved a friend, who was come, as it were, to my aid and support, however little she might be really willing to help. In my confusion of mind I turned to Muriel. Had all difficulties been smoothed away, I might have been thinking at that moment only of Gray.

But Muriel's sleep was not a very sound one, and my presence was making itself felt. She grew restless, stirring as one does when becoming gradually aware that another being has come close. Abruptly she turned her face upward and saw me. I said nothing. Her brown eyes widened in surprise and then in recognition. She whirled to a sitting position.

"You!"

"How are you, Muriel?" I asked in what I tried hard to make a courteous and kindly manner of speaking.

And then she said so queer a thing as startled me out of my assumed complacency.

"Selden, there is a man in this house whom you and I must kill."

XII

It seems to me to have been as strange a thing as I had so far encountered that I did not find it strange for Muriel to say that she and I must become partners in a deed of murder. I do not mean that the murdering itself seemed, at that time and in that place, to be a thing of the commonplace, but that her claiming of my help appeared so natural as to evoke no surprise. If Ormond Ormes were to be slain, I did not intuitively think it queer that she asked me to help her do it.

Why was this? Was it because I myself stood in need of a friend? I do not think that a sufficient answer. I think it far more likely that the partnership between Muriel and myself must once have been far deeper and more sincere than either of us had supposed. It did not occur to me to suppose, either, that Ormes had "wronged" her in the sense that it would have at once occurred to my Victorian father to assume it, had he stood in my shoes. Muriel was not the woman to go about killing men for the sake of her "honor." Muriel's honor was a greater thing than her bodily chastity, and if she trusted a man's promise and the man broke it, she was far more likely to despise herself for her feckless folly than to cry the man's villainy in the public ear. Nor did I now surmise that she wanted my aid in any such trumpery cause. I knew without asking that the crime Ormes had done, or contemplated doing, was a real crime and a substantial one, and not a lover's perjury.

Yet it is no less queer that, for all my knowledge of the woman's character and ability to take care of herself—to defend, that is, her self-respect, I was jealous of what I suspected had happened between her and Ormond Ormes. I do not excuse myself. Neither do I wholly condemn my emotions. They were human enough, however vulgar. I shall content myself with setting down a true record of what happened. That, I fancy, will be enough.

"That's as it may be," I said. "Have you any notion of when it's to be done? Or where, or how, or why?"

"But what are you doing here?" she demanded.

"I might ask you to reply first to the same question, since I saw you arrive in his car, with him, this morning, and while you had reason to think that his wife was in the house."

"Yes, I did. I came here with him for the purpose of seeing her."

"I know you did. I heard your conversation in the library. Besides, I know more about the rest of it than you do."

"You did? You do?"

"Yes. If I hadn't known what I did, and if you hadn't been so well able to handle him, I suppose I'd have stepped out and knocked him into a corner. Habit of thought and action, you know. As matters were, I waited. Now I've just left him. I've taken the liberty of telling him that you are my wife."

"You have? Oh, Selden, I'm so glad you did that!"

"Thanks for being glad. A week ago you'd not have been, perhaps. But you'll be willing to back up my statement, then?"

"But where is Agnes Ormes? You seemed to hint that——"

"She's dead."

"Dead!"

"In a car in the garage yonder. I found the body a little while back. I was there when you and Ormes arrived."

"But— Oh, this changes everything!"

"I'd be obliged if you'd tell me about it. I hate being kept in the dark, and I've had to unravel so many mysteries, during the past day or two, they've begun to pall. Suppose you tell me, without wasting time, for we've very little time to waste, let me inform you, why you came here, what you intended doing, and why you want to kill this man Ormes."

"You said you knew all about it."

"So I did. And so I do. I'm checking up on what I've heard and learned for myself."

"Oh! Well, there isn't so very much to tell you. I met Ormes about a month ago. He at first wanted to make love to me. I'm on the stage; they all do, of course. That's why I divorced you."

"I know," I said. "Go on."

"But I kept him guessing. You and I had parted. I threw love out of the window. I'd made up my mind that since men are willing to pay well for a pretty woman's kisses, I'd get all I could for mine. I'd heard that Ormes had money. But it developed that, like everybody else, he was in need of cash. So I listened to a scheme he proposed for getting money out of his wife. It seems that he married her some years back under circumstances that . . . well, I don't know the details, but she forced him to marry her to save a scandal. Then she forced him to put a hundred thousand dollars in Government bonds into her hands. He showed me letters from his aunt and sister supporting the story. Besides, Gray admits it's true."

"So it is," I interrupted, "except that she didn't actually force him to marry her. But that's of no consequence. Go on."

"She didn't? I was afraid of that. But I'm not excusing myself. I needed money. Ormes needed money. We agreed to come here together, with me helping him to get back something that seemed to belong to him. That's all. As I say, I don't excuse myself. He told me that he simply must have fifty thousand to stave off a petition in bankruptcy. I was to come here, represent myself as having married him a year prior to her own wedding and claim seventy thousand for my silence and my promise to obtain a divorce immediately and quietly. He got me a marriage certificate, forged, of course. It's dated at a town in England——"

"Ah!" I exclaimed, involuntarily. Then I added: "He's got friends there, I've heard. It isn't the first time he's procured forged documents from England. But I'm sorry to have interrupted you."

"So we came here and I was to see her and demand the money. Twenty thousand were to be mine for helping him in this . . . this blackmail. Now you say she's dead. It changes everything."

"But what did he do . . . here . . . that made you want him killed?"

"He called his sister in. We talked——"

"I know. Go on. What happened?"

"Gray, the sister, wouldn't agree to the plan. It seems that she had been in favor of it, but now, for some reason, she's changed her mind. I couldn't learn why."

I wondered why Gray had admitted to me at the breakfast table that she had at first joined in the scheme, and had not also told me of later rejecting it. For she must already have rejected it at that time. Was it because she wanted to take the blame upon herself, blame for the proposed blackmail, thus shielding her aunt and her brother? I considered that Gray might have been capable of such generosity. Muriel was speaking again.

"Ormes was furious. He pleaded, he stormed, he threatened. But she merely sat and looked at him. Then she left the room. As she was going out she whispered to me that I'd better come up here."

"You didn't . . . immediately?"

"No. Ormes told me he had something else to propose. It was . . ."

She paused. She rose from her seat on the bed and came near to me and looked me squarely in the face. Then she went on:

"I didn't mean that you and I were actually to kill him. That was only a way of saying that he ought to be killed without mercy. What did he propose? I suppose he thought that because I'm something of an adventuress, and had already agreed to help him in a fraud and with blackmail—I suppose he thought I'd do anything, if there was a little money in it. This, he said, was an alternative scheme he'd had in mind for some little time, in case the other should fail. Well . . . he proposed that he shoot a certain man whom he said was staying here, a fool bookworm, he called him, and I didn't know, then, that he meant you!" I started violently, but controlled myself. Muriel continued: "And that he then shoot his wife, also. He'd put both the bodies together in Agnes's room. He'd swear that he and I had come here suspecting she had a lover, and had found you with her. The rest was to have been done, apparently, in a fit of jealous fury. I was to pose as having come here with him because I had had reason to think that the man might be my husband and— Do you see? He and I, two wronged spouses, were to join hands in punishing you and Agnes, two erring spouses. That's the way it was to be made to appear at the trial. But did he know that the man he was proposing to kill in cold blood was actually my husband? That is, excuse me, had actually been my husband? I didn't know it, then. I got away from him and ran up here to Gray. Why, the man must be mad! How could he get away with such a plan as that? But Gray wasn't in. Then you came."

As for myself, I shall not attempt to describe my feelings of that moment. Horror was dominant, naturally. But it was so mixed with other emotions that my brain danced and I felt dizzy. Through it all came gradually a thrill of having triumphed. The crazy Grayce had done that which delivered Ormes into my hands . . . and Muriel's. The securities, for which he had been willing to murder his wife and me, might now be his for the taking, unless she had otherwise disposed of them in a will. Muriel had betrayed his schemes to me, and Gray had refused, at the last, to join him in blackmailing his wife. Barbara would stand on my side; at least, I thought she would; and I suspected that Hobbs, if he could be convinced of Ormes's villainy and incipient madness, would not oppose me. Into my brain was slowly coming an idea for the solution of most of our problems, disposition of Agnes's body and a logical reason for her disappearance, without any need of her husband's suicide.

I was confident that I could prove my own innocence of Agnes's death, whatever Hobbs and the rest might say against me in testimony. Grayce was not dead, as I had feared she might be at the time of finding the result of her work in the garage. The bloody finger prints on the car and on Agnes's dress and shoulders could be made to show that Grayce had killed her. And I did not think that Ormes, with his pressing need for money removed, would lightly allow himself to become known as the son of one murderous maniac, even though he must be published as the brother of another. Nor would he be likely, now, to seek my death in an attempt to fasten a criminal guilt upon his wife and me, since Muriel, the tool he must have for such a business, happened to be my own wife and not antagonistic to my interests. Moreover, how could he account for Agnes's slashed throat, even if he carried out his scheme and shot her dead body through heart or brain?

Thus I reasoned, not quite logically, I fear, during the few minutes I continued standing in Gray's room, and while Muriel turned away from me to seat herself again on the bed and bury her face in her hands. For it must be understood that I could not well leave Ormesby until this matter of the disposition of Agnes's body had been cleared away. Could I go, leaving Ormes to remove all traces of his sister's work, then to call in the police and charge me with that bloody deed? I was a mere adventurer, as Muriel had called herself an adventuress. And, as I have said before, or hinted, even though I might be able to establish my innocence, by aid of the further secrets I held, still it would mean disgrace among the people I had consorted with, and might again consort with if ever my financial standing improved. Moreover, after being hunted across the States, what if I were caught and brought back to face a charge of being accessory, either before or after the crime? I might not be able to prove innocence of that. In the first place, it didn't exist. I was really guilty of it, and I continued being guilty of it with every moment I maintained silence. No, summing it all up, hastily enough, I grant, and no doubt illogically, yet with the best reasoning I had time for, it seemed to me that, like Macbeth, I had become so deeply involved in blood as to make it easier and safer to wade across the stream than to attempt a turning back.

And Muriel's position was not greatly different from my own.

But what was Ormes about? Already he might be in the garage, working destruction upon the evidence which Grayce had left there. For I believed him to be more than half way to madness, and his family pride and fear of disgrace might drive him to any insane hazard. Or, alone where I had left him, he might be already dead by his own hand.

"You stay here," I commanded Muriel. "Have you had any breakfast? No? I'll find Hobbs, or Gray, and have something brought to you here. But you musn't be seen by any other person, if it's possible to keep you out of sight. Stay here and lock this door behind me."

I went to the door and opened it and looked out into the hallway. No one was in sight. Then I remembered something.

"Did you know that Gray has a twin sister?" I asked.

She had followed me, and now she was standing very close to me. She shook her head. It came to me that she was not thinking. As I rapidly sketched the situation for her, and for all the astonishing things she had so lately learned, she was not listening much to what I was telling, nor was she thinking of the inmates of Ormesby.

Muriel had tried divorce. It had, so far, brought her nothing but insult and hard work. Now, meeting me here, in a place of danger, I knew intuitively that, if I opened my arms to her, she would come into them. All the old relationship might be then picked up and renewed where it had been broken off. And for a moment I was tempted to welcome her.

Yet I refrained. After all, she had deserted me when most I needed her. And Gray's face had come between us in the interim. Say what you will, no man easily forgives desertion. I stared into Muriel's eyes. And she read in my gaze that I would not receive her. She turned away, then, smiling a little wryly in the way that women love. And I went out of the door, closing it gently, yet firmly, after me.

Ormes was still alive in his room. I did not trouble to knock at the door, but opened it and saw him there and entered. He sat in a chair by the window, seemingly in deep thought. If he heard me, he gave no sign of it. I stood inside the threshold of the door.

"Ormes," I said, "I've heard enough of your doings and intentions to justify me in shooting you here and now, like a dog, and as you'd have shot me."

It was a silly way of approaching the man, villain though he undoubtedly was, considering the heavy trouble which lay upon him. He roused at the sound of my voice, turning toward me a face from which all color and expression had fled away. It passed through my mind, fleetingly, that the near strain of insanity in his blood might well have proved too much for his brain in this crisis. And I now think that if ever a man was near to madness, while still retaining sufficient grip on sanity to be reasonable and accountable for his words and deeds, it was Ormond Ormes in that moment. But my speech, rude as it was, had sufficed to recall him to the world in which he lived. Slowly, as I waited there, watching him, something of color reappeared in his cheeks and a gleam of interest returned to his vacant eyes.

"There's a dead body in your garage," I said, since it seemed to me that he might have forgotten it. "I'm going to telephone to the authorities to come and take cognizance of it, unless you do so."

"Eh? What's that? No, don't do that. Wait. Let me think. For God's sake, don't do that, Seaverns! I'll—I'll—let me think! Leave me alone, and let me think."

"I did leave you alone. You haven't been thinking. You've been brooding. Come! Snap out of it! Something's got to be done at once."

"I thought you agreed to help me."

"I did. I will, if you'll do something sensible."

"What can I do?"

"Well, for one thing, the crazy person who did the killing must be surrendered to an asylum. It can't be avoided any longer. You've got to face it, Ormes."

"No. Wait! There's a way. I can hide her—the body. I've thought of it. If you'll help me, I'll——"

"You mean, you'll put her down the old cistern? Well, I won't help you do that. It's too risky."

"What do you want?" he demanded, dully, rising and coming close to where I stood.

"Want? Money, you mean? Nothing at all. I'm not trying to hold you up. I wouldn't take your money, even if you had any and offered it to me. But Hobbs and his wife, if they don't already know, will know very soon. And there are too many others. Besides, your sister Grayce can't be depended on to hold her tongue. I know it because I know how freely she talked to me, about you and about your father. There's nothing to be done, except report the death. You'd better come and do it with no more delay. Every minute we wait makes it look the worse, for all of us."

He hesitated, scanning my face, from which, I suppose, he took no more than evidence of my determination to force him to do as I bade. Nevertheless, I will not deny that, for a moment, I was half tempted to take his money. I would have kept silence in any event, if for no other reason than I could not have talked without involving Muriel and Gray. But this man had plotted to kill me for his wife's bonds. It did not seem entirely unjust that I should make him give me a part of them, provided they could be found. And the thing he proposed might well have been accomplished.

Hobbs could be bought, or perhaps his loyalty would keep silence in any case. I would be bought . . . apparently. Grayce, being crazy, must be confined closely in the house, where her tongue could not reach a stranger's ears. Or, if it did, then he must be made to see that her words were the ravings of a disordered brain. Gray and Barbara would say nothing. Muriel, reunited to me, would hold her peace. It was a wild risk; and yet such risks are taken every day, and every day they succeed, despite editorial writers and moralists, who try to make us believe that murder always outs, though even they have not the effrontery to claim that it is always punished. It is true that I had overlooked Mrs. Hobbs, and that oversight might have been fatal to everything.

But I conquered the temptation, which, as I said, was not more than half an enticement. I had seen enough of crime and of the effects of crime, of late, and of the terror that lives after the hiding away of crime and does not ever leave the hider in any peace. Moreover, Muriel had been forced near enough into the commission of the crime of fraud. I had no stomach for making her join me in another. Now that she had returned to me (do you think I needed her spoken promise to be aware that we could be united again?) I was determined to help her, despite my own poverty and despite her feminine hunger for luxuries. And I was determined, further, to wrest a living somehow from this bank-rupt world. I am no philosopher, and I am no economist; but it seemed to me that a generation which had taken such a beating as mine had ought to be afraid of any determined man who had the courage and the effrontery to cry "Boo!" If it became neces-sary to commit crime to obtain money, well, I might not later refuse to commit it; but it would not be the criminal action sug-gested by Ormond Ormes.

He had, as I said, approached me and he now stood scanning my face as if for a sign of my yielding to his desire. I gave him back look for look, resolved to make him understand that I could not be bought to do his bidding. And he must have read the un-spoken resolution that stared at him out of my unswerving eyes. Abruptly his self-control was gone. He flung out his hands and rushed at me, his pale face contorted and suddenly flushed with fury. I had no time to avoid his rush, nor to draw the pistol from my pocket, even if I had remembered having it there. I swung at his chin and missed, as he closed in on me. Then his long arms were around me and I could only grapple with him as he flung his insane strength upon me and bore me backwards against the wall. And I went down beneath his rush and his weight and we rolled together across the floor of the room.

I fought with all the force I could muster to grip him by the throat and choke him into senselessness. But he caught my arms under his own and hugged me with the hug of a grizzly, pinning me against him so that I could not free a hand. Over and over we went, knocking chairs and small tables from their places and making noise enough to rouse the entire household. I expected that the clamor of the fight must bring Hobbs to my help within a very few minutes. I would shout to him that my antagonist was insane. For by this time I knew that I was going to need the aid of someone if I were to escape from that fight alive. Ormes was a bigger man than I, and he gripped me with all of his maniac's power, crushing out my breath against his heavy chest. Nevertheless I thought, for an instant, that he could do me no great harm, and that if he was imprisoning me in his arms, also I was holding him and preventing his escape. But in a moment I saw that he was trying to reach my throat with his teeth! The lycanthropy within him, the madness of the wolf, which had been in his father and was now in his sister, was come uppermost into his own frenzied rage. The Thing which he had feared had conquered him at last! He wanted to tear my flesh and to glut his lust for blood by drinking mine!

How long we had tossed and tumbled about that room I do not know. I felt the strength going out of me, along with the air from my lungs, which I could no longer renew. His iron muscles held me in a hug that I could not possibly break. His terribly blotched and twisted face was just above my own. I butted at his teeth with my head, and the blood sprang from his crushed lips and ran down over his chin.

But help was coming. I heard the voices of women, screaming in terror within the room. I heaved my body upward with the last ounce of strength remaining in it, striving to hurl my enemy into such a position as would enable the others to drag him off me, or to hit him over the head with some implement or weapon. In the next instant I knew that his sharp and nearing teeth would close upon my throat. Then a blow descended upon him from above, a blow so great that I felt something of the impact even through his body. He started back from me. His muscles stiffened rigidly, then as suddenly relaxed. After that he fell forward upon me and I was aware of the taste of warm and salty blood upon my mouth.

XIII

I did not entirely lose consciousness, but the world swam before me dizzily, then went black for a while. I was aware of several persons moving about me; of the body of my enemy having been lifted off my own; of someone bending over me and examining me as if for wounds. Then I heard Hobbs's voice.

"I don't think he's much hurt. He'll be all right."

I struggled and opened my eyes.

"I'm all right now," I gurgled, for my throat had been pretty severely constricted in Ormes's grasp and the cords and muscles would not function properly at once.

"Lie still and rest. Get back your strength," said Hobbs, soothingly.

Whereupon, I sank back onto the floor and lay quietly there, hearing Hobbs, with Gray and Muriel, moving around me. I knew that Ormes lay beside me, a little to my right. He lay still, and I wondered about it. None of them addressed any word to him, nor did they approach him to give him aid. Looking back on it, I suppose that the entire scene occupied only a few minutes of time, though to me it seemed that long hours must be passing. At last I heaved up onto my elbow, opened my smarting eyes, blinked a while, and coughed. But I knew that I was not greatly hurt, and I would no longer allow the hand on my chest to press me back.

"I'm all right," I said, gruffly. "Where's Ormes? What's happened to him?"

Hobbs bent over me until his mouth came close to one of my ears.

"He's dead," he whispered.

I said nothing. It seemed perfectly natural that Ormes should be dead. He had been crazy and he had been bent on killing me; but as my head cleared I began to suspect that Hobbs had killed him. I wanted to know about it. The servant, seeing that I was bound to rise, helped me to a chair. Swiftly now my eyes cleared; my power of speech came back; and as the blood receded from my brain, I began once more to be sharply aware of everything and everybody in the room.

Hobbs, somewhat dishevelled, stood before me, a little at one side. He was very pale and his hands opened and closed nervously, while there was a spasmodic twitching about his mouth and eyes, and one shoulder hunched upwards in a peculiar way. Gray stood before a window, her back to the room. She seemed to be crying, for her hands covered her face, though I could not hear sobbing and her body did not move. Muriel was beside her, one arm around her waist. The latter turned her head, now, and stared at me with wide and frightened eyes. Ormes lay on his back in the middle of the floor. Someone had spread a towel over his head. It was a large towel and heavy, and it was stained with blood. Several other bath towels, wadded into a red heap, lay near to Ormes. They had been used, apparently, for soaking up a pool, for the boards of the floor about the mass were streaked and smeared with blood. The small rugs which had covered the floor were twisted into rolls or torn into rags and a great many pieces of furniture were either lying over on their sides or were jammed against larger pieces. The room looked as if many more than two men had done battle within it. My own clothing had been ripped into ribbons, with scarcely enough of it left to cover me decently.

"What did you hit him with?" I muttered.

Hobbs did not answer in words, but contented himself with pointing toward a table nearby. On it stood a bronze elephant. It was about nine inches high. I did not go and examine it, but I knew that it would be very heavy and that it could have crushed a man's skull like an eggshell. I had no difficulty in guessing at what had happened. Rushing into the room, seeing that his master had me down and was choking me, that my face was even then purple with congestion and that Ormes was about to sink his teeth into my throat, Hobbs had no time in which to deal gently with the maniac. He had snatched up the bronze ornament and had struck out with it. He had not meant to kill. But the sharp points of the trunk and tusks had penetrated my antagonist's skull and the weight of the metal behind them had crushed in the surrounding bony area. Ormes must have died instantly. When I later examined the elephant, I saw that shreds of brain tissue were still clinging to the curving trunk. I did not then question Hobbs as to details, of course, but he told me afterward that my reconstruction of the killing had been a good one, only adding that he had first tried to separate us by pulling Ormes away from me. When this had proved to be impossible, he had seized the elephant and struck the man's head with it, never thinking to do more than stun him.

And now there were two dead bodies at Ormesby, and the problem of what to do with them had more than doubled in complexity. I got to my feet, my head whirling with the effort and needing several seconds for it to clear. Then I drew Muriel toward me by a crook of the finger.

"Take Gray to her own room and make her lie down for a while," I said. "I'll get some other clothes, somewhere, and think what's got to be done. Then I'll call you."

She nodded and led Gray out of the room. Hobbs had already guessed my predicament.

"I can lend you some clothes, sir," he said.

"Can you? Thanks! I'll go with you at once and change. I don't dare be seen in this condition, in case anyone comes here. Leave all this as it is. We'll lock the door."

We did so, Hobbs giving me the key, which I returned to him, bidding him put it into his pocket. He was about of my own size and he gave me a suit of gray serge that fitted me well enough for all present purposes. I had stopped in at my own room and picked up clean linen. Soon, bathed and presentable, in the event of any stranger, or of Doctor Barnes, coming to the house, I joined Hobbs in the dining room, where we once more had recourse to Ormes's whiskey to quiet our frayed nerves.

"Have you notified anyone of the . . . the accident?" I asked.

"No, sir. I was waiting, sir, for your advice."

"I suppose the police must be told, and at once. I don't think, Hobbs, that you need worry much about clearing yourself. It was a clear case of assault to overpower a maniac and . . . and to save another person's life."

"Yes, sir."

"Do you know, Hobbs," I asked, watching him narrowly, "what has become of Mrs. Ormes?"

"No, sir. I haven't seen her since she came into my wife's room this morning. I have been wondering what has become of her."

If he had been to the garage and had seen Agnes's body there, he gave me no sign of it. I resolved to take Hobbs fully into my confidence. For already I was forming a plan for disposition of the dead bodies, and I thought that Hobbs, committed as he now was to my side by having killed his master, innocently or otherwise, was an accomplice on whom I could rely. If it be said that I ought to have called the authorities immediately, I can only reply that the investigation they must have made could have done no one any good. Two persons had been killed at Ormesby, within a few hours of each other, and yet neither had been slain by sane premeditation. Nothing could come of such an investigation as the police and the newspapers would have made, save trouble for everyone at Ormesby, trouble of worry, trouble of expense, trouble of disgrace. It might be that the difficulties before me would prove to be too great to be surmounted. But I was not yet ready to call in the police.

"I know what has become of her, Hobbs," I said, and went on to tell him of how I had come upon the corpse.

He was much shocked, I could see that. Yet he maintained an outward calm, so that I began to augur much from his ability to hide his feelings.

"It was the news of his wife's death," I said, "that drove Ormes mad. I went to his room to tell him of what I had found. He at once accused me of killing her. I didn't kill her, Hobbs. I had nothing to do with it. You must come to the place with me, in a minute or two, and you'll see the marks of the murderer as plainly as I saw them. But Ormes insisted that I surrender to him. I argued, thinking he was willfully trying to fasten a crime on me in order to save his own sister."

"Ah!" breathed Hobbs, though I suppose that he had already suspected Grayce.

"So he attacked me. But I must tell you, first, that the news reached him at a bad time. The poor fellow was driven half frantic by other troubles. He had come here this morning— By the way, do you know that the woman who came with him is Mrs. Seaverns?"

"No, sir, I haven't heard her name, sir."

"Yes. She was coming up from town, in any case, and since he had to come suddenly, he offered to bring her, which she accepted. But the reason for his visit is this . . ."

Whereupon I spun Hobbs a story of how Ormes, faced with bankruptcy, had come here to demand of his wife the surrender of securities and jewels sufficient to save his financial structure. He had not seen his wife, for the reason that she had left the house before the arrival from New York, and had been killed by Grayce in the garage. I told Hobbs frankly that I had had all this from Barbara and from Gray, both of whom had expressed to me their concern for Ormond's sanity in his trouble. Then I went on to explain to the man how Ormes, driven to desperation by the news I brought, had attacked me murderously, first shouting that I had killed his wife. The tale was largely true. I did not think it necessary to give him the exact truth as to Muriel, nor as to Ormes's connection with her. I could not see that it would help anything to put Hobbs in possession of the secret of Ormes's plot against Agnes, while I could not reveal that against my own life without telling him more of Muriel's association with the dead man than I cared to. Upon the whole, however, I made out a credible enough story, the more easily as Hobbs had himself been witness to Ormes's insane frenzy just at the last. (Indeed it is not likely that he would have attacked the lunatic with the bronze elephant had it not been necessary to save me from those ravening teeth of his.) Hobbs had seen Ormond's father's madness, and he had seen something of Grayce's. He was soon to see more of it. He had no difficulty in believing that the insane taint in the Ormes blood had come uppermost in Ormond, as indeed it had at the last.

"So there it is," I said. "We can call the police and have a full investigation, with mobs of curious people tramping through the place and over the grounds, worrying all of us half to death, asking questions, prying into everything, stealing pictures and photographs and anything else that's loose, with great scare heads in all the papers, disgrace, ruin, humiliation, all that, with you and I, in the meantime, sitting in jail, gnawing our nails and being beaten perhaps by big policemen administering the third degree to us. . . . Or we can hit on some other plan."

"What do you suggest?" asked Hobbs, who had gone a shade paler as I pictured for him the scenes to follow, and who now, in this extremity, dropped his air of the servant to speak with me as man to man.

"You helped Ormond put his father's and mother's bodies down the old cistern, didn't you?"

"My God, how did you know that?"

"Oh, I've been around, Hobbs. I saw, the moment I entered this place, that something was wrong. So I made a few quiet investigations. Besides, I had reason, even then, to think that Ormond was slightly wrong in the upper story. Do you know why I'm here? I'm here to write a sort of history, for Ormes, to comply with a provision in his Aunt Matty's will. If the will had been complied with, Ormes might have inherited a hundred thousand dollars that went to some historical society, I understand. But when he hired me to write the book for him, using the books in the Ormesby library for material, the time set by the will had already expired. His Aunt Barbara will tell you that he insisted on having the book written anyway, claiming that he could have the will set aside. Is that exactly the reasoning of a perfectly sane man?"

Hobbs agreed that, under the circumstances, it did not seem to be so. Then, again, he asked what I proposed.

"I'm thinking," said I, "that you and I together might hide Ormes and his wife Agnes in the same way. You put the . . . the others . . . down the iron pipe, didn't you?"

He nodded.

"We could do the same. We could say that Mrs. Ormes got into her car and left the house and never returned. We could say that Ormes, threatened with financial ruin, must have secretly done away with himself in New York, or elsewhere. What of it? Unidentified men are found every day in New York, picked out of the river, or out of the subway, or just found in alleys."

"What shall we do with his car, standing now just outside the door?" asked Hobbs.

"Oh, Lord! There's a difficulty, sure enough!"

And indeed, as I considered it, the problem of disposition of that automobile seemed nearly insurmountable. Human bodies can be destroyed, by quicklime or fire, and there are other means of getting rid of them. But how to efface all traces of an automobile? There are records kept of engine, body and factory numbers, of designs, models and the like, records especially kept for tracing cars when they have disappeared. Cars do, of course, disappear, and some of them are never heard of again. But even the hub cap of a known make may supply such a clew to police officers as will lead to discovery of something which has been thought well hidden. What we had to do was so to dispose of that car that no one, finding it, or any part of it, should connect it with the one which had been registered in the name of Ormond Ormes.

"There's one thing in our favor, Hobbs," I said.

"What's that?" he asked. "If there is, I'll certainly be glad to hear of it."

"It's time," I replied. "I can't see that we've got to do everything in a minute. Ormes won't be missed in New York for a day or so. That is, perhaps he won't be. It depends on the story we concoct and tell here whether Agnes's disappearance ought to be reported today, tomorrow, or . . . never."

"There's a bank up in the woods," he said, slowly, "where the mountain comes down and makes a low cliff above the level ground. He might drive his car there, set it close under the cliff, then have a landslide to cover it up."

"And the tracks of the wheels on grass and soft ground?"

"I don't know, sir. Maybe we could cover 'em with rakes or shovels."

"Well, we'll have a look at the place. But now, where are those dogs? For you and I must go to the garage."

"They're loose," he said.

"Can you pen them?"

"I'm afraid I can't. I've tried it, several times. They won't obey me. They let me alone . . . usually . . . but . . ."

"Then Gray must do it. Besides, we can't do anything here without her knowledge and consent. Come, let's go to her room. By the way, Hobbs, where's your wife?"

"Lying down in bed, sir. She's going to be ill, I'm afraid. She gets so upset whenever there's trouble around. If it wasn't for that, her throat wouldn't bother her so much."

"She does, eh? Then whatever we do, we musn't let her know everything."

"No, sir. No need to, sir."

I grew immediately afraid that the sickly Mrs. Hobbs might thereafter do or say something to ruin any plan we might make and carry through. Nevertheless there was small time to give to the problem her conduct might set for us. From his suggestion of a place of concealment of the Ormes car, Hobbs himself seemed to be entering wholeheartedly enough into my partly formed scheme.

Together we climbed to the third floor, where I knocked on Gray's door. Muriel opened for me. Gray sat in a chair. She had been weeping; her yellow eyes were red and swollen. Hobbs and I stood before her, and I struggled for words in which to begin.

I do not see that it will serve any good purpose for me to set down every word and argument the four of us used and proposed. I should have been surprised had Gray not fallen in with my half-formed design. I had seen enough of her to suppose that she dreaded an investigation and the consequent disgrace as much as her brother had dreaded them. We agreed, then, soon enough on the main details. Hobbs and I would take the bodies to the mouth of the pipe, push them into the hole, then throw down a sufficient quantity of lime to cover them. After that we must carefully cover every trace of violent death. All clothing, towels, rugs— everything, in short, that bore the slightest stain of blood, must be gathered up and burned in the incinerator which adjoined the kitchen. This was the device built into the house and designed to consume the household's garbage and other refuse. Muriel it was who thought to remind us to remove all keys and other metal objects from pockets, since such articles could not burn; and that all garments ought to have the buttons cut off them before consigning them to the flames. Ormes's room was to be rigorously set to rights, and the work of doing it must be performed by Gray herself, with Muriel helping her, since it ought not to be entrusted to Mrs. Hobbs, even though she could be driven to leave her bed and do it. It appeared that Gray, more than I was coming to do, suspected Hobbs's wife of a moral weakness that might very well break under even slight questioning. Lastly, Hobbs and I must go to the garage, after Agnes's corpse should have been taken out of it, and carefully wash away every stain of blood, from the garage itself, and from the floor, body, brake rods, transmission housing, and upholstery of the car. It was most fortunate that the little coupé was upholstered in leather, and not in mohair or some equally permeable material.

With the two bodies thus disposed of, Hobbs and I were to drive the car to the place mentioned by him and there in some way bury it, either by throwing down enough earth with shovels, or by undermining the bank so as to induce a landslide. We had no explosives with which to overthrow it, and we dared not purchase any. In the event of suspicion falling upon us, the fact that we had bought explosives must convince any investigator that we were lying, even if he had no other clew. Then tomorrow morning, and not before, Gray would drive into Tiltown and report to the authorities there the disappearance of her brother and his wife. She would say that he had come to Ormesby about daylight, bringing my wife from New York on a visit to her husband. That he had briefly stated his unexpected visit to have been necessitated by a desire to consult with his own wife on some matter of finance. That he and Agnes had driven away in Ormond's car, ostensibly for the purpose of talking while driving about the countryside. And they had not returned. No great uneasiness had been felt until after nightfall. Gray herself, though slightly anxious, had retired earlier than usual, having a nervous headache; she had fallen asleep and had not awakened until nearly dawn. Thereupon, finding that her relatives had not returned, she had telephoned his residence and his offices in New York (which Gray, of course, was to do), learning that no one there had seen him since Friday evening, it being now Saturday. This would make Gray's report to the police fall upon Sunday morning.

After that there would be nothing to do but wait. Ormes's business associates would probably send a representative to Ormesby to consult with Gray and with Barbara. No doubt the police would also visit the house, now and again, questioning and prying. My own business there was to be stated as that of a friend who had consented, at Ormond's request, to look over his library for the purpose of estimating its value in the event of his deciding to dispose of it. Thus we planned, desperately, sticking to truth where we could do so without becoming involved in admissions we dared not make, and only inventing where necessary. We knew, all of us, that we were taking terrible risks. The slightest slip would precipitate an investigation which would bring down our entire house of straw about our ears. Everything depended upon the authorities, and Ormes's creditors and partners, obtaining not the least hint that he and his wife had not disappeared in the manner we were to relate.

How wild a thing it is to undertake the concealment of a violent death! Not one of the four who had been slain at Ormesby had been killed maliciously by anyone sane enough to suffer for the deed. Except, of course, that the elder Ormes had been done to death by his son in protection of a woman. Yet here we all were, two of us outsiders with no apparently vital interest in fostering the pride of this family, bound by such secrets as filled that silent house with ghosts, and intent upon the burial in hugger-mugger of yet more corpses! All for the sake of this family's crumbling pride! When I look back upon it, I think that we must, all of us, have been more than a little mad. I could have refused, and Muriel could have refused, to join Gray in her fixed resolve to hide the madness which had wrecked her tribe. Yes, and Hobbs could have refused. There was really no good reason why we should have taken the risks we all agreed to take merely for the sake of pandering to this girl's fear of scandal. If the three of us had stood together and had told the truth, no more harm than inconvenience could have come to us, perhaps, though we should have crushed Gray and Barbara and have made it impossible for either or both of them longer to reside at Ormesby. Yet we

did take those risks. We did join hands in trying to hoodwink the
police. We did agree to conceal the fact of the deaths and to aid
Gray in destroying the bodies. We did, in short, become criminals
by conspiring to thwart justice and by refusing to report those
deeds of violence.

Well, let me be honest! We did all that for Gray's sake, it is
true, but we did it even more for our own. I know that I was mor-
tally afraid of scandal, as much afraid of it as Gray herself was. I
dreaded questioning by the officers of police as much as or more
than Hobbs did. I feared, more, perhaps, than any of the others,
that we might not be able to establish our innocence, were we to
be charged with crime, or with being accessories to crime. As for
Muriel—well, I cannot answer so well for her as for myself, naturally, but I thought then, as I still do, that she became one of us
because she found me to be one of the conspirators. It was what I
had called, up there in Gray's room, habit of thought and action.
She had left me and she had divorced me. But she had been my
wife. Now, facing danger with me, she stood beside me as she had
not stood when the danger threatened only her comfort and love
of luxury. There was, I thought, some extenuation in that.

"Where is Grayce?" I asked.

"She was fast asleep when I looked in there an hour ago," Gray
replied. "I'll look in again before I leave the floor. She—well,
she'll probably sleep like that until tomorrow."

"And Barbara?"

"I had to tell her there'd been a fight. I must go and tell her
now that Ormond is dead."

Hobbs and I went straight to Ormond's room for the purpose
of taking up his body and carrying it to the "crypt" at the foot
of the winding stairs. We dared not leave it in any of the other
rooms. In all probability it would have been quite safe to do so;
but our imagination saw dangers where they probably did not
lurk, even as they in all likelihood failed to seem then where they
were. I was thinking that, much as I loathed such work, I would
far rather do it than do what Gray must. Muriel accompanied us,
and after we had wrapped the corpse in a sheet, so that blood
might not drip onto the carpets and floors, and had borne it out
of the door., she set to work to remedy the appearance of the

room. Half an hour later we all came together, quite by chance, in one of the small drawing-rooms on the ground floor.

"I've told her," Gray said.

"She wasn't . . . shocked?" I put in, for Barbara's attitude interested me deeply.

"She . . . she bore it bravely enough. In fact, she seemed relieved. Maybe you know why? She said she had feared for some time that Ormond's brain was failing, and that Agnes meant no good to any of us. She's always claimed that Agnes doesn't belong here, you know. And then she asked what we intended doing with . . . with the bodies. She wants all of us to come to her room."

We went. There were questions asked and answers given, but I shall not detail such matters. The only thing of any consequence spoken in that gathering was a speech made by Barbara. Here are her words:

"You're all fools to think you can get away with such crude work as that. Don't you realize that Ormond's disappearance will cause his business associates to hire clever detectives to learn where he went, or what became of him? Or, if they don't, his creditors will. We shall have 'em here, questioning us separately, and they'll be bound to find flaws in any story we can hatch. It won't do. Besides those bodies must be disposed of in a manner more becoming to—that is, I mean, both the bodies must be disposed of in some entirely different way. Now listen: Someone's said that Doctor Barnes is to return here about seven this evening, to give Alice her first injection of vaccine. Where is Ormond's car? Still on the driveway? Put it into the garage at once, and lock the garage door. When the doctor comes, you three must be sitting downstairs, on the lawn, chatting. You must appear entirely at ease. I'll be here in my room. I'll show no excitement, if he stops here, as he usually does. Hobbs will admit him and take him up to Alice. Barnes will be able to testify, afterwards, if need be, that nothing was wrong at the time of his visit. If he asks after either of the Ormeses, you're all to say that they went for a drive through the hills. That is, one of you is to say that, the others are to remember it and back it up, if need be. Don't say it, don't mention either of their names, unless his question obliges you to. After he's gone, Mr. Seaverns and Hobbs will take both the bodies out and lay them near the kennels. *Then let the dogs loose upon them!"*

"Good God!" muttered Hobbs, while the same expression, or similar ones, showed in the shocked faces of the rest of us.

Barbara glanced round the circle, asking us haughtily with her eyes whether we had any better suggestion to offer. Since none of us said anything, she resumed her orders. But I could not help noticing that her eyes had in them something of the same red gleam which I had seen, and more than once, in Grayce's eyes, and had seen in Ormond's eyes at the last, and had seen in the eyes of the portrait of the dead man whose unclean ghost yet walked in the house of the Ormeses.

"After the dogs have torn the bodies for fifteen or twenty minutes, one of you—no, two of you—Seaverns and Gray—who will be out in the grounds, will scream several times. Hobbs will rush out of the house. You will all shout, then, and make as much noise as you can, and Gray will lead or drive the dogs back into their pens. Then Mr. Seaverns will rush to the telephone and call the doctor again, and also call the police. You will say that a horrible thing has happened. That the dogs have just dragged down and killed Ormes and his wife. By the time people get here, if the brutes have done their work as thoroughly as I think they will have, there will be no one to ask how Agnes's throat came to be cut."

"Well enough," I objected, "but the dogs won't have been able to put that hole in the man's head. What's to account for that?"

"It's well you thought of that," she said, favoring me with her little, brittle, hard smile. "Let me think a moment."

Horrible or not, there was not one of us who could not see that Barbara's idea was worth a score of such plans as that on which we had thought to proceed. Already we had a witness, in the person of Doctor Barnes, that the dogs at Ormesby were vicious creatures which would, on occasion, with or without provocation, attack even the persons living there and with whom they could be supposed to be perfectly familiar. The doctor had said that the brutes ought to be got rid of. I could truthfully testify that Ormes had been afraid to alight from his car, on the night of my arrival with him, until his sister had called the beasts to heel.

All of us could swear that Agnes had been afraid of them. The entire plan, if carried through with resolution and with natural- ness, ought to succeed, provided that Barbara, or any of us, could think of something to account for that great hole in Ormond's skull.

"This," said Barbara at last, "is the best I've been able to think of, so far. If I get a better idea later, we can change the plan. But one of you—Hobbs, you—will rush out into the grounds with an axe or a hatchet in hand. You will kill one of the dogs—brain him—with it. And you will kill several of them, if you can. You will say that the wound in Ormond's head was caused by aiming a blow at one of the dogs and striking his dead body. This whole thing will depend on how well all of you can act. You can't re- hearse it. But you can do this: live the parts you're to play after the doctor's arrival. Then, perhaps, you'll be able to tell your story with some appearance of truth. The thing isn't perfect. It shouldn't be ... quite. It must look, then, too much like a plot. But for God's sake, or your own, or for Hell's, do the best you can. It's your only chance. And may Satan have mercy on all of you."

Again I started, as I think the others must also have done, except, perhaps, Gray. I saw her smile grimly at the woman who had used such expressions. This gentle Barbara must have looked deeper into the Pit, and into human hearts, than any stranger could well suppose. But Gray seemed not astonished.

It was after four o'clock, and there was no time to be lost. Hobbs and I went at once to the garage, carrying pails, water and sponges. We took care that no one should be passing on the road below us while we traveled between house and garage. There we laid the stiffened form of Agnes Ormes on the floor, while we at- tacked the interior of the coupé with our sponges and water. In an hour we had removed the last least trace of gore from inside and outside of the car, and from the garage floor. I knew that a scientific investigation, with proper instruments and appliances, must reveal traces which we had not removed, could not remove. But all our efforts were to be bent upon preventing the necessity for such an investigation. The stockings I had found, my own torn and bloodstained clothing, one or two of the small rugs from Ormond's room, and the filthy blankets from the little room at the rear of the second floor, all these were carefully burned in the incinerator. The towels and the sheet used to wrap Ormond's body in could not be burned until we had removed that body from the house to the lawn. Hobbs was detailed to make it a special duty to see to it that all such articles should be consigned to the flames as soon as they should have served their purpose and before the dogs should have been let loose.

Both Gray and Muriel spent some little time in the dead man's room, putting things to rights there, removing broken chairs and tables to the lumber room in the attic and replacing them with others. Gray had gone at once to the kennels, after leaving Barbara. She reported that the pack, which had not been fed all day, came eagerly to her whistle and that, finding no meat awaiting them, one or two of the more surly brutes had behaved badly. They would all be ferocious with hunger by the time we offered food to them. And all this helped to assure us that they would not hesitate to tear the corpses literally in pieces, as soon as they should have been released upon them. Grayce, said Gray, slept soundly in her bed.

There seemed, indeed, to be but two bad flaws in the plan. It might very well be that the hole in Ormond's head would excite more suspicion in the police than could be allayed by Hobbs's story of the chance blow; and since *rigor mortis* had already set in, it might be that the coroner or some other medical sharp would give it as his opinion that the torn bodies had been dead longer than they should have been. But we had to take these chances, great as they were. The scheme was certainly not perfect.

But we did not overlook placing a small axe in the kitchen, where Hobbs could most easily snatch it up on his way to the rescue—I do not write that word ironically!

Much later in the afternoon (indeed, I was on my way to my room to remove some of the grime I had accumulated in doing my part of the work) I paused for a moment before mounting the stairs. Why I paused, I do not remember. But as I stood there in the hallway, something touched my throat!

I was not mistaken. The sensation was unmistakable. A swift cold touch, as of metal or thin claws. It was a repetition of what I had felt upon first entering this house. Then it had come to me in darkness. Now I felt it in the full light of day.

Do you say that I was mistaken? That I imagined the thing? That my nervous state induced the fancy? If you account for the sensation in any such rational way, you do what I myself endeavored to do, after my first astonished and affrighted gasp, and as I gathered courage together and mounted the broad stairs.

Oh, yes! But what of the tall thin man, dressed entirely in black, who strode swiftly and silently down the hall in my direction, seeming to have come from Alice Hobbs's room, and vanished into the little room where hung the evil portrait?

I did not follow him. I should have done so, undoubtedly. If a stranger were walking about in the house, I ought to know his business there. But I did not follow. Instead, after what seemed a long while, I went to the door of Mrs. Hobbs's room and knocked. There was no sound from within. I turned the knob and looked in.

The woman lay in her bed, her face as white as the sheet beneath her chin, her eyes fixed and staring. She was unconscious. I saw that when I had entered and gone close beside her. And the bandages around her throat had been partly ripped away!

XIV

It was a silent dinner to which three of us gathered, a dinner which Muriel had prepared and which Hobbs, once more the perfect servant in word and manner, served to us at table. I do not know what may have passed through the minds of those others; for myself, I had already begun to lose heart. With lessened action came time for thought. The difficulties thought conjured up loomed very large. It was in vain that I quoted for my own benefit all the copybook maxims pertaining to courage and the proper use of it. My spirits continued steadily to sink until, with dinner over, I must have been pulling as long a face as the Knight of La Mancha himself.

How much of this depression was due to my recent experiences in the hallway upstairs and in Alice Hobbs's room, I cannot

say. No doubt they contributed mightily to it. Nevertheless I
believe, today, that my pessimistic attitude had been induced
more by the suspicions that were slowly forming in my brain
with regard to Barbara Ormes than by any other happening
or thought. Something was wrong with the woman! Lovely as
her face was, I had seen in her eyes and in her smile the hint, the
merest ghost, it is true, yet not to be mistaken, of something
more terrible that Grayce's lunatic frenzies, more shocking than
Ormond's murderous schemes and efforts, more diabolical than
even the ghosts which walked at Ormesby.

Mrs. Hobbs had regained consciousness while I stood unde-
cided beside her bed. She looked up and saw me. Gradually the
blankness went out of her eyes. Then a flash of terror came into
them. That also faded. After all, she had not been physically injured. And she herself might have disarranged the bandages
about her throat. But there was in the whole aspect of the poor
woman a hunted look. It was not a look so much of fear as of
despair, as I have seen it in the face and bearing of a man about to
be hanged. She was doomed, and she knew it, and she had aban-
doned hope. And when hope has left the breast of any human
being, that being is already, though he or she may still move and
breathe and think, that being is already as one dead.

"Are you all right?" I asked. "You have been having a bad
dream." And I smiled at her.

"Don't let ... her ... come here ... again," the woman gurgled,
and she spoke out of the corner of her thin and twisted mouth.

"Her?" I gasped. Was Grayce abroad again?

"Yes! She ... she ..." Her words died away.

"Yes?"

"She'll kill me! I know it! Oh, I'm so afraid of her! But it's no
use ... no use ... no use!" she sobbed, though her eyes were dry
enough.

"Have you seen nothing of a man, then?"

She shook her head. I was in doubt as to whether she heard or
understood me.

"But she'll— Oh, please don't let her come near me!"

"No. We won't. We'll watch out for you. You'll be all right now.
It's lucky I came in when I did. But now everything's all right. You

feel better?" She nodded. I bent over her and rearranged the bandages. "You don't want anything?"

"No, only . . ."

"I understand," I said, soothingly. "But we're all very busy just now. I'm needed downstairs. But she—the woman—is locked in her room. You hear?"

She nodded, though her eyes went to the door and a look of fear came again into her face.

I reassured her again, and as well as I could. I must humor her, I supposed, in her fancy that a woman had visited her. I knew that Grayce slept soundly in her room. I knew that neither Muriel nor Gray had been lately above the ground floor. And I was certain that Barbara sat alone in her chamber. And yet . . . Barbara? Was it possible that she . . . ? But I could not answer that.

None the less, I had become more convinced than I had yet been of the reality of the figure I had seen in the hallway as I mounted the stairs. It was the figure of a man, and I knew it to be the figure of Ormond's father. And when I speak of it as a "reality" I mean, of course, that it was an objective ghost, not a phantasm of my disordered brain. And yet, after all . . . Was it a ghost? What if it were the man himself in the flesh? What if the Undead walked . . . ?

And did this man, this Undead Thing, move always where Barbara . . . where Barbara . . . ?

Whatever Gray felt, and however much she may have doubted our chances of success, her iron will sustained her throughout dinner and throughout the time which followed. She had given way to tears earlier in the day. Now her inflexible pride appeared to have lifted up her courage, and not by word, nor by a sigh, nor by so much as a look of terror or doubt in her yellow eyes did she betray the slightest hesitation or wish to yield. Her resolution nerved us all, somehow, and shamed us out of weakness and a wish for failure.

Sitting together on the lawn, with Hobbs within easy calling distance inside the house, we discussed in low tones every detail of the work before us. Ormond's car had been driven into the garage, the door of which had been, of course, closed. I estimated the time when we could expect sufficient darkness on this clear evening, supposing that it would have descended upon us, though not upon the hilltops, by eight o'clock, or a little later.

Mrs. Hobbs had not been told anything by her husband, save that she was to remain quiet and hold her tongue, both then and at any later time. Barbara had elected to remain secluded in her room. But Hobbs reported that he feared his wife was developing a slight fever, so that new complications threatened, should the woman say in delirium anything which might attract the suspicions of the cynical Doctor Barnes.

As for myself, though I forced my brain to take cognizance of what was going on around me and to formulate questions, and answers to the questions of my companions, I was more intent upon the problem of Barbara's conduct than upon anything more directly pressing. I had not said anything to the others of what I suspected. What, indeed, was there to be said? And could I tell even Gray of the apparition I had seen of her dead father? In that hour I did not think I could. But I could not rid my thought of fear, nor my body of desire for action—action, I mean, relative to investigating the meaning of the sight I had seen and the suspicion I had partly formed.

It was arranged that Gray must accompany the physician, when he arrived, and remain with him in Alice Hobbs's room until he had treated the patient and then had left her.

The doctor arrived at a few minutes past seven o'clock. Bringing his little car to a stop under the old porte cochère, he skipped nimbly out of it, nodded in the general direction of Muriel and me, then was admitted by Hobbs and disappeared from our sight. Gray, who had previously entered the house, would accompany him up the stairs. I had risen and bowed to the visitor; now I resumed my seat, gave Muriel a cigarette and lighted one for myself.

"When he goes," I said, "you and I will have become engaged in something of a kind we never thought, once upon a time, to be engaged in."

"Yes. This depression in business is having strange results. We can't blame it directly, of course, and yet, if it hadn't brought us here, we wouldn't have become involved in such things."

"It will have made an entirely new world, Muriel," I said,

"when it has passed." I spoke, I confess, more to ease the tension of my brain than to say anything of consequence. "It's not only your life and mine. It's changed something in the lives of everyone in the country, maybe even in the world. Which reminds me.... What are you thinking of doing ... afterwards?"

"If we go through this without being arrested, you mean?"

"Yes."

"What are you thinking of doing?"

"I'm not thinking. I don't know. It doesn't matter much, I suppose."

"Doesn't it matter? Then I don't know either."

"But——"

"No! I've tried that. It didn't work. At least, it didn't work satisfactorily. I thought, at first, that it was going to be great fun, with half a dozen men dancing after me. I enjoyed the liberty, just as you did, too, if you'd admit it."

"I might have enjoyed it more," I said, bitterly, "if I'd had cab fare and enough money to buy a decent dinner, now and then. As things were, I——"

"I know," she interrupted, softly. "I'm sorry, Selden. But I wasn't really happy. Having fun isn't being safe. And I'm intended to be safe, if I'm to be happy at all. I'm that kind of woman, I guess. It seems to me that right now, in spite of all the things threatening us, and in spite of poverty and all that threatens hereafter, it seems to me that I'm safer with you ... here ... than ..."

Her voice trailed away. I was tempted to answer in words calculated to bridge the chasm between us. For that such a chasm existed, neither of us would, I think, have denied. It had been one thing to see Muriel, after the divorce, in town, to take her to dinner, to make love to her in her apartment. Then the doing of it had smacked of romance. There was then no notion in either of our brains that we should ever marry again, for all that we talked idly of it as perhaps happening ... some time. But now, with the woman offering again, as certainly she was offering, to come back to me legally as my wife—well, I hesitated. I do not defend my attitude. Neither do I wholly condemn it. She had made it plain that she wanted a reconciliation. Perhaps I manifested a streak of cruelty in allowing her to do this without encouragement. I do not know. Besides, under the conditions we faced, love-making would have been no less than heartless. Within a short distance from where we sat there were two stark corpses against which we meditated the foulest of violations.

None the less (let me be as honest as I can be) I do not think my words were checked by any such considerations as I have mentioned. I was afraid . . . of the ghost I had seen, that Thing Undead which haunted Ormesby and seemed to be looking on with approval at such deeds as I was beginning to suspect were done by that vampire's sister. I was afraid of the dangers which threatened us, of Muriel's honesty, of my own desires. In that moment Gray's face, handsome in fixed resolve, rose before the eyes of my mind. I searched for words in which to reply to Muriel, but found none. I suppose I did not wish, earnestly, to find any. Nor did she speak again. She had made her advance. If I received it in silence, what could she further say or do? The time dragged.

Doctor Barnes and Gray came at last out of the house, and stood together, for a moment, chatting on the steps before the door. I knew at once, from her manner, and from the glance she flung at us, that everything had happened according to our desire. The medical man made as if to enter his car, then hesitated and engaged in some earnest talk with her. I caught the word "dogs" and later the worthy doctor's "dammit!" Abruptly he stepped away from her, tossed his satchel into the car and came toward us. I sprang to my feet, introducing Muriel and the man. For an instant I had hesitated. Then I named her as "my wife, Mrs. Seaverns." I saw a dry little smile cross her mouth.

"Haven't you any influence with this unreasonable woman, Mr. Seaverns?" the doctor demanded.

"I'm afraid she thinks she knows her own mind," I answered. I had guessed at something of what he intended saying. "But if there's anything I can do——" I broke off, laughing a little.

"I want her to get rid of those damned dogs. Somebody's goin' to get badly mauled. There oughta be a law against keepin' savage brutes like that."

"Oh, they don't bother people who have any business here," Gray objected, while I marveled at her ability as an actress.

"Well," he said, helplessly, shrugging his narrow shoulders, "have it your own way. They ain't my dogs. But you mark my words, you're gonna be sorry, sooner or later. Some day they'll chew somebody up bad. Good night! I'll be up tomorrow. The patient may be a bit restless tonight. I left something to quiet her, if she is. But if her fever rises, you'd better call me."

"Yes, doctor," murmured Gray.

He turned away and she walked with him part of the distance to his car. Then they separated and she came back to us. He entered the car and drove away, a shower of sparks streaming from the fouled exhaust of it.

"He will treat Alice every day for fourteen days," said Gray.

"I'm very glad of it," said I. "His being here every day will keep the police away. And vindication of his prediction will make him very friendly to all of us, even if he allows himself to be a bit superior. He'll be willing to believe himself right, if only to show us how wrong we were. This doctor is invaluable."

After that the minutes dragged again. Eight o'clock came, and still it did not seem dark enough for our purpose. Fifteen more minutes dragged their dreary way into eternity. I ran to the house, to find Hobbs drinking whiskey in the dining-room. I forbade him to take any more, while at the same time I poured myself a stiff portion and downed it. But at last it was eight-thirty and beyond all question too dark for anyone passing on the road below to see us at work in the grounds.

Hobbs was ready. Together, carrying torches, we descended the winding stairs and lifted the body of Ormes. Muriel came after us, with a small pail of water and a sponge, to remove any smear of blood that the wet towels may have left upon the cement floor. Gray was with her, lighting her with a torch. Hobbs and I carried the stiffened corpse out through the kitchen, from which Mrs. Hobbs had disappeared. We laid it down on the grass outside, compelled to rest and catch breath. Then, lifting it again, we bore it to a point half way between the garage and the kennels, laid it there, removed the sheet and the towels, which Hobbs immediately took to the incinerator, where he burned them, waiting long enough before the door of the burner to see that they were entirely consumed.

In the meanwhile I had gone to the garage and had pushed

back the door of it. Muriel followed me there, also, prepared to clean up any stains that might be left on that floor when we should have carried Agnes's body out of the building. Gray had taken up her stand near the kennels. The dogs, scenting her presence near them, set up a sharp yelping and growling, begging to be fed. Through the darkness I saw their evil eyes, red and menacing, as they leaped against the fence or sniffed for a hole along the bottom of it. As soon as Hobbs came back, it was the work of but a moment to carry Agnes to a point close beside the dead body of her husband. Muriel, behind us, closed the garage door. Then she ran to the house, where she burned such cloths and rags as she had used and stained, washed her hands and made ready for the part she was to play later. In the meanwhile, as part of her routine of the moment, she visited Grayce's room and Barbara's, seeing to it that everything there was quiet. One mistake we had made, and it later came near to wrecking us: we had not thought to appoint Muriel to visit Mrs. Hobbs during this time, though we should have anticipated that the woman must be aware of something out of the ordinary and be made nervous and frightened.

But all being ready outside, Hobbs returned to the kitchen, carrying with him a bloody towel that had been under Agnes's head as she lay on the garage floor. Also he resumed his coat, which he had laid aside while helping me. He was next to appear as the servant who had been on duty ready to serve drinks, if they had been called for, or to answer the door-bell or the telephone.

Gray stood beside the gate to the kennels. I could not see her face in the gloom, but I guessed from the rigidity of her figure that she was near the breaking point. I did not fear, however, that she would give way to emotion before she had completed her work of loosing the dogs and urging them onto their dead victims. What I dreaded was the reaction which might very well make her hysterical at a later time, when we should have called in the police and the neighbors and when every word and gesture of each of us would be scanned and remembered and, if possible, used against us. But there was now no turning back.

"Loose them," I commanded.

She turned to unbar the gate, and I pulled my revolver from a pocket, not doubting that I might have to use it in the next second. I intended, in any case, to shoot a dog or two before dashing to the telephone and calling help.

The brutes sprang through the opening almost before the gate had cleared a way. Gray, caught behind it by the impact of their rush, was thrown violently against me and into my arms. They closed about her, and the dogs surged through the gate, turned and came toward us. Gray straightened quickly. She knew that not even she dared show any weakness before their ravening jaws.

"Keep close behind me," she commanded, starting away toward where we had laid the corpses.

I followed. I dared do nothing else. Even as it was, more than one of the great beasts snapped at my heels, one of them even catching a leg of my trousers in his teeth and ripping it from knee to bottom. It was Hobbs's garment, but I was glad of the mishap, since it would lend color to my story of having fought with the dogs in a vain effort to drive them from their prey.

But now we were close beside the bodies. The dogs ran to them and sniffed at them. For some reason they would not attack. They circled, snarling furiously and darting back from the scent of the blood. I had not, so far, had leisure to sympathize very deeply with Gray in her ordeal. But in that moment my heart went out to her in pity. I had stepped in front of her, indicating the cadavers and endeavoring to sick the dogs on to tear them. But they would not obey me. They mistook my desire and prepared to rush at me instead. Gray was forced to take the last horrible action.

She did it! I don't think that I could have done it, in her place, but Gray called upon some hidden reserve of strength and did the unnameable thing. She bent right over her brother's body, her outstretched finger almost touching his face, and directed the dogs by name to the eating of their meat! And they understood her at last! And they fell upon the carcasses and began to tear them!

Gray screamed, straightening and reeling backwards into my arms again. But it was not yet time for her to scream. The dogs *must* have time to tear those corpses limb from limb. I tried to stifle her screams, but she wrenched herself free from me and ran screaming toward the house. And I, excited as I was, and stricken dumb with fear and horror, yet took time through it all to commend the realistic terror in her screaming and the mortal abandon of it. But I quite forgot that I ought myself to be joining my screams to hers.

It was Hobbs who saved the day in this respect. As it happened, not a soul ever heard the horrid din we made . . . we and the dogs. Not even the reports of my revolver reached anyone's ears. But if we had not shouted and screamed, if we had not fired shots, if the dogs had not replied with furious yelpings and snarlings, and if anyone *had* chanced to be within earshot, then our carefully laid and utterly heartless plan must certainly have failed.

Hobbs, supposing that Gray's premature screaming was his cue to issue forth with his axe, did so. Gray left my arms, staggering and stumbling away from me toward the house where, I learned afterwards, she fell at Muriel's feet in a dead faint. I saw Hobbs's white face as he ran toward me through the gloom, and I caught a flash of light reflected from the blade of his axe as he whirled it through the air above his head. A dog yelped sharply, the yelp ending in a deep wet gurgle. Then Hobbs, the stoical, the stolid, the reserved, went completely wild.

Cursing like a man demented, he flailed about him with the axe. I dimly saw two more dogs cut down with it. The pack, sensing that they were being attacked, left the dead bodies and drew back for a moment, preparatory to rushing these new enemies. I sang out to Hobbs to leave them and come into the house. Whether he heard me or not, he gave no sign of it, but sprang toward the dogs and cut at one of them again. But if he were not himself dragged down and killed by the furious brutes, he would end by dispatching so many of them that there might not be enough of them to complete the terrible work we wanted done. I darted up close behind him, narrowly missing being brained by that whirling axe of his. A long dark brute flashed through the air, launched straight for Hobbs's throat. He went down under the impact of that spring, with the dog on top of him. Then he screamed again, this time in terror and not in rage. I thrust the muzzle of my revolver against the dog's ribs and pulled the trigger twice. And then, out of the struggling chaos of legs and arms and flashing teeth, I dragged Hobbs and jerked him onto his feet.

He was dizzy and dazed. But I gave him no time for recovery. There was none to give. Throwing all my weight and strength against him, I propelled him in the direction of the house. He had lost his axe. Another dog came for both of us, and again I could not miss, being so close. Then we were clear of the pack, the remaining members of which returned to worrying and tearing the meat we had provided for them.

At the kitchen door we halted and turned about. The pack was fighting above the carcasses, raising a hell of sound. Hobbs retched horribly beside me, making spasmodic efforts to vomit. My own brain was reeling, but I was not physically sick, as Hobbs was and as I had been upon coming face to face with the naked and bloodstained Grayce.

But more work awaited me. I pushed Hobbs through the door, following him inside. It was my part to telephone the doctor and to call the police from Tiltown. I found, however, that Muriel had already done it. I was glad enough that she had taken this duty from me. I doubt that I could, at that time, have played the ghastly hoax another step.

But after we had rested a few minutes, Hobbs went in search of another gun. Then he and I again issued onto the grounds. We must be engaged in striving to kill or drive off the dogs when the help we had summoned arrived. Nevertheless, afraid of killing too many of the beasts before they had finished their work, we did little more than fire a shot or two among them, trying to frighten them into dragging their victims farther and farther away from the vicinity of the garage and house. And we did succeed in killing two more of the creatures before the police, racing madly in a large open car, swept in from the road below.

They joined us with drawn guns. The beams from their torches showed them enough of the human fragments strewing the ground to make them fighting mad. The dogs, knowing themselves overmatched, and partly satiated now with the meat they had wolfed down and the blood they had lapped, broke away, making for the hills. Only two of the original dozen escaped, however, and those two were shot and killed on the following day by hill dwellers who had bruited among themselves a story that the entire Ormesby pack was mad.

But the scheme had succeeded. By the light of the torches we found and gathered up the poor fragments of what had once been living persons. The women, with Grayce among them, and as white and terrified as the rest, had huddled together in Barbara's room. To questions of the police, Hobbs and I stammered a tale of seeing Ormes and Agnes return from their drive. They had put their car in the garage, the dogs being then penned up. Later, I said, I had lost sight of them, but Hobbs tremblingly told of seeing them making their way toward the kennels. The next thing any of us had known was the screaming of the woman and man as the pack bore them down. Then Hobbs and I had rushed out, I with the gun I had been carrying as protection against the very dogs I was now called on to shoot, Hobbs with the axe which had been standing in the kitchen. The tale seemed plausible enough. The bodies were literally torn limb from limb. The clothing was reduced to bloody and mud-smeared rags. The hole in Ormes's skull, noticed at once by one of the policemen, was explained by Hobbs in the manner we had plotted. Doctor Barnes, who had arrived a few minutes after the police, put in his word of "I told you so." There was nothing visible to anyone which lent the lie to our story. Hobbs's agitation, my own, and that of the women weeping and wailing in the room above, all these were signs of no more emotion than we must have displayed had the thing befallen as we said it had. The police bundled up the battered and torn corpses in blankets and sheets, loaded them into their car and drove away with them to the undertaker's rooms in Tiltown. Doctor Barnes found occupation for his professional services in attending to Hobbs and myself, both of whom were scratched by claws and bleeding from the cuts of slashing fangs. Moreover, having attended to us, he had still to administer sedatives to the hysterical women.

How the news of this horrible happening had spread among the dwellers of the hills, I shall never know. The police had scarcely arrived, however, before strangers began to appear. Some came in cars, others on foot. Some were people of fashion from the neighboring country houses, others were natives of the Berkshires. I begged of the police chief that he leave one of his men with us, as protection against these intrusive strangers, who pushed and crowded into the house as if it were no longer a private dwelling but some public place. This policeman, very sympathetic in the midst of our tragedy, went outside several times and drove the people away. I heard him haranguing the crowd, trying to shame them into some kind of orderly conduct, but when they continued trying to slip past his men and enter the house, he directed the officers to use clubs against them. That scattered them quickly enough. He returned to tell us that he would leave one man with us, but that he himself and the rest must return to Tiltown, since they comprised the entire protective force of that community.

With our policeman tramping round and round the house, chasing idlers out of the grounds and threatening to shoot trespassers, we began, at last, to find some quiet. Gray had led Grayce to the latter's room, where the two of them now were. Barnes had ordered Barbara into bed, and she, without protest, obeyed him. Muriel visited Mrs. Hobbs, going from there to the kitchen on some errand, then joined Barnes and me, where we stood talking in the front hallway. I was having difficulty in convincing the good doctor that Gray had promised to rid Ormesby of the remaining dogs on the morrow.

"Pshaw!" he cried. "They ought never to have been here. This would never have happened if she'd taken my advice in the first place. But they've always had a savage pack here. I shouldn't be s'prised if she gets another."

I replied with something, I have forgotten what it was. Muriel, as I said, came from the rear room and joined us. The front door opened and the policeman guard came in, reporting that all seemed to be quiet outside. Perhaps five minutes, not more, passed while the four of us stood there, discussing the recent happenings in low whispers.

Then Hobbs, whiter than his own shroud will be and clad only in trousers and shirt, since he had not fully resumed the clothing he had been forced to remove for the doctor's ministrations, burst upon us from the dining-room. He halted, seeming to be about to speak. But speech failed him. He could only lift an arm and point with it back along the way he had come. It was evident from his manner and agitation that something had happened in the kitchen.

Leading the way through the dining-room, I heard the others following me. Nothing was in the latter room, and I began to think that Hobbs might have been frightened by the same spectre I had seen. But he caught up with me and, still quite unable to speak, urged me toward the kitchen, gibbering unintelligibly beside me. So I went on.

A short passage led from the dining-room to the kitchen. It was not greater than three feet in width, so that while two persons could have walked abreast along its length, they naturally would prefer to go in single file. Hobbs stumbled along behind me, clutching at my arm, and after him came the policeman, the doctor, then Muriel. And I stopped dead and stared before me, glad that I was not alone. The kitchen was a shambles.

Seated in a chair, over the back of which her head had fallen, so that her slashed throat gaped open, with a thick stream of blood still springing from the severed arteries, was Alice Hobbs. Beside her on the floor lay a long red knife. She had slashed her left wrist and the under side of both knees. Then she had cut her throat. She would be dead within a minute or so.

Doctor Barnes and the policeman, more accustomed than I to such scenes, pushed past me and went to the dying creature's side. I stepped staggeringly aside, my hand clutching at the kitchen table.

Something drew my eyes to the door opening to the stairs which rose from the kitchen to the neighborhood of the servants' room. Barbara Ormes stood there. In the light which shone full upon her, she stood very straight and rigid, her eyes fixed upon the woman before her. She did not glance at me. Abruptly her lips opened and the red tongue came lickingly out between them. Then I saw that there was froth on her mouth, as there had been on the crazy Grayce's mouth last night. And the eyes with which she stared at the horrid sight were as red as are the eyes of a wolf in darkness!

I shuddered. I well-nigh cried aloud. I clutched harder at the table for support. All this had occupied but a second of time, yet in that brief interval I had looked deeper into a woman's soul than a sane woman ever permits any man to look.

Something was under my fingers. Mechanically I picked it up

and glanced at it. It was a folded bit of paper. It was a note of some kind. Without thinking much of it at that moment, I thrust it unseen by any of the others into a pocket of my trousers.

But a few minutes later, while the officer again telephoned the police at Tiltown, I found an opportunity of examining the note. It had been written with a pencil.

"Harry—I kilt Mrs. Ormes. And now she won't let me alone. She will kill me, I know it. She cheated me and hid them from me. Maybe they are in the old iron place I don't know. I cant tell. Im glad to get out of this. Good by.

Alice."

XV

A coroner's jury, having reviewed the remains of Ormond Ormes and Agnes, his wife, identification of which had been made by a succession of witnesses, beginning with Gray and ending with the policemen who had carried them to Tiltown, and witnesses to the manner of their deaths having been sworn and examined, the said jury had no difficulty in arriving at a verdict of accidental death caused by dogs owned by the deceased. It was by no means a surprising verdict. How could they have found otherwise? There was no reason to suspect that reputable persons, such as were the witnesses examined, had conspired to do away with the bodies of their friends or relations in any such manner as that described. One or two questions, put to and answered by one of Ormes's business associates, proved that the man was on the verge of bankruptcy. No suspicion, then, that he might have been killed for his money entered anyone's head. Our story that he had taken a long drive with his wife, probably for the purpose of discussing their financial affairs, seemed perfectly plausible.

The bodies were returned to custody of the nearest of kin, and Gray at once gave instructions to have them cremated. That part of the business was over. We could, we supposed, draw quiet breath for a while.

But suppose the police had come into possession of the note I had found on the kitchen table at Ormesby? If Alice Hobbs were afraid of one of the women about her, then there was cause for a further investigation of her suicide. If certain bonds were concealed on the premises, then Ormes may have been trying to find them, and this effort on his part may well have led to his murder by someone interested in keeping the bonds from him. And if Alice Hobbs had killed Agnes Ormes, then we had all lied, and the way would have been open for a full and complete investigation. There are moments when I shudder to think of how near we came to destruction from that cause.

As to Mrs. Hobbs herself, there was never the slightest doubt as to the means of her death. Even the police were convinced that it was clearly a case of suicide, with a motive of despondency induced, perhaps, by illness, even of temporary insanity caused by horror and fright following the terrific ending of her master and mistress.

Hobbs had his wife's body cremated along with the others, and a single funeral ceremony sufficed for the interment of the three pots of ashes.

The rest of us returned to Ormesby . . . and to horror!

There is no doubt about it, human intellect is no match for human imagination. While yet swift action drove us in that house, we had no time for thinking. But let no man suppose that his moral nature can readily become hardened to the terrible deeds his hands may have had to do. I speak, of course, of fine-grained people, of men and women somewhat above the level of the brute. We had not been an hour at Ormesby, following the funerals, when the ghosts came out of their nooks and crannies and gibbered at us from the shadows of every room and passage.

Only Grayce, of all the six of us, seemed not to suffer. She appeared to be quite sane. She moved about the house, humming to herself and doing small tasks as if she had not a care in the world. As, indeed, she had not. Yet she was fully aware of nearly all that had taken place. It was not that her memory had blanked out for her the deeds of her own madness. She probably knew, even, that she had herself attacked the poor woman whose suicide must have been induced by fear of Grayce. For all this, however, she evinced absolutely no remorse. Doctor Barnes, who had seen but

little of Grayce in the past, said to Gray that her sister's vivac-
ity astonished him. He had caught only furtive glimpses of the
crazy girl in past years, since she had never been ill, supposing,
as a medical man should, that she was probably not very bright
and kept out of sight from a pathological access of shyness,
while the family allowed her to so hide herself because they were
ashamed of her. Now, however, seeing her as full of life and spirits as a young woman could well be, and seeing that she was quite
as personable as Gray herself, the good man admitted himself
somewhat puzzled by Grayce's former attitude.

Gray, meanwhile, grew pale and thin. Lying awake in my bed
at night, I frequently heard her walking the floor, unable to lie
down and sleep. It was not Grayce who walked. More than once
I had slipped up the stairs and listened at Gray's door, and I knew
that it was she. And if Gray's nerves were to break and hysteria
come upon her, I had small doubt that the lycanthropy in her
blood must come to surface and have its will with the girl. After
that, by so much as she had been saner than her sister, she probably would become the more dangerous. I dared not think of all
that. I must leave Ormesby before that calamity fell upon it, and
Muriel must go with me. Whether she wished to go or not, and
whether we were to live together, or were not, she must leave
Ormesby not later than my own leaving.

So I told myself. Nevertheless, I lingered there; and the days
passed and grew into weeks and then into months. It was nearly
the middle of October. I had returned to the house with the
Ormes women because I could scarcely leave them alone immediately after having been so closely associated with them in deeds
of horror. We all told ourselves and each other—all but Barbara,
who merely smiled and said nothing—that a short time would
bring about such a readjustment of life there as human beings
must make with each other and with their surroundings if they
are to live at all.

But Hobbs was a broken man. I did not think he grieved, over-
much, for the loss of his wife. I did not believe he had deeply
loved the woman. It was the terrible end she had put to herself,
and at so terrible a time, which had unnerved him, that and the
things he had been obliged to carry through with me. And I had

not yet showed him the note Alice had left. It was addressed to
him. I had, perhaps, no right to withhold it. But while he stood
within danger of apprehension by the authorities, I dared not add
to the burden this additional weight of horror must put upon the
man. Whatever loyalty he entertained for the Ormes family, it
must have been somehow strengthened by the innate contempt
which the sane feel for the insane and for those with lunatic blood
in their veins. Hobbs, servant as he was, could yet in a way look
down upon his employers, since pity, is a form of contempt. But
to reveal to him that his own wife had been also insane, that she,
too, had contracted the hideous lycanthropy which made a wolf
of her, lustful to tear out the throats of living victims and to drink
of their blood and to gnaw at their quivering flesh, that, I feared,
might well prove to be too much for poor Hobbs's already shattered nerves. So I did not tell him of the note prior to the inquest,
and after that I still hesitated to do so. For what had Alice meant
by "cheated"? And what by "the old iron place"? Here was fresh
mystery. Was Hobbs himself in some way involved in it?

Yet there was probably a greater danger in keeping the note
to myself. I am not made of iron. The thing was fast growing
to monstrous proportions; it was a symbol of all the secrets at
Ormesby. I could not live with those secrets and remain the man
I had been. I must assert myself and leave this house, despite
Gray's eyes and regardless of Barbara's frankly voiced plea that I
remain. There was, for one thing, Muriel to consider. And there
was, for another, Gray.

Gray was in love with me. Why shouldn't I say it? I am not
ashamed of it. She did not make such overtures as Grayce had
made, nor such frank invitations to join her in an intrigue as Barbara's eyes and attitude spoke of. None the less, since a thing like
that is always known to either the man or the woman who is the
object of affection, I knew that Gray loved me. No, she did not
speak, nor would she speak for many a long day. Perhaps, even,
if I were to remain silent, she might never speak of it. But what I
knew, I knew; and I could not continue (at least, I told myself this)
living with her in the same house and long refrain from yielding
to her unspoken call.

As for Muriel, she had said nothing of leaving Ormesby. Nei-

ther had she said that we—or either of us—ought to remain. I
was not quite sure that I any longer understood Muriel. She
saw, as I was well aware, Grayce's open preference for the only
man of her own generation with whom she had ever shared a
single secret. Yet I do not think that Muriel troubled herself to be
jealous of Grayce. She must have seen that Barbara ignored her
presence to the extent of stroking my face and throat in playful
fashion whenever she happened to stand or to sit near me, a position I avoided as well as I could. Nevertheless I hardly think that
Muriel could have been angry with Barbara. She, Muriel, knew
well enough that I could not sleep for thinking of Gray, pacing
all night back and forth in her lonely room upstairs. She knew,
too, that I left my bed and stole up there to listen, for she had
several times opened her door and seen me prowling. She could
not have supposed that I prowled with the intention of seeking
an entrance to her own chamber. Yet, knowing Gray as she did,
she could not have imagined that I sought entrance there, either.

For all that, and for all that pity and concern for Gray led me
by day to give her tender words and soft glances, the thought that
Muriel must be taken away from Ormesby gave me no peace. I
said to myself that I no longer loved the woman as I had once
loved her. I swore in my heart that I loved Gray Ormes. And yet
for all of that, I knew that Muriel must be shielded and safe. She
herself had said that she must have safety to live happily. She had
of her own volition deprived herself of such protection as I could
give. And I could not, for my life, rid my brain of the notion that
I must shield her now and hereafter. Explain that on any logical
basis, if you can.

Moreover, as I have said, I no longer quite understood Muriel.
For if she was not jealous of her companions at Ormesby, and I
could not think her so, then why did she treat me, of late, with
such marked coldness and disdain? Nor could I attribute this attitude to anything of "the woman scorned" by my refusal to accept
her frank offer of a new marriage. She had lived with me too long
not to have borne many such rejections of her advances. It might
have been different had we never before been man and wife.

But how could we leave the place? At least, how could I leave
it? If I left it, I should live every day of my future life in terror

of the hand of the law. At any moment Grayce might become mad again. Nor could I hope that insanity would long delay its mastery of her sister and her aunt. Hobbs also. Some day Hobbs would be as mad as his wife had undoubtedly been at the last, if he did not put an end to himself as she had. How could I go away and leave all that? I had neither money nor prospects. That, in itself, might not have held me there, though it could make it uncommonly difficult for me to go. But I was still young enough and strong enough to suppose that somewhere must be waiting for my hand a work that a man could do. No, it was not altogether reluctance to leave the warmth and the shelter and the decent food.

I had been once to Pittsfield, performing an errand for Gray. The journey and my business there occupied me not more than two hours. Still, though I believed myself to be enjoying my interval of freedom, I drove homeward at breakneck speed. So many things might have happened! I should not have been astonished had I headed into the drive at Ormesby to see a policeman's car under the porte cochère and to learn that I was under arrest.

Nor was this fear groundless. It might have happened. It might happen at any hour of the day or night. How could I be sure that Doctor Barnes would suspect nothing amiss? How could I be sure that Ormes's creditors, who were now carefully investigating his affairs, not only in New York but at Ormesby, would not stumble onto an inkling, at least, of the truth? He might have left any kind of letter or note among his papers. I lived over a powder mine, and I was fast losing the ability to "take a chance," which had carried me through the things I had done and helped to do. Every day Barbara was growing more reckless. It began to seem to me that she would have welcomed discovery. The secrets within her had nearly reached their full time and must some day be delivered at whatever cost of shame and pain. And every day Gray's eyes grew more sombre and more hollow and her wide lips more silent. And Hobbs went about his duties like a man dazed. And the animated Grayce's singing and laughter rang ever more lewdly and demoniacally in my tortured brain.

Nor could Muriel, perhaps the least affected of any of us, live long in constant contact with such ghosts as walked at Ormesby and be in no wise changed. There was already growing up in her a bitter cynicism which had never before shown itself to me. She sneered at me and snubbed me, making her manner all the more pointed and poignant by the tenderness with which she treated Barbara and Grayce and Gray.

Muriel had certain duties. All of us had work to do. It had been agreed that no new servant should be brought to Ormesby, at least for a while. Hobbs cooked for us and performed all duties incident to the work of the kitchen. But he could not be everywhere; he could not do everything; and the general house-keeping was divided among the women. Upon me devolved, more and more as the days passed, the handling of Gray's finan-cial and business affairs. She required me to pay bills, to consult with tradesmen, to undertake the overseeing of the estate. It was I who dealt with her brother's executors and with his business partners and with his creditors. She gave me a power of attor-ney to act for her in small matters, and then she broadened it, broadened it repeatedly. She insisted that I use her money, with-out troubling to consult her about it, or even to account to her for it, for the defraying of such minor expenses as Muriel and I could not help incurring.

I did not think then, nor do I think it now, that Gray did all this to bind me to her in the way a woman naturally wishes to bind a man when she loves him. Nor did I then think, though today I am not so sure of it, that Muriel was jealous of Gray.

But it was undoubtedly becoming more and more difficult to live comfortably at Ormesby. We had not buried our troubles. On the contrary, we had, as it were, loosed a new swarm of them out of the graves we had dug. Murder will out. We had not commit-ted murder, but we had done things of whose consequences we stood as much in dread as if we had intentionally slain Ormond Ormes and Agnes. Terror dogged our heels and tore at the ends of our tortured nerves. The approaching footfalls of one of our company set the rest a-tremble. The distant opening or closing of a door threw us into a funk. We dreaded going alone into cer-tain rooms; we feared what we might encounter in any and all of the halls; and yet we slept so badly at night that, one and all, we roamed those halls and haunted the library and could not keep

away from the room in which Ormond had met his death. I had
stumbled against Hobbs in the front hallway, and I had encountered Barbara in the little room where I had found Alice Hobbs
lying on that filthy pallet. She came to me and stood close against
me for the space of a moment. The beauty of her face and body
tempted me to clasp her against my breast, despite the loathing I
felt for her. But then, with a brittle little laugh, dry and crackling
as twigs on winter ground, she slipped away into the darkness.
She did not go into the hall. And I did not learn, until afterwards,
that she could pass from that chamber to her own room through
a passage similar, though shorter, to that which led from my
apartment to the room where hung the portrait of the avidly evil
eyes.

Once I entered Ormond's room at three in the morning,
thinking I had heard a noise there. It had been made by Gray. She
was dressed as she had been during the previous day, and she was
standing in darkness in the middle of the room. I saw her only
dimly, yet I knew it to be she. When I entered she brushed swiftly
past me and climbed to the third floor without a word. Shudder-
ing in spite of myself, for something I had not seen but had felt to
be showing in her face, I crept back to bed.

One silent night, awaking out of troubled dreams, I snapped
on a light and ran to the mirror on my dressing table. I had had
a feeling that someone had been very near me; and my first
thought was that one or another of the Ormesby women had
stolen to my bedside and kissed my throat, as on the first night of
my lying in that bed. But if the thing had happened, the woman
had not bruised the skin by sucking it. Perhaps it had not happened. None the less, the skin of my neck tingled slightly, but
continuously, as though it had been chafed. I do not say that this
sensation was not induced by nerves. It may very well have been.
But my nerves were not befooling me into thinking that I was
smelling the odor of a woman's body.

I went to the little closet. The smell there was unmistakable,
for my olfactory sense had become so acute of late that I had a
great many times detected the recent presence of a woman in a
room, now empty, which I had entered. And this in spite of the
fact that none of the women at Ormesby was addicted to the

use of perfume. And this in spite, also, of the fact that all of the women at Ormesby were clean of person.

I felt drawn along the passage. I did not require a light, for I knew the way well enough now. I dreaded going on, into the room where the portrait still hung. Yet I could not turn back. Something drew me along that passage in spite of my horror and disgust. I knew that the eyes of that man on the wall would be shining through the darkness with the same devilish and redly malevolent glare I had seen so many times. I knew that those eyes would follow my every movement. I knew that they were even now looking at me through the door of the closet in which I stood and trembled. I would have given ten years of my life to have been able to turn back and creep under the covers of the bed. But I could not do it. I was drawn forward by a force stronger than my fears. I opened the door and looked into the room.

There were the eyes! I had never seen them so menacing, so triumphantly ablaze. But also there was something else. I could not make it out, at first. Then, gradually, I saw that it was a woman's naked arms. One arm embraced the wall on either side of the portrait, and against the breast of the portrait was a woman's head. Her face was pressed to the canvas as it might have been pressed to a man's chest or throat. And her nude body clung to the wall lasciviously, ecstatically, in so deep an abandon that she neither heard me nor noticed me.

Released, after I do not know how long a time, from the spell which had drawn me forward, I stole back through the passage to my own room. It had been Barbara Ormes, brought, at long last, to this avowal of that love for which her brother had killed his wife and been in turn murdered by his own son. I could no longer doubt that Barbara had taken from that bite in her throat the strange virus which made a wolf of her. She, too, must have blood from the bodies of living persons to maintain her horrid and precarious hold upon consciousness and the world. No wonder that Undead Thing which had been her brother followed her movements about the house! I knew, at last, what poor Alice Hobbs had meant when telling me that she had been afraid of a woman. No wonder the eyes of the man in the portrait had gleamed in evil triumph!

On another occasion, also at night, though this was a night when the wind howled through the hills like giant wolves, I, who had not been able to sleep after midnight, distinctly heard my name called from somewhere. The voice had seemed to come from below stairs. It had sounded like a man's voice, though Hobbs should have been asleep in his room. I listened. The call was not repeated. Yet I had not been asleep, nor had I been dreaming, and I knew that the sound had not been caused by the wind. Someone had plainly shouted my name—"Seaverns!"—and it had been a man who had done it. And the name had been shouted, not spoken in that inaudible voice which one hears sometimes, inside the brain itself.

Snatching up a bath robe, I pulled it swiftly on and went out into the hallway. The house creaked and groaned in the wind. There was so much noise all about it that I could not have heard a tiny noise within. Therefore I did not stand and listen for one, but went directly to Hobbs's room. I could hear no breathing from a sleeper in there. I turned the handle of the door and opened it. Hobbs lay there, covered to the chin with a sheet, and that he slept soundly I could not doubt. I turned away.

Down the stairs I went and through the dining-room and thence into the library. With every step I shivered. Ghosts? Do you think a man grows used to them and ceases to shudder when he feels them near? Do not think, then, that I strode boldly into that library. On the contrary I crept in stealthily, fearfully, dreading what I might find. For that voice might have been Grayce's deep voice, and if she had called me thus in the angry night, it meant that she was abroad again, raving and in search of living blood. But there was nothing in the library which could have brought me there, nor was there any person.

None the less, Grayce, if it had been she, might be now in the passage behind the books, but I would not seek her there. Wherever she was, she ought to be found and forced to go back to bed, yet I could not drive myself to go and look for her beyond that panel. Down at the foot of those winding stairs we had laid Ormes's body. Now, unreasonably and yet persistently, I felt that it was again lying there. I knew I had not strength of will to go and look. If Grayce were down there, then she must stay there alone.

But I did go and look. It wasn't a matter of willing myself to do so. It was simply that my feet moved in that direction, and this in spite of any will within me to keep them from so going. I could not help myself. Little by little I approached the panel. Reluctantly and yet surely my hand went out and pressed the spring which opened it. My feet moved into the passage as by the urging of some unseen force. Certainly it was not by any driving of my brain. It was very dark in there. There was not the slightest sound to tell me that any living thing waited in that gloom ahead. Slowly I groped my way along the passage and came to the head of the stairs. Down there, at least, I would not go. I swore it to myself as a man swears he will not throw himself over the cliff before him. And I do not remember moving down those iron steps. Yet, somehow, I went down them.

By the time I had come to the first landing, I had died a thousand deaths. I would have given my right hand to have escaped the necessity of going farther. It seemed to me to be a cruelty greater than my flesh could stand to force it to go farther. But I went on. It must have taken me many minutes to reach the bottom. But I did reach it. I had willed my body to go in the opposite direction. Yet it took me to the foot of those winding stairs. I stood in the crypt in darkness so absolute as to seem a palpable thing.

There was nothing there. Feeling all about the walls of the crypt, I learned that there was nothing there. Nor any person. Just where my feet stood, Ormes's body had lain. I knew that, though I could not see my position with relation to the stairs.

Stooping over it in that inky blackness, without groping over the floor and with as sure a grasp as if I had seen it plainly, I picked up a small object from between my slippered feet. It was soft to the touch, and silky, as if it might have been a piece of stuff, shredded and raveled with much chafing. I could ascend the stairs, now. Nothing held me any longer. Swiftly, then, I mounted them and ran through the passage and came again to the library. I found a lamp and lighted it. I examined the object I had picked up from the floor of the crypt.

It was a lock of human hair! It was a piece of the scalp of Ormond Ormes! It must have become torn in some way from his broken head, and Hobbs and I must have overlooked it in lifting the body to carry it up and lay it outside for the dogs to tear.

But how had it been able to draw me so unerringly from my bed to find it in that darkness?

And how had it been able to call me by my name?

XVI

Such was my life! Such, in brief outline, were the lives of all of us at Ormesby. Of necessity, such a situation could not long endure. Something, somewhere, must break. Gray might go mad. Barbara was already more than half way there. Grayce must come, sooner or later, to another period of frenzy. Hobbs was rapidly cracking. My own nerves, though I was yet a young man and owned to no bodily weakness, could not long stand the strain that was being put upon them.

It was not only that ghosts walked in that house of Ormesby. If that had been all, one might have escaped their evil influence by leaving the place. But where could one go to be out of reach of ghosts that had longer arms than memory? And how leave a place to which one was tied with stronger bonds than fear? Muriel could not go away, for all her aversion to me. She had threatened to leave and she could not do it. Hobbs could not go. He had already been away, and he had come slinking back, after two days, trembling and gibbering and begging to be allowed to remain. I could not leave. I dared not leave. To be out of the house so long as one hour filled me with an abject terror. The ghosts that walked in the house of the Ormeses were the ghosts that walked in the souls of men.

As I have said, such a situation could not long continue. And as it happened, the first moves made to relieve the tension were moves made by the lunatic Grayce. She had begun by talking more freely with Muriel than she perhaps intended. To all appearance, as Muriel afterwards maintained, the girl was quite sane at the moment. They two had met by chance in the library and had seated themselves there. Grayce had begun the conversation by asking, rather abruptly, whether Muriel intended staying much longer in the house.

"Why, I hardly know," Muriel replied. "I suppose we ought to be leaving."

"We?"

"Yes, certainly. We're married, you know," and I suppose she smiled at Grayce in the unconsciously superior manner affected by married women everywhere. The statement was not true, but only Gray and Barbara were aware of the real situation.

"I know you are, of course. At least, I've heard you are. But what of that? He doesn't care for you, you know."

"Indeed?"

"Really he doesn't. He's my lover, you see."

"*Is* he? You astonish me!"

Muriel looked sharply at the other to be sure she was not about to slip into one of her fits of lunacy. But Grayce appeared to be calm enough.

"Yes, he is. I don't think he quite knows his own mind, but . . ." Her words died away. She sat dreamily gazing into distance. There was a little smile playing on her lips.

Muriel who, for all her present dislike of me, knew that I could not be so great a fool as to make love to such a creature, thought it best to humor Grayce. She did not contradict anything, but waited for the other to proceed. She might learn something.

"Poor Selden," Grayce went on, after a time, "I'm afraid he's very hard up. At least he was. Fortunately he now has enough for both of us."

"He has?" For it was perfectly well known to Muriel that I owned nothing but the suit of clothing given me by Hobbs; and she knew, also, that Grayce owned nothing at all.

"A hundred thousand. It's in bonds, I believe. Don't you think that enough?"

Muriel agreed that it ought to be enough for the present. But a hundred thousand dollars? And in bonds? A hundred thousand in bonds was what Ormond Ormes had given to his wife.

"What kind of bonds are they?" she asked, casually. She did not wish to arouse any suspicion in the girl's cunning, if clouded, mind.

Grayce declared she did not know the kind of bonds. She supposed they might have been issued by the Government. What difference did it make? Bonds were bonds, you know.

"Oh, none," said Muriel. "None at all. But where does he keep them? For surely they're not kept here at Ormesby?"

"Well, they're in a safe place," said Grayce with great complacency. "He'll know where to look for them when the time comes."

Muriel, seeing a gleam of suspicion enter the other's eyes, decided to drop the subject. But she repeated what she had heard to Gray; and Gray, troubled, came to me with it.

"It's not impossible," I told her, "that Grayce may have learned something about those bonds Agnes had. I hope you don't suspect that I——"

"Of course not! But why should Agnes have kept them here at Ormesby? I'd think it much more likely they're in some safe deposit vault."

"Still, no one has been able to find any record of such a box among her papers, or a key anywhere among her effects. Mr. Paget and the creditors' auditor have been looking high and low for just such a key."

"But where could she have hidden them? This is a large house, of course, and it's old and all that, but really there aren't many places where a package of bonds could be safely hidden so that no one could find them."

"That depends," I told her, "on how thoroughly one searches. Why, they might be lying at this moment behind some of the larger books in the library. If so, if they were left, apparently carelessly, in plain sight of everyone. . . . Well, you remember Poe's 'The Purloined Letter'?"

"But that was the work of a very clever person. Agnes was anything but clever. It would have been the greatest folly, in her opinion, to have tried to hide securities by revealing them."

"I grant that. None the less, I'm becoming more and more convinced that those same securities are somewhere at Ormesby."

"You must have a reason for thinking so."

"I have. I'll show it to you. For I'm also about convinced that the time has come to tell you the truth about Agnes's death."

"You mean——?"

"I mean that your sis— that Grayce hadn't anything to do with it."

"Then who——?"

"It was Alice Hobbs."

"Are you quite sure of that?"

"Perfectly." And I took from my pocketbook the folded note I had found on the table.

"Why this . . . this changes everything!" cried Gray, her eyes shining in excitement induced, I supposed, by proof that her sister must be held guiltless of murder. "For don't you see what it means? 'She cheated me.' That must have something to do with those bonds we were speaking of. Oh, you're perfectly right, Selden. They're here at Ormesby. If only we knew where to look."

We sat down and discussed possible hiding places. I was by no means as firmly convinced as Gray had immediately become that the bonds were meant by the wording of the note; but I owned myself, nevertheless, willing to accept such a supposition as a working hypothesis. For, so far as either Gray or I could imagine, there was no manner in which Agnes could have cheated Alice Hobbs, unless Alice had become in some way the accomplice of Agnes, with a promised reward out of the only money which Agnes was known to possess in considerable quantity. More-over Alice had written "she hid them from me," and the "them" certainly appeared to mean the things in respect of which Mrs. Hobbs had held herself to have been cheated. And they were in "the old iron place"?

"At least," I said, having re-read the note slowly and aloud to Gray, "we needn't waste time looking behind books and such things."

"I keep thinking," she remarked, "of an iron kettle, though 'the old iron place' hardly fits as description of such a thing. Then there's a spot up in the woods where we've always thrown old scraps of tin and iron. But surely she wouldn't have put them there."

"Do you suppose Hobbs could help us? For she wrote as though he'd know what she meant. I haven't told him about this note. I've hesitated to do it for more reasons than one."

"Yes," she nodded, slowly, "I think I understand you. And I also think you've been wise. Just the same . . ."

"Oh, he's a right to know, of course, provided he can take it."

And then we discussed this further matter of Hobbs's reaction to the knowledge we possessed. In the end we broke off our talk without having come to any definite conclusion. I promised Gray, however, that I'd have a look at the scrap dump she had mentioned, while she declared herself ready to search attic, basement and all cupboards and closets to satisfy her notion that an iron kettle would prove to be the thing we wanted.

As to our actions in the event of finding the treasure, we held one purpose in common. That was to turn the securities over to the creditors or their representatives, who had in some way become possessed of a vague knowledge that assets in large amount were yet missing. Two or three of these men yet lingered in Tiltown, visiting us almost daily and pestering us with inquiries. Their questions were, to say the least of it, embarrassing. Each of us went in hourly dread lest one or more of the others betray something which might lead to an investigation which must bring down upon us the heavy hand of the law. To find the bonds and turn them over to Paget and the rest and thus to rid ourselves, as we hoped, of these spies—that, it seemed to both Gray and myself, would be well worth the loss of the value of the bonds to us.

I could not help thinking, for a moment, how naturally Gray and I worked together in double harness. And it may be that I sighed a little, upon leaving her company, to think that the time was surely approaching, even if slowly, when she and I must part forever. But enough of that!

I searched, then, the scrap heap I have mentioned, while Gray busied herself in rummaging through the house. We were obliged to work very quietly and unostentatiously. Neither of us dared let any of the others suspect our purpose, since we had reasons to suspect the discretion of all of them. I do not mean that they might have tried to hinder us, or that they might have objected to our intention to turn the bonds over to Ormond's creditors. It was, rather, that our companions, with the exception of Muriel, had suffered so severely in their nervous states as to be quite untrustworthy. They were already carrying secrets enough, and to spare. We dreaded lest the addition of even one more to the load should prove to be too much. It is true that the people of the town had not, as yet, shown themselves to be very inquisitive. Doubtless they would begin to betray this very human character-istic before many more days had passed.

With all this, however, it almost seemed as though each of us at Ormesby were engaged in a private hunt for the bonds. I have spoken of how I encountered this one, or that, wandering alone, at dead of night, in various parts of the house. And now, when I came upon any of them anywhere about the place, that woman, or Hobbs, if it were he, started and turned hastily in another direction. Even Muriel acted thus unaccountably. Hith-erto, in our married life before the divorce, on those occasions when temporary little quarrels had come between us, she had been wont to stare me out of countenance, with that silent hurt look which some women know so well how to put into their eyes. And in those days I was frequently made to feel that I had been brutal to her, and then I'd beg her pardon, make love to her, and peace would be restored between us. But now she would not glance at me at all. She avoided my eyes as if she, and not I, had been guilty of the things which were driving us apart. And this, in some unaccountable way, acted upon me to convince me that it was actually I who had done the wrong, whatever that might have been. It was as if she were so sure of my guilt she had no need to vindicate herself before me, or to bring me to woo peace with her in order to save her feminine pride. She gave me no chance whatever to justify myself. And I was mystified and, in spite of everything, I could not bring myself to secret acknowl-edgment that I was not deeply hurt.

Let me make all clear in this matter of Muriel. I had wavered for a time before Gray's dominating and somewhat mysterious charm. Even now I thought of her tenderly and pitied her for the fate which had overtaken her family and herself. I had more than once been tempted to lay myself at Barbara's feet, a slave to the exquisite beauty of her face. More than that, I was tempted, by what abysmal demon within myself I do not know, to become her slave for worship of that very evil which I knew to be within her and which called to me to put by decency and pride and revel down to death in forgetfulness of all that has gone to create such civilization as we have. And despite Muriel's notion to the contrary, I had not escaped a longing to throw myself into Grayce's crazy arms, spend what little of life might remain to me in one delirious orgy with her, and then die and be done with it all, glad only to go out of the world and be at rest. Yet through all of this, I had never ceased entirely to think of Muriel as of the woman I had once loved and whom I might love again could I be convinced again of her truth and steadfastness. Besides, let her present aversion and dislike be the result of what they might, I did not doubt, in the deepest part of my heart, that she still loved me. Nor do I lay that wholly to masculine vanity. She might leave me again . . . oh yes! I could well imagine her doing that. But that she would always be, at bottom, my woman in such a way as she would never be woman to any other man, somehow I could not seriously doubt that. And it hurt, now, when I saw her turn coldly away from me with no slightest sign of a desire for reconciliation. I had rejected her offer of that very thing. Now, however, it hurt because she no longer seemed inclined to make such an offer.

The situation was rapidly becoming more than I could bear. Perhaps, even, the state of my relations with Muriel had lately made it possible for me to give Gray merely a sigh, no more.

"You treat me," I told Muriel one day, stepping between her and the door, so that she could not leave the little drawing-room in which I had trapped her, "as if I were some kind of criminal. What's come between us? I mean, what more than usual?"

"Let me pass," she began, icily, "I——"

Then, abruptly, she changed her mind. "Come with me," she commanded.

She passed me and led the way up the stairs and into the room formerly occupied by Agnes Ormes. As I have said, Muriel had been using it since Agnes's death. I stood just over the threshold, wondering why she had brought me there. Without a word she pulled open a small drawer in Agnes's ornate desk, took from it a package of brown paper, and thrust the package into my hands.

"Open it," she said, simply, turning away from me to stand before one of the windows.

The package was not tied with string or anything else. The paper had been rolled loosely around whatever object it contained. It was the work of but a moment to disclose a sheaf of bonds. They were Government bonds; and there were a hundred of them, or so I estimated their number during the few seconds that elapsed while I stood examining them.

"Where did you find 'em?" I asked.

For answer she went again to the little desk and out of the same drawer in which the bonds had lain took another piece of paper. This also she handed to me, saying curtly "Read it." I read:

"Dear Mrs. Seaverns I come to you because I haven't no place else to turn to I am a wronged and a unhappy woman if ever they was one upon this earth. Things has got to such a pretty howdy-do that something desprit must be done soon. I take this means of writing terrible wrongs. Please forgive me and overlook the manner. Them bonds had disappeared entirely from the old iron place where she kept them in the pipe that leads down to where the poor dead folks reposes in peace I hope, God rest their souls. Your husban has got them safe and soun in his room. They lies safe and soun under the bath tub in his room which I didn't clean this morning like I'd ought to have. Goodby. Don't grieve for me to much. It is better so, to write the wrongs done me.

Yrs respectively,
Alice Haskins Hobbs.

"The old iron place"! It seems queer to me now that the large iron pipe had never come into my mind as a possible hiding place. But then, just as I had said to Gray might be the case, the most obvious place of concealment would be that in which we might never think to look. It appeared that either poor Alice Hobbs had removed them and placed them under my bathtub, before killing Agnes Ormes or immediately after that; or she had seen Agnes change the hiding place. That bathtub stood on four short legs; it was not of the modern pattern that sits flat on the floor.

But why had either woman put the securities into my apartment? And why had Alice informed my wife of what had been

done? Had she become convinced that we, the strangers at
Ormesby, were the only persons there who should escape alive
from the clutches of the Ormesby curse? She might have thought
that the sisters and the aunt of Ormond were doomed as he
had been. Or it may have been that she had long nursed a secret
grudge against all members of the family, not an uncommon
thing with servants of a certain mental stripe. It might even have
been that her hatred of Agnes had extended itself to include the
others. It might have been that she hated her husband. Whatever
her motive, it was clear that she had wanted Muriel and me to
have possession of the wealth which she must have fancied she
could never herself enjoy. And it could only have been a disordered brain that stressed the disappearance of the bonds from
"the old iron place" to add, the next moment, that they were to be
found under my bathtub.

To my questions Muriel replied readily enough. She informed
me that she had found Alice's letter in Agnes's room, pinned to
a pillow of the bed, quite as if Alice had been a reader of old-
time murder tales. Muriel had entered the room for some little
thing soon after the finding of Alice a suicide in the kitchen. She
had then visited my room and had taken the bonds from under
the bathtub. She had immediately placed them in her own bed,
under the mattress, where they had been safe from the prying
eyes of the creditors' people, intending to inform me of the find.
But circumstances had prevented her doing so until the next day,
and by that time she had become somewhat suspicious that I was
in some way conspiring with Grayce to rob the rest of the family
of their rightful property. I had, of course, been keeping a very
watchful eye on Grayce, remaining much in her company, since I
dared not let her speak privately with any of the strangers at the
house. But Muriel, sensible as she really was, was yet a woman.
Jealousy had had its way with her, even when she had told herself
that she was not jealous. She had not hesitated to conspire with
Ormond Ormes to gain possession of the bonds, quite willing
to believe his tale of needing his own property to stave off bankruptcy. Yet she could find it in her heart to condemn me for what
she assumed was a contemplated theft. I know that we are all, at
bottom, ready to blame others, rather than ourselves. Neverthe-

less I think that Muriel's unconscious jealousy was at the root of her manner and actions.

"For all I could tell, you were really going to cut and run with Grayce," she argued as we sat and talked, the bonds lying unnoticed on the floor between us. "I wasn't jealous. I don't think I was. I've been jealous often enough to know the feeling of it. But I did think you might want to go away with Grayce for a long enough time to— Oh, don't you see? All of us hate this house. How could you or any of us be blamed for wanting to leave it? And if you took Grayce away with you and took the bonds, too, well, I supposed you'd not abandon the girl. I couldn't think that of you. So the thing might easily have become permanent."

"Yes," said I, slowly, "this depression has made changes in all of us. You'd not once have thought such things of me."

"I'm sorry, Selden. I don't really think them now."

"You'd not have thought them at all, if . . ." I did not finish. But she read my mind.

"Yes! I deserve that, I suppose. If I'd not been weak enough to. . . . Yes, you're right. But I'm not going back to the stage. No matter what may happen, I'm not going back."

"I don't wish to act the prig," I told her, for I was feeling, at that moment, very much like one. "Come! No one is above temptation, at some time, especially when poverty helps the tempter. I'm not holding anything of that divorce business against you. And I'm not saying that I myself haven't been tempted to do the very thing, with Grayce, that you thought I might. So . . . well, all's even between us, isn't it?"

"Is it?" And there was a sudden gleam in her eyes. "Whatever we may have been tempted to do," I told her, "we're together again. It isn't the being tempted that kills respect and . . . and love. I love you now. I've never ceased loving you, I think. We'll start again . . . somewhere. We'll be better people for having been through all this."

But I did not go to her at once and put my arms around her. I am glad we did not coax passion, at that time, to do for us what reason was more slowly, yet more securely, doing.

For I had begun to understand something of Muriel's motives and to see a little way into the recesses of her mind. That which had appealed to me as inconsistency and which had almost dismayed me, now resolved into something resembling consistency when it appeared that she had crushed down what she had supposed was her natural feeling of jealousy to excuse what she had taken to be my own wish to escape leaving Ormesby a pauper. That jealousy had been working, of course, all the while. And it had really been no more than a jealous fear that there might have been an understanding between Grayce and me which had caused Muriel to remain silent on this matter of the bonds all these weeks and months. None the less, if such a vice as jealousy can be made to serve one's better instincts and to help one in the doing of generous deeds, then I do not see how it is entirely to be despised and condemned. Fear, also, is a vice, but it was fear, and very little else, that made the first man out of some whimpering ape.

I do not know how long we talked, but in the end everything was clear between us. Watching me as she had during the past weeks, she had become convinced that I was secretly searching for the bonds. But Grayce had declared me to be already in possession of them. Was it Grayce, then, who had removed them from "the old iron place" to hide them beneath my bathtub? If she had done that, then she had done it between the time Alice Hobbs had penciled her first note to her husband and this later one to Muriel. Was it Grayce who had "wronged" Alice Hobbs? Had Grayce been hand in glove with Agnes against Alice? Muriel confessed herself to be sorely puzzled, as I now admitted myself to be also. For I had supposed that Barbara might have done everything which Alice spoke of as a wrong against her.

"After I heard from Gray," said Muriel, "that both of you wanted to find the bonds to turn them over to Ormes's creditors, I purposely left them in my traveling bag, and that in your room. But you probably thought I left it there only for the purpose of drawing you to return it and thus giving me a chance to. . . . Do you see?" I nodded; I suppose I may even have blushed! For I had returned the bag, and I had thought that very thing. And I had been so distant and formal as to have precluded any attempt on the woman's part to enmesh me in the toils of such passion as I knew she could arouse. But she continued: "I reasoned that if you had missed the bonds from under the tub, you'd look through the bag. But you didn't. You merely handed it back to me. So I began to think that you must be entirely innocent."

"Well," I answered, "since all's clear between us, let's try to keep it so. It's quite true that I've been hunting for these things, as has Gray. We'll go now and give them to her, and she can turn them over to her brother's creditors. And then I mean to have a look into that famous iron pipe, where Agnes must have put them at the first. I've a feeling that there's still something undiscovered in that old well."

Muriel accompanied me in search of Gray. A few words, together with Alice's letter, sufficed to show Gray how the bonds had come into Muriel's possession. But I—masculine as I am! —was astonished upon learning how little was necessary to convince Gray of Muriel's reason for withholding delivery of the bonds until this moment. Say what you will, women have an understanding of all things affecting the heart which men seem never to attain.

Gray went immediately to the telephone and called Mr. Paget, who had returned to New York. He promised to come at once to Ormesby, in company of the investigating auditor, to take possession of the securities and to render a proper accounting and receipt for them. And then I descended, alone, to the crypt, intending to examine that iron pipe.

I carried with me a hammer and a small chisel, thinking to chip away the mortar which fastened the pipe in place. But when I had carried a folding step-ladder down there, I learned that there was no mortar to be chipped away. The pipe pierced the brick wall without binding of any kind, though there was evidence that it had once been cemented in place. By moving it a bit more than an inch into the wall, I was able to disconnect it at the uncemented joint and thus to remove and hold in my hands the end piece of pipe. It was a heavy piece of iron, but it was not above twenty inches in length. A woman, by exerting her strength, could have slipped it aside and then replaced it. It could have concealed the small package of bonds effectually enough. But now it was empty. Yet I could not rid myself of a feeling that the old cistern still concealed a mystery. Nor do I think this feeling was caused by my knowledge that it contained the bones of the elder Ormeses.

But I had learned the means whereby Barbara had been able to come into the crypt after I had left it. To slide down that pipe from its opening in her room, and then to remove the loose end piece and to drop to the floor, that was a feat requiring great strength and agility. Yet she must have done just that. No sane woman could have done it. But Barbara was not sane!

I saw that I could not break through the wall without larger tools than I had at hand. I must go and fetch others. Perhaps, also, I might call Hobbs to my aid.

Passing through the library, on my way to the shed adjoining the kitchen, in which most of the larger tools were kept, I heard a motor stop at the front door of the house. Paget could not yet be arriving from New York. It might be a tradesman from Tiltown. Of late, as if in contempt of the persons who still dwelt at Ormesby, following all the queer doings there, I had more than once noticed that drivers of trucks and delivery wagons did not trouble themselves to use the service entrance. Nor, so far as I knew, had any of the Ormes women protested against this want of courtesy. Nevertheless, suspicious as I had grown to be of every small happening in and about the house, I found myself hastening toward the front door, intent on learning something of the arriving person or persons before he or they should have been admitted. In this case I reached the door before Hobbs, who might have been busy somewhere on one of the upper floors, could come to open it. I opened it. A policeman in uniform stood there. I recognized him as the chief of the police of Tiltown.

"Howdy, Mist' Seaverns," he said, appearing to be somewhat embarrassed. "Nice day."

"What can I do for you, Chief?"

"Well—where's all the Ormeses? But maybe I better talk to you first."

"What's happened?" I demanded, premonition of some disaster seizing me on the instant.

"A bad accident's happened."

"Who's hurt?"

"Miss Ormes . . ."

"Gray?"

"No. . . . I ain't sure, but I think it's the other'n. And your man Hobbs. Kilt."

"What? Where? How?"

"Yep. Both dead. It's pretty bad. I seen the bodies myself. Hobbs musta been drivin'. He run the car over Mohawk Slide. Went down more'n a hundred feet. Ever'thing busted to flinders. Miss Ormes was jammed again' him so hard she had her teeth sunk plumb into his throat when we got down to 'em."

"Good Lord!"

"Glad I found you here. You can help me break the news to the other folks. Gosh! Looks like hard luck's tryin' to git the best o' this fam'ly, don't it?"

I had turned back from the door, signing to the officer to follow me into the house. I wanted to hide my face from him, and was glad of an opportunity of turning my back, even though I should have allowed him to pass me while I held the door for him. But I dreaded lest he see that the horror I naturally felt at such news was much tempered by relief at losing from among our midst the two weakest of our members. The secrets of Ormesby would hereafter be the better kept. I do not say that I felt no sorrow for poor Hobbs. I think I must even have experienced a stab of pity for Grayce. But I will not protest that relief was not my dominant emotion, now that both Grayce and Hobbs were forever silenced.

My elation was, however, of short duration. As I opened the door which gave into one of the parlors, I started back from the threshold, treading on the officer's foot as I did so.

A man was standing just before me. He remained there for an instant, fronting me, his horridly red and glaring eyes alight with something that looked like triumph. Had I not seen that look in the eyes of the portrait upstairs?

Then the *thing*, for I knew it was *not* a man, turned away, crossed the room swiftly, opened a farther door, and went through it, the door swinging noiselessly shut behind him.

"Who's that?" It was the police officer behind me.

"One of the . . . one of the auditors, I believe," I managed to say. "They're still checking up. . . ."

"Uh-huh." I was very glad of the Chief's interruption. "Funny lookin' feller, though. Looks a lot like old Mr. Ormes used to look."

My friend the policeman said something further, but I shall never know what it was. My knees had gone very weak beneath me. I knew now, past all doubting, that the *thing* I had seen was not a subjective vision. Others could see it, also. That *undead emptiness* actually walked in the halls and through the rooms where people lived!

XVII

It appeared that Hobbs had been on his way to Pittsfield, sent there by Barbara with several small commissions. Why he had consented to allow Grayce to accompany him, without, at least, notifying me, we, of course, could now never learn. No doubt she had presented herself, ready to go, at the last moment. Perhaps she had wheedled him, alleging that she desired to ride but a short distance and would walk back. Whatever the reason, we could none of us doubt that she had flung herself upon the man and had bitten into his throat, thus causing him to lose control of the car, so that it plunged through the heavy railing above Mohawk Slide. Knowing what we knew, we must seem to accept the theory of the police that the fall had hurled the girl against the man in such manner as to cause her teeth to become embedded in his neck. But we ourselves could accept no such harmless notion.

Gray had her sister's and Hobbs's bodies cremated, as she had had those of Ormond and Agnes—yes, and poor Alice Hobbs, also.

Doctor Barnes, whose visits to Ormesby had ceased, following Alice's death, stopped one day as he was passing the house. He did not ask to see any of the others, and it was I alone who talked with him. He informed me that so many tragic endings in the Ormes family had caused no little gossip and wonder throughout the countryside. But the good man gave no indication of supposing that those deaths had not been caused by accidents due entirely to impersonal agencies. I was left with the comforting assurance that as he thought, so thought the people. I had noticed curious eyes turned upon me when I had entered Tiltown, on the few occasions of my going there, but I had not seen a single glance of hostility, nor even one of suspicion. Whatever troubles beset us, we were not, it seemed, to be pestered by the community in which we moved.

And now we were faced with the necessity of arranging something definite with regard to the future. With Hobbs gone, Gray and Barbara both refused to import another servant. The three remaining women took turns at the cooking and at keeping the house in order. Yet I fear that a scrupulous housekeeper, had such a person visited us, must have found not a little to cavil at.

Gray began to speak of selling the place. With what she should realize from such a transaction, together with her private funds and such little money as Barbara still possessed, she would take her aunt to England, buy or lease a cottage in the country, preferably somewhere in Devon, and there live quietly the rest of their lives. I doubted whether Gray should be able to accomplish that, with Barbara beside her. Moreover, Barbara herself, when the matter was broached to her, refused to consider it. She would never leave Ormesby, she declared. And while they two remained there, neither Gray nor Barbara would willingly allow Muriel and me to leave. We repeatedly declared that we must go. We protested that we could not remain living as pensioners under their roof. We were, I think, fully resolved to go, sooner or later. We had been half a year at Ormesby, and—for such is our human nature—the place had become, in spite of the horrors it held for us, something like home. We had no other home. The world outside still groaned under poverty, striving blindly to win back something of the wealth it had lost. We knew that if we left Gray's roof, we should be plunged again into a bitter struggle for mere bread. Let me confess at once, then, that while I said and repeated that we must be going, yet I had, so far, made no active effort to get away.

I had begun, shortly after the last of the funerals, poking and prying into the masonry of the old cistern. My hands were soft and I soon found them covered with blisters, yet by dint of perseverance I at last succeeded in removing enough of the wall to

permit of forcing the *upper* half of my body through the opening.

Down there all was, of course, absolute blackness. A damp and
nauseating odor rose from the pit and rushed through the whole
house, bringing Gray and Muriel down to learn the cause of it. I
had not informed them of what I was doing. I should have been
as well pleased had they both remained to the last in ignorance of
it, but now I was obliged to explain my work. Gray remonstrated
vigorously. She argued, later and privately, with me that no good
could possibly come of opening what she called a tomb. Let the
dead lie undisturbed in such grave as they had together. And I,
to please the girl, for after all it was her house, put back in place
the bricks I had removed, though without mortar, and remained
away from the cistern for several days. Yet I could not avert my
curiosity for very long. A fascination which I could not explain to
myself drew me down there.

It was about the time of Christmas, I think, or a little after that,
when I found an opportunity of working there undisturbed by
any of my female companions. I carried with me, this time, a
powerful flashlight. Having again removed the bricks I had loosened, I worked my head and shoulders through the aperture and
played the beam of the torch over the bottom of the well. That
bottom appeared to be not more than fifteen feet below my eyes.
It was covered with what looked like fine white dust, the remains
of the quicklime which Hobbs and Ormond Ormes had thrown
down to cover and eat away the flesh and bones of the latter's parents. The walls of the pit were perfectly dry, in spite of the damp
smell that came from below. And there was no slightest sign of a
body.

Yet—stay! Something was there. I returned the beam of the
light to the spot I had noticed, and studied it carefully. I was looking straight down upon it, which was a disadvantage to me. Was
I seeing bones—the bones of a human arm and hand? Or was I
looking at a mere impression left in the lime by what had once
been bones? I could not determine. Long and long I gazed at that
place on the bottom of the cistern, gradually coming to think
that I was looking at actual bones. But whether this were the
case, or not, that appearance of bones must be finally and for-

ever destroyed before I could rest secure in any bed by night. No stranger's eye must ever be allowed to see what I was seeing. It would be necessary for me to enter the well and remove the relic, if relic it was, or so to disturb the hardened lime as to efface the impression made in it. It was not work that I could enjoy performing. Indeed, so great was my unreasoning horror of the place that it must have been quite the middle of January before I could fully make up my mind to delay no more, but to enter the pit. And all this in spite of the fascination I had felt, and continued to feel, and which drew me, almost every day, to descend those stairs. That fascination had been pulling me down there from the very first.

I shall not detail all my pains and exertions in getting into the well. I was obliged to desist frequently, owing to the near presence of Gray or Barbara in the library above. But at last I had knocked together a ladder sufficiently slender and, as I hoped, sufficiently strong to bear my weight. Carrying with me nothing but my torch and a heavy hammer, I went into the pit.

Arrived at the bottom, I very soon found that the figure of an arm was no more than the thick paste formed by quicklime after being exposed to dampness. Striking a portion of it with the hammer, it shattered inwardly, showing me that it was hollow. The bones it had once covered had been completely consumed. And there were no other bones, or parts of bones, anywhere. I made quite certain of that. The crusted lime lay flat on the ground all about me. Only in the case of this one right arm and hand to a point several inches above the elbow had the lime retained the shape of the human remains it once had fed upon. That it had been the right arm I could see from the shape of the hand. That it had been the arm of the man, and not of the woman, I decided from the size of it. The fist was doubled, save that the index finger pointed straight out along the line of the hand and arm. I shuddered, suddenly recalling how Grayce had said that her father had died with that finger beckoning to her and to the son who had killed him. It had beckoned them as if inviting them to join him in death. Well, two of them had gone to him, now, and the pointing index finger seemed to my disturbed imagination to be still beckoning. Perhaps for Gray and Barbara? It seemed somehow like a denunciation. And somehow it was like a threat.

But I wanted to leave that noisome place as soon as might be. I had come down there to efface the last telltale traces of a deed of violence and blood. I set about destroying the shape of that high relief with the hammer. The lime cracked and crumbled under my blows. I worked methodically, beginning at the upper portion of the arm and proceeding toward the fist. I had got as far as the wrist, pounding on and breaking up the lime to either side, of the upraised portion, so as effectually to remove all semblance to a human arm. I now smashed that accusing finger and beat into powder the material on all sides of it. Then I was at the fist. The first blow of my hammer shattered it, though it did not yield inwardly with so hollow a small sound as had the other portions. I struck again and then again. And then I made out, under the light of my torch, that something within the fist had offered sufficient resistance to prevent the hammer from crashing down directly against the stone flooring of the cistern. It was something of a white color. It was something rounded. At last, fearing to touch it before I had made out plainly what it was, I saw that it was a piece of ordinary paper, wadded into a tight ball, having been clenched in the dead man's fist, and now still preserved as paper by the fact that when the bones which had held it disappeared the lime had already hardened over and above it. It had not been touched by decay.

And there was writing upon it. So much I clearly distinguished. But I could not read the thin lines of ink. I dropped the thing into a pocket of my trousers, straightened, and carefully examined every square foot of the floor and walls about me. Then I turned away and scrambled up the ladder and emerged into the little room just as Gray, Muriel and Barbara came down the last of the steps and stood before me.

Barbara was very pale. There was a drawn look on Gray's face. Even Muriel seemed badly frightened. I was amazed. It was almost as though that final destruction of the mere semblance of an arm long dead had frightened these women, and that when they were at a distance from the work I did. But I was myself conscious of an uplift of spirits, and I smiled into the faces before me. But I did not immediately inform them of what I had found within that hollow fist.

"You're safe?" cried Muriel.

"Safe? Of course. I assure you I am able to negotiate a little—"

"But why did you shout like that?" Gray demanded.

"I didn't shout."

I saw them exchange glances.

"What's happened? What's frightened you?" I demanded.

"Someone—or something—yelled like—like—" Gray began, stammeringly.

"I thought you were being ... murdered," Muriel said. Her face was paler than usual.

"No, it was a cry of triumph," declared Barbara, and she smiled as she said that, evilly. And she put forth a hand and would have stroked my throat had I not darted back out of reach.

"I'm sure I didn't make a sound," I said. But then I began to consider that I had to calm two badly frightened women. Also, it was barely possible, I might have cried out unconsciously upon discovering the paper in the dead man's fist. "But perhaps I did, after all," I said. "For I've discovered something. Come up to the library and we'll have a look at it."

The writing was not wholly effaced. It was faded, but with a reading glass I made out enough of it to guess at the rest. I cannot say, however, that it much enlightened either Gray or me upon any of the mysteries still surrounding us. It was as follows:

"My dear son: Before I go whence I shall not return, I feel I must warn you against a woman who is capable of doing [here was a single word of which I could not be sure. I took it to be "great"] mischief. The bon[d—?]s which I have concealed in the old iron place were [taken—?] from her. Give them to her when the time is ripe. She is, as you very well know, A ."

That was all. That was entirely all. The letter ended in the middle of the sheet of paper. No dash followed that "A" as if the writer had wished to abbreviate a name. The writing broke off as abruptly as though the man who had penned it had been violently interrupted. Had he then crumpled it, angrily, or fearfully, into a wad? And had he carried it, thus crushed in his hand, throughout the last of those mad scenes which ended in his death? If he had not done just that, how had I found it where I had found it? I imagined that here was one small mystery which might remain forever unsolved.

Then there was again that phrase used by Alice Hobbs, "the old iron place." I had supposed, and Gray had agreed with me, that Alice had meant the loose end piece of that iron pipe. But if the writer of this unfinished letter, and it must have been Ormond's father, since it was plainly a man's writing and began with "My dear son," had meant that pipe, then the bonds he had concealed there must have been removed before Alice Hobbs had learned of the hiding of still others in the same place, or had herself hidden others there.

Yet stay! Why might not the two groups of bonds have been one and the same? Why might not the hundred thousand Ormond was said to have given to Agnes have been those left in "the old iron place" by his dead father? For surely that "A" had been intended for Agnes.

No, not so, for Agnes had become Ormond's wife. Had she become his wife after being perhaps the mistress of the father? Here was a further mystery. Barbara had declared that Agnes had not, in Barbara's belief, sought marriage with Ormond. Had the supposed wrong he had done her been really a wrong done by his father? Agnes had struck me as being a woman who had been, or might easily become, an adventuress. Nevertheless, if my present half-formed surmise were a correct one, then her reluctance to marry the son might be in some part explained.

Still, "A" might have stood for Alice. Why not? Alice Hobbs was certainly in some way involved in this matter of the bonds. Alice had made use of the same phrase as had the elder Ormes in speaking of the hiding place. Alice had slain Agnes Ormes and had penned a note alleging that the murdered woman had done her a wrong. Alice it had been, at the last, who had succumbed to the hideous madness of lycanthropy, which had afflicted the father of the Ormeses; and if there were any basis of truth in the old tales of the werewolves, then Alice might have contracted the disease from having been bitten. . . . I did not care to pursue that reasoning further. Yet why might not that "A" have been intended for Alice Hobbs?

Of course, it might have been meant for a lower case "a" and not a capital letter. I did not believe this to be the case, however. The writer was evidently an educated person. He would have been careful of such things. And it was very plainly a large "A", even though a small one had been meant.

These were all mysteries to which I could find no answer. For all I could see, they were mysteries which might never be solved, if, indeed, there were anything of good to be gained by solving them. But there was one mystery which made it imperative that a further search be made in that house, and that was the hiding place of the bonds which had been put aside for "A". I was coming to think that "the old iron place" was not, after all, the iron pipe. I represented this to the others. Muriel was not, or pretended not to be, interested. Gray agreed with me. It was only Barbara who protested against a further search, declaring that the money did not exist. She even went so far as to say that, even if it should be found, it might bear a curse against the finder. I was about to offer some argument against this superstitious aversion. I suppose I must have smiled in scorn of it. At any rate, Barbara abruptly changed her mind. She faced me defiantly.

"Very well," she said, calmly enough, though her eyes flashed in her pale face, "I'll show you where it is. I know. But I'm not to be blamed for what may happen."

"We'll try to prevent anything happening," I said, fatuously enough, as I admit.

"*You?* How can *you* prevent it? But come!"

Without another word she turned and walked toward the secret passage and the secret stairs that led to the little room in which hung the picture of her dead brother. The rest of us followed, no one speaking. Arrived in the room, I stepped toward the only window and threw up the shade. It had been drawn so long that when I moved it a thick cloud of dust descended from the roller. I turned away, toward Barbara. She was again facing me.

"Remove the portrait," she commanded.

I glanced keenly into her eyes. They were alight with a look which I had come to know only too well since I had lived at Ormesby. For a second I thought of endeavoring to persuade her to desist; I had a notion that I myself might come here later and remove the portrait, since there must be a wall safe concealed behind it. But then I saw that the woman was determined. Matters had gone too far to draw back. I verily believe that I could have stopped her only by exerting my strength against her and forcibly carrying her out of the room. She swayed for a moment on her feet. I both feared and hoped that her resolve was broken and that her strength would fail. But she mastered her emotion swiftly, drew herself to her full height, stretched out her arm and pointed toward the picture.

"Take it down!" she ordered, regally.

I did so. After all, I could see no harm in doing it. I stepped close in front of the thing, grasped it firmly by the frame on both sides, lifted it slightly, so the cords by which it was suspended were freed of their hooks—then almost dropped it! For I could have sworn that a foul and sickening odor of *breath* came from the vicinity of the painted mouth! More than that, I *felt* a movement of air against my face, as though the portrait had exhaled forcibly against me!

But I mastered my fright. How far this mastery was due to pride before the women present, I do not know. Perhaps it was altogether due to them. Perhaps, had I been alone in the chamber, I might have left the thing undisturbed, finding some excuse for leaving the room. As it was, I again took hold of the frame, this time lifting the picture from the wall. Then I turned and set it down against that wall opposite the single window. And I was careful to turn the painted face to the wall, so that those baleful eyes should not look on at what we did there.

Sunk perhaps an inch in the plaster of the wall behind the picture, I had seen a small iron or steel door. It was the door of a common kind of wall safe, a bit old-fashioned, no doubt, but still in use in houses fifty years or more of age. There was a steel handle, and in the middle of the door was a single knob. Evidently Barbara knew what the combination was, for she was spinning the knob before I had quite completed my task of placing the painting out of the way.

"I never knew that thing was there," murmured Gray.

Barbara must have heard her. "There are a number of things

you don't know, my dear," she said, her voice brittle and hard. "I'm going to show you some of them, and to tell you others."

She continued spinning the knob, though more carefully now. I remember wondering whether she actually knew the combination, or was merely carrying through some silly bluff. Maybe she would abandon the safe, declaring it to be out of order and only to be opened with a bar or a cutting torch. Perhaps she would assert that she had forgotten the figures. But then I distinctly heard a tiny metallic click, as of tumblers falling. Barbara left off turning the knob. She wheeled and faced us.

"Now I'll tell you things," she said.

She was deathly pale. Her face, drawn with an inward emotion, looked far older than I had even seen it look. But she did not falter, nor did her dry and brittle voice tremble.

"When I open that door, I die," she told us. "You don't believe it? But I know that it will happen. My brother said so, years ago. He told me that some day I'd open it, and that then I should join him. Now I will open it."

I may have made a slight movement toward her. I do not now remember. She went on:

"There aren't any bonds in that safe. There are bones there, however. That's what the note said—"bones." They are the bones of a baby. My brother was the father of it. That's why Ormond insisted on marrying Agnes. He thought it was Agnes's baby, by his own father. But he was mistaken. The baby was not hers. But the blood of that infant . . . can any of you guess what happened to that . . . blood?"

She glared at us, seeming to be seeing all of us at once. My own blood ran cold. I felt sweat breaking out on my face. What monster from the primordial void had lurked all these years in this woman's soul to be now having his will of her?

"You don't believe in werewolves. You're all very modern, aren't you? You know so very much! But let me tell you that my brother is here . . . now . . . in this room, looking at all of you. He's alive . . . as much as any of you. You, Seaverns, have thought —for *I* know —that you've been seeing ghosts. I tell you that my brother walks in the flesh, that he breathes, he lives, he still loves!"

And I, God help me, had I not smelled the breath, the fetid breath, of the monster but a few minutes before?

Barbara's voice fell to a low register, almost as low as that of Grayce.

"My brother and I are one and indivisible; where I am, there he is also." It shot through my brain that I had seen the spectre of the elder Ormes only when Barbara must have been about some of her fiendish business. "Now he calls to me, and I go to him. It wasn't Grayce who killed that fool Agnes. I did it. It wasn't Alice Hobbs. I taught her to say that. I made her say that. But it was I who killed the woman. Now I am tired of all this. I—do you hear? —I caused Hobbs to run that car off the road, because it was I who sunk my teeth into his throat, even though Grayce may have seemed to be doing it for me. You, Seaverns, you are mine. I've already marked you. You shall never escape me. I'll follow you wherever you go. You can't go so far, you can't hide so securely, that I shan't find you. And you others, too. Some day . . . some day . . ."

She broke off. I stood rooted to the floor with horror and with fear. I licked my lips, the tongue seeming dry and swollen as I thrust it forth. I managed to glance at Gray and Muriel. They both seemed rooted to the ground. Neither spoke, neither seemed capable of speaking. Barbara laughed suddenly. It was not a pleasant laugh. I should not like to hear the like of it again.

"And now I'm going. I'll not say good-bye to you. I'll see each of you again . . . perhaps . . . tonight!"

Before I could have stopped her, she whirled and wrenched open the door of the safe. There was a deafening report. I was hurled backward by the shock of a blinding flash and a heavy cloud of smoke. When I recovered some use of my muscles, no more than a second later, I saw that the woman had half turned from the wall and was facing me. Her little hand had gone to her breast. Through the delicate fingers of that hand trickled a thin bright stream of blood. And in the next instant, with what was unquestionably a happy, triumphal smile, she fell forward onto her face. When I reached her side, she was already a corpse. That is . . . if . . . if . . . God grant she had not told the truth!

And then, and I am as certain of it today as I was in that

moment, there rang through the house such a shout—or yell—
or whooping scream—as I had never heard, and as I pray I shall
never hear again. Then all was as silent as the grave.

"That," muttered Muriel, after a while, "is the second time I've
heard that."

XVIII

Once again there were policemen moving busily through the
rooms and corridors at Ormesby. Once again a curious public
stared from the road below and strove to penetrate into the
grounds and house. Once again a dead body had gone in a car to
the little undertaking rooms in Tiltown. Once again the flesh and
bones of an Ormes were burned to ashes.

They were all gone, now, all save Gray. That old wolf, that
elder Ormes, had succeeded in wiping out his clan as effectually
as if he had shot each of them through the heart. Only Gray remained of the lot of them.

And it was curious, now, when nearly everything could be
shown and nearly everything told, that the police should have
exhibited so much suspicion of the three of us who were left
alive. For days they questioned us, separately and collectively.
They ransacked the premises. They did not fail to descend into
the crypt and thence into the cistern, and they were curious as to
why lime should have been thrown down there. Gray answered
that the cistern had been damp and foul, and that the lime had
been put in to sweeten the ground. That seemed plausible, yet
they doubted, or appeared to doubt. They could not understand,
they maintained, why I had removed bricks from the wall, hint-
ing that I must have intended thrusting Barbara's murdered body
through the opening. Why had I constructed the ladder, which
lay still in the hole? Why had I ventured down into the cistern?
They measured my shoes and compared them with the foot-
prints to be seen at the bottom of the pit, though I had not denied
being down there. I protested that I had two reasons for my investigation, one, to learn why the cistern leaked, and, two, to search
for treasure.

For it was at this point that I produced the note I had found in the dead hand. I pointed out that one word might be read either as "bonds" or "bones", and that I had suspected it to be bonds, substantiating my theory by calling attention to the fact that we had actually found bonds to the amount of a hundred thousand dollars' worth, which we had immediately turned over to Ormond's creditors. Nothing of this could be denied, yet the police hesitated to accept my story. Why had I carried down a hammer into the cistern and then proceeded to smash the encrusted lime in one place and in no other?

There was certainly nothing to substantiate any theory that we, or any of us, had murdered Barbara Ormes, or even intended doing so. We were all fingerprinted, of course, but, equally of course, none of our fingerprints could be found on the heavy old pistol in the safe, or anywhere about the interior of the safe. I had had sense to see to that. After the first shock of dismay, following the explosion, the death of the woman, and the hideous shouting which had rung through the house, I had mastered my nerves enough to lead both Gray and Muriel immediately out of the room, so that nothing should be disturbed before the arrival of authorities, for whom I had at once telephoned. Only in this respect did I lie under questioning on the matter of the note: I said (and I had instructed the others to maintain) that Barbara herself had found the note among her brother's forgotten papers. I explained that Ormond's aunt, recognizing the ancient family nickname of the "old iron place" as meaning the safe which had been so long concealed behind the portrait that even Gray did not know of it, had led us thither, had worked the combination, and had been shot dead for her pains. But what had we thought to find in the safe? I stated that we sought treasure. But at this point Gray interrupted, hesitatingly and with a reluctance to speak which seemed natural enough, in view of what she was to tell.

"Mr. Seaverns tells the truth," she said. "He was looking for bonds. I, too, thought, at first that the note meant that. Afterwards I began to be less sure."

Q. "Why was that? What made you change your mind?"

A. "I thought the word looked something more like bones than bonds. And I remembered——"

Q. "Yes? Go on. Remembered what?"

A. "That my brother had had . . . before he married Agnes . . . that there had been some kind of . . . difficulty. I never knew, definitely, but I've always thought that——"

Q. "Well?"

A. "That she had had a . . . a baby . . . before . . ."

I saw the questioners exchange glances. If there had been a child born out of wedlock, it seemed plausible to them that it might have been slain and its body tucked away into the forgotten safe.

To be brief, Gray's story supplied the police with a theory that a baby had been killed; that Ormond had been the father of it; that Agnes had been the mother; that Ormond's father had been privy to the crime; that the older man had wanted to warn his son of the danger he ran in continuing his intrigue with Agnes; that the mysterious wording "before I go whence I shall not return" had probably meant simply "before I die, as any man may, at any time, die"; and that we—Gray, Muriel and myself—having found the note among Ormond's papers, were perfectly justified in supposing it to have referred to bonds, and in having attempted to find such valuable securities. They mulled this over for several weeks, but in the end accepted it and granted permission for the tiny bones of the infant to be cremated.

It is true that there had been some talk of sending an investigator to England for the purpose of looking into the records there of the deaths of the elder Ormeses. But nothing came of this. Such documents and letters as Gray could show seemed conclusive enough. Ormond Ormes, insane though he may have been, even at that time, had been cunning enough to have done his work well. And eventually the matter was dropped.

We were left in peace, indeed, but it was a peace of the body only, not of the spirit. Surely we had enough to disturb our sleep at night, we who could not obliterate from memory a single horror that we had seen and known. But this was by no means all. For now, when any of us showed a face outside the Ormesby grounds (and there were many reasons why we must, occasionally, go beyond them) we were the subjects of hostile stares. The people had formerly looked upon us with pitying eyes. Now they were definitely against us. We were undesirables. They wanted us out of those hills. Tragedy stalked at our heels, evidently, and that quiet community was afraid of us. Nor could we much blame the people for this attitude. If we could not be positively connected with the causes of death in the cases of so many of the Ormeses, we had stood, at least, too close to those mysterious doings. It was as if we were ourselves bewitched. It was as if we might, at any moment, bring down calamity upon the heads of the inno-cent. The time had arrived for the three of us to leave Ormesby. We knew this and set about making plans to go.

Gray renewed her resolve to leave America. She would repair to England, perhaps to France, buy a little cottage somewhere in the country, and seek among flowers and books the rest she had been denied in her native land and in the home of her fathers. As for Muriel and myself, we had no plans, save only that we were determined to put Ormesby far behind us. And save only that we intended to become again legally man and wife. We dared not do that at present. We had posed as married; it would have brought down again upon us an investigation by the representatives of law if it had become known that we had lied in this matter, as it might very well have become known had news of our application for a license to marry been made public.

Gray wanted to divide her little fortune with us, but we could not consent to that. We did allow her to give us the coupé which I had once driven and in which Agnes Ormes had met her death. I did not think that the car, at any rate, was haunted. Also, we ac-cepted from her, as a loan, a few hundred dollars to enable us to live until I should have found something to do.

For the madness of the Ormeses had at last put out of my heart all desire I had once had to make Gray my wife. Gray had been dear to my dreams, once, and I had come very close to asking her to share my future life. But I had not done it, and now I no longer wanted to do it. It was too late for that, forever. Moreover, I do not think that Gray herself, though she had loved me, would have consented to marry me. Gray has never married any man. She knows what taint she carries in her blood. Gray Ormes, whatever the rest of her tribe may have been, is not the woman to transmit that taint to her posterity.

Naturally, I had turned back to Muriel. She had returned to me. Whatever had taken place in New York, I could not deny that she had risked liberty and disgrace to stand beside me at Ormesby. Moreover, I knew that my love for Muriel had never quite died, though it had been hurt and had slept. Divorce or no divorce, I had never entirely ceased to think of her as my wife. And she, as she had told me that evening on the lawn, could find no safety in the arms of a man she could not love.

Into the little car we loaded our few belongings. Gray, who had not yet been able to sell anything, either Ormesby itself or the furnishings, put all her affairs into the hands of a trustworthy agent with instructions to get what he could. I imagine that a good many hunters of antique beds and chairs secured bargains to tickle their collectors' hearts; and I wonder sometimes whether they would enjoy possession of those articles if they knew their histories.

"Good-bye," said Gray as we were on the point of leaving. "You have both been better friends to me than I have deserved. I hope everything good comes to both of you. But there's one thing you ought to know. I've put it into a letter to you, Selden. Don't read it now. Don't read it before you stop for the night. Promise me that?"

Of course I promised. I knew that if the secret in the letter were anything I ought to know at once, Gray would have told me in words. So I slipped the letter into an inside pocket of my coat and did not open it until we had ceased driving for that day and were comfortably settled in a tourist's cabin. Then I read it. It bore no superscription.

"The truth of it is, I do not know anything about a baby belonging to Ormond and Agnes. I said what I said because it seemed necessary. But the child really belonged to Barbara. And it really belonged to her brother, that is, to my father. You who know so much of the secrets of Ormesby, should know that last shameful thing also. But how could I have told that to the investigators?

"I was never told this, but a woman knows some things without words. Barbara bore the child in that little room where you found Alice Hobbs. The blankets had never been removed. She would never permit anyone to enter that chamber. No one attended her, except Alice and the man. And whether the child was born dead, I do not know. I heard a baby's cry, for I was listening. It may, of course, have died soon after that. But . . .

"You will destroy this, of course. This secret belongs, with so many others, in the grave. But you now know, at last, why Barbara insisted on opening that safe. Something must have snapped in her brain. She knew that her baby's bones were in that place. But she wanted to join . . . well, all of them. There is no knowing the human heart. As there is no limit to the height of it, so also there is no bottom.

"And now, good-bye again, and forever. I shall keep no single scrap of paper which can, in any way, implicate you, or either of you, in anything which has happened. For I live over a mine. It may be that I shall be allowed to die peaceably. I cannot know, naturally. But if not, then with me shall have ended the family of Ormes as well as the curse upon it."

So Alice Hobbs had been privy to a secret more shameful and more carefully concealed than almost any of the others? It may well have been, then, that the final "A" of that old wolf's letter referred to Alice and not to Agnes. What should Agnes have had to do with Barbara's baby? Why should Agnes have been the dangerous woman of whom Ormond was being warned? But this secret of Alice Hobbs and of her relations with Ormond's father —there was now no way of solving those mysteries satisfactorily. Nor did I wish to solve them. Whether Agnes had been the mistress of the father before becoming the mistress and later the wife of the son, I could not see how the determination of that could in any manner be of the slightest benefit to either Gray or ourselves. Let the dead past bury its dead. None the less, it seemed plausible that Alice's statement that "she cheated me and hid them from me" might have had reference to something, perhaps securities, which Agnes, by becoming Ormond's wife, had obtained, and which Alice, as the price of her silence with regard to Barbara's baby, might have considered belonged rightfully to herself. Indeed she may have been promised a sum of money, or its equivalent, by either Ormond or his father. With Alice "cheated," with her tongue silenced by time and the removal of evidence, it might have been that Barbara had only then begun to persecute the woman, hence the "and now she won't let me alone." So, egged on by her own hatred and by Barbara's diabolical cunning, she had at last murdered Agnes Ormes. For that is what Barbara must have meant in saying that she had been the slayer. She had confirmed such an hypothesis by adding that it was she who had done away with poor Hobbs. In brief, she had meant that the actual slayers had been her agents.

I shall not reveal the name of the state in which we finally settled. I do not see that it concerns anyone. Suffice it that we came, after devious wanderings, to a thriving little town in a smiling valley nestled between tremendous hills. And there we halted and went forth in search of some means of livelihood. Almost at once I made the acquaintance of a hustling young fellow who wanted an older man as partner to assist him in his filling station business. I seized the opportunity presented, invested such few dollars as remained to us, and today, if any of the fellows from the M——— Club should motor out our way, it isn't at all unlikely that I may fill their tanks with fuel and speed them on their journey. But as for myself, I would not return to the city and the ways of cities for all those fellows' collective wealth. And Muriel wholeheartedly agrees with me in that.

I do not think I am given to superstitious fancies more than another man; certainly I am not more dastardly before the grisly fingers of fear than another man who has done what I have done and seen what I have seen. And certainly, also, I have not been haunted by Barbara Ormes's undead body, for all her prediction that I should be. Whether the fire did for her what the stake did for the larvae in older times, I do not know. But if she meant that I should never be able to put from mind the horror of her deeds, or efface from my soul the scars her gleaming teeth have left there, then she spoke the truth.

As for this matter of superstition, naturalistic hypotheses are not lacking to account for a good many of the happenings at Ormesby. None the less, I cannot find reason to accept any of them as fitting all the facts. Say, if you will, that I dreamed or imagined the figure of the man I saw in the hallway just before I entered Alice Hobbs's room to find the woman unconscious and with her bandages disarranged. Upon coming to her senses, she had spoken of a woman of whom she was afraid. In my ignorance I had then supposed she raved of some spectre of her dream. Yet Barbara had actually been with her a few moments, previously. This I now know from my memory of having seen Barbara's look while she stood at the foot of the back stairs and gloated on Alice's dying form.

And if I had been the victim of hallucination in the front hall-way, what of the policeman who stood behind me and saw the same thing? Not very long before that happened, Grayce had flung herself upon poor Hobbs. And did not Barbara confess that people died at Ormesby because her agents killed them?

For where Barbara Ormes went, there went also that apparition of the brother who had loved her and who directed his human agents through her!

Barbara spoke truly when she said that her brother and herself were one and indivisible. Too much has been substantiated in the realm of dual personality to permit of being dogmatic when denying the reality of many mysterious events. Too much has been dredged out of the mud at the bottom of the human soul to allow anyone to toss away with shrugs the legends which have come down to us and which, discount them as much as you will, must yet have had some basis in actual human experience. If the Tiltown policeman and I saw exactly the same thing, at exactly the same time, and if the thing we saw acted for both of us in the same way, then there is no alternative but to accept the appearance as an appearance of reality. We can test reality in no other manner.

And what of the manner in which Barbara, apparently so delicate and frail, plunged into the great pipe and slid down it? No sane woman would have done that. No sane woman probably could have done it. Yet Barbara did it. She might well have killed herself, had she misjudged distance and dropped into the well. But she checked her descent at the right moment. She removed the loose piece of pipe and then replaced it. She must have done all that many times, in the past, to have acquired proficiency at the doing of it. Why? For mere amusement? Did she know that I had but just left the crypt? I do not know. But I do not see how her feat could have been accomplished at all were she not either herself some kind of larva or under the guidance and instruction of that monstrous brother of hers.

Then there was the typewriter which wrote quite of itself. It is true that I saw this happen but once, and then with but half an eye. It is true that only one key was moved. Moreover, that movement *might* have been caused by some peculiar vibration in the building, or in the floor, consequent upon my treading upon a loose board of it. And yet . . . *try* making one key, and no more, move from any such cause! It cannot, in my opinion, be accomplished.

Again, it will be remembered that I took that portrait from the wall and stood it on the floor against that wall opposite the one window in the room. I well recall setting it down as carefully as one usually handles a work of art. In brief, I did not drop it. I recall, also, that I so placed it as to leave the face of the picture toward the wall; I did not want those baleful eyes staring at me as I worked.

Then came Barbara's horrid revelations. Then came that swift wrenching open of the door to the safe. Then came the explosion, and then the shock and bustle following the vampire's collapse and death. And then the dismay caused by that infernal yell.

I am quite certain that none of us touched that portrait after I stood it against the wall. How, then, is one to account for what happened to it within the next very few minutes?

Yet there it was. When I led Muriel and Gray through the door, so that nothing within the little room should be disturbed before the police arrived, I chanced to glance down at the picture and I saw then that the canvas had fallen out of its frame. A few moments later, when I returned to the room for the express purpose of investigating this, the canvas was nothing but a small heap of dust. And that dust was entirely white, like ashes. And it was as hard and brittle to the touch as though it had been composed of lime slaked years before.

And then, too, there was that horrible triumphant shout!

Sometimes I wake in my bed at night, and always Muriel wakes beside me, waiting for that shouting to be repeated. . . .

THE END

www.ingramcontent.com/pod-product-compliance
Lightning Source LLC
Chambersburg PA
CBHW012207030726
47494CB00023B/2553